THE KEY

'Was you at the inquest?'
Garth nodded.
'What did they say?'
'They said it was suicide.'
'Why?'
'Because he was found in the church with the
the door locked and his key in his pocket.'
Cyril gave a scornful laugh.
'I reckon there was another key all right,
mister.'
'Oh, yes—there are other keys. The
Rector has one. Mr. Bush the sexton has
one, and Miss Brown who plays the organ
has the third. They were all accounted
for.'
Cyril said 'Coo!' And then, 'They don't
'arf believe things, those blokes at
inquests. I could tell them something
if I liked. And would they believe me?
Not 'arf, they wouldn't! I'm not a
clergyman, nor a sexton, nor Miss Brown.'
Garth was leaning against the wall with
his hands in his pockets. He eyed the
flushed cheeks and bright blue eyes and
enquired,
    'What could you tell them?'
    Cyril came closer.
    'Something about a key . . . '

**Also by the same author,
and available in Coronet Books:**

Pilgrims Rest
Miss Silver Comes to Stay
The Brading Collection
The Gazebo
The Case Is Closed
The Clock Strikes Twelve
The Listening Eye
The Girl In The Cellar
The Fingerprint
Spotlight
The Chinese Shawl
The Catherine Wheel
Watersplash
Vanishing Point

The Key

Patricia Wentworth

CORONET BOOKS
Hodder and Stoughton

Copyright © 1946 by Patricia Wentworth
First published in Great Britain 1946
by Hodder and Stoughton Ltd

Coronet edition 1953

Fourth impression 1984

Printed and bound in Great Britain for
Hodder and Stoughton Paperbacks, a
division of Hodder and Stoughton Ltd.,
Mill Road, Dunton Green, Sevenoaks,
Kent (Editorial Office: 47 Bedford
Square, London WC1 DP) by Cox and Wyman

Typeset in Times by Fleet Graphics, Enfield, Middlesex
Printed and bound in Great Britain by
Cox & Wyman Ltd, Reading

CHAPTER ONE

There are traffic lights in the middle of Marbury where its two main roads cross. Michael Harsch came up to the edge of the pavement and saw the orange light go on. Having lived the greater part of his life under German rule, he made no attempt to cross before the red, but stood waiting patiently just where he was until the lights should change.

Of the two roads, one runs as straight as a ruled line, set with pompous examples of Victorian shop architecture. The other comes sidling in on a crooked curve and shows an odd medley of houses, shops, offices, with a church and a filling-station to break the line. Some of the houses were there when the Armada broke. Some of them have put on new pretentious fronts. Some of them are no better than they should be from a cheap builder's estimate. Taken as a whole, Ramford Street has a certain charm and individuality which the High Street lacks.

Michael Harsch, waiting for the lights, looked idly down the irregular line of houses—a tall, narrow one running up to four stories with a dormer window in the roof; the square front of a shabby hotel with its sign of the Ram swinging tarnished just over the heads of the passers by; farther on a little squat, two-storied house with its old woodwork painted emerald green, and over the door in gold letters two foot high, the word *Teas*.

He turned back to the traffic lights, and found them green too. If he had crossed then, a great many things might have happened differently. Yet the moment came and went without anything to mark it out from other moments. His mind was divided between the purpose which had brought him to the crossing and the realization that he was tired and thirsty, and that a cup of tea would be pleasant. If he crossed now, he would get the four-forty-five to Perry's Halt and catch the bus to Bourne. If he waited to have some tea, he would miss his train and the bus, and be late for supper, because he would have to walk across the fields from the Halt. He hesitated, and as he did so the lights changed again. He turned his back on the crossing and made his way down Ramford Street.

He had without knowing it taken the most momentous decision

of his life. Because green changed to orange at just that time three people were to die, and the lives of four others were to be deeply and radically altered. Yet there was nothing in his mind to warn him of this. And perhaps—who knows?—a warning would have made no difference.

He went a little way down the street and crossed over. Here again there was a decision to be made, but this time it hardly cost him a thought. The little green tea-shop had put the idea of tea into his mind, but it had no attractions for him. He went up three steps, crossed a tesselated space, and entered the dark, narrow hall of the Ram. Nothing more inconvenient could have been devised. There was a staircase, there was a booking-office. There were two barometers, three cases of stuffed fish, and the grinning mask of a fox. There was a grandfather clock with a gloomy face and a hollow tick, there was a marble-topped table like a wash-stand with gilt legs which supported a pining aspidistra in a bright pink pot. There was an enormous umbrella-stand, and a small oak chest. There was no light, and a smaller amount of fresh air than one would have believed possible. A smell of beer, damp mackintoshes, and mould appeared to be indigenous. It had a bouquet and a richness not to be attained in less than fifty years.

There were six doors. Above one of them were the words *Coffee Room*. As Harsch approached, this door opened and a man came out. The room was lighter than the hall. The light fell slanting past an ear, a cheekbone, a tweed-covered shoulder, and struck full upon the face of Michael Harsch. If the man who was coming out of the coffee-room checked, it was no more than anyone might have done to avoid colliding with a stranger. He certainly did not draw back, and before a breath could be taken he had gone past and was absorbed into the gloom.

Michael Harsch stood still. He thought he had seen a ghost, but he was not sure. You have to be very sure indeed before you speak about a thing like that. He had had a shock, and he was not sure. He stood looking into the room but not seeing it. Presently he turned and walked back into Ramford Street. When he got there he stood and looked about him, up the street and down. There was no one in sight whom he had ever seen before. Ghosts don't walk in the day. He told himself that he had been mistaken, or that his nerves had played him a trick. He had been overworking —it was a trick of the nerves, a trick of the light—light slanting like that plays tricks. There were too many things in his mind, in his memory, waiting for just such a chance to give them the illusion of a present instead of a past reality.

When he had satisfied himself that there was no one in sight he began to walk back towards the traffic lights. He had forgotten that he was tired and thirsty. He had forgotten why he had gone into the Ram. He thought only of getting away from Marbury, of catching his train. But he had lost too much time, when he reached the station the train was gone. He had an hour and a half to wait, and the long walk over the fields at the other end. Supper would be over before he got home. But Miss Madoc was so kind —she would see that something was kept hot for him. He filled his mind with these everyday trifles in order to steady it.

When he had crossed the road and was at a safe distance, a man in a tweed coat and a pair of grey flannel trousers came out of the little newspaper and tobacco shop next door to the Ram. He looked exactly like dozens of middle-aged men in country places. He went back into the hotel with an evening paper in his hand. To all whom it might concern he had just stepped out to buy it. He went back into the coffee-room and shut the door. The only other occupant looked over the top of a cheap picture paper and said,

'Did he recognize you?'

'I don't know. I think he did, but afterwards he wasn't sure. I went into the tobacconists' and watched him through the window. He looked up and down, and then, when he saw no one, he wasn't sure—I could see it in his face. He didn't see you, did he?'

'I don't think so—I had my paper up.'

The man in the tweed coat said, 'Wait a minute! When you get back you can find out what is in his mind about me. He's had a shock, he is doubtful, but you must find out what is the state of his mind when the shock has passed. If he is dangerous, steps must be taken at once. In any case it is very nearly time, but if it is possible without too much risk he should be allowed to complete his experiments. I leave it to you.'

Michael Harsch sat on a bench at Marbury station and waited for his train. His mind felt bruised and incapable of thought. He was very tired.

CHAPTER TWO

Michael Harsch came out of the hut in which he had been working and stood looking down the tilted field to the house at

Prior's End. Because the work on which he was engaged was dangerous, and there was always present the possibility that it might end itself and him quite suddenly in a puff of smoke, the house was nearly quarter of a mile away. The hut was long and low, a shabby-looking affair roughly creosoted to withstand the weather, but the door through which he had come was a very solid one, and the line of windows not only carried bars but were secured inside by strong and heavy shutters.

He turned to lock the door behind him, pocketed the key, and then stood again as he had done before, looking out past the house to the lane which followed the slope, and the line of willows which marked the trickling course of the Bourne. The village of Bourne was out of sight, all except the top of the square church tower. On a fine day the weathercock glinted in the sun. But there was no sun to-night. Dark hurrying clouds overhead where a wind blew—high up, unfelt below. Strange to see the clouds drive when not a leaf was stirring in the hedgerow or among the willows.

Unseen forces driving men. The thought went through his mind, tinged, as his thoughts were apt to be tinged, with something deeper than melancholy, more austere than sarcasm. Forces driving men, unseen, unfelt, unguessed at, until the storm broke in darkness and shattering confusion.

He lifted his face to the sky and watched the driven clouds. A man of middle size, standing crookedly to save the leg which had been crippled in a concentration camp, the habitual stoop of his shoulders less noticeable now that he was looking up. His hair, rather long and still very black, was barred by a white lock which followed the line of a scar. His features had no markedly Jewish look. They were thin, and drawn so fine that it was only a second or a third glance which would probably decide that they had once been handsome. The eyes were beautiful still—brown, steadfast eyes which had looked on many things and found them good, and then had looked on other things and found them evil. They looked now upon the sky and upon those hurrying clouds, and all at once he straightened up, standing evenly upon his feet. For a moment ten years dropped away—he was a young man again. There was power in the world, and he had the key to it. He began to walk down the field to the house.

Janice Meade was in the little sitting-room which had been built on at the back, perhaps a hundred and twenty, perhaps a hundred and fifty years ago. It jutted out into the garden and had windows on three sides of it—casement windows, each with a cushioned window-seat. The rest of the house was very much older. Some part of it must have been standing before the old Priory had fallen or been battered into a heap of ruins. The house fetched its name from those far off days. It was, and always had been, Prior's End. The lane that served it served no other house, and ended there, just beyond the gate.

Michael Harsch came through the house, stooping his head where the low beam crossed a crooked passage, turned the handle of the sitting-room door, and came in with something of the air of a man who comes home. Janice was in the window-seat, curled up like a mouse, with a book held close to the glass to catch the light. She always reminded him of a mouse—a little brown thing with bright eyes. She jumped up as she saw him.

'Oh, Mr. Harsch—I'll make you some tea.'

He lay back in a long chair and watched her. All her movements were quick, light, and decided. The water was hot in the kettle; it needed very little to bring it to the boil again over the blue spreading flame of the spirit-lamp. He took a biscuit and sipped gratefully from a cup brewed just as he liked it, very strong, with plenty of milk. Glancing up, he saw that she was looking at him, her eyes bright with questions. She would not ask them in any other way—he knew that—but for the life of her she could not keep them out of her eyes. His answering smile made a younger, happier man of him.

'Yes, it has gone well. That is what you want to know, is it not?' His voice was deep and pleasant, with a marked foreign accent. He reached forward to put down his cup. 'It has gone so well, my dear, that I think my work is done.'

'Oh, Mr. Harsch!'

The smile was gone again. He nodded gravely.

'Yes, I think it is finished. I do not mean altogether of course. It is, I think, a good deal like bringing a child into the world. It is your child—you have made it—without you it would not be there at all. It is flesh of your flesh, or, like this child of mine, thought of your thought, and between its conception and its birth there may be many years. With my child, it is five years that it has been in my thought night and day, and all that time I have worked with all my might for this moment when I could say, "Here is my work! It is fulfilled—it is perfect! Look at it!" When it is grown it will do the work which I have brought it into the world to do. Now it must have nurses. It must grow, and be strong. It must be schooled, and tutored.' He reached his hand for his cup again and said, 'The man from the War Office will come down to-morrow. When I have finished my tea I ring him up. I tell him, "Well, Sir George, it is over. You can come down and see for yourself. You can bring your experts. They can see, they can test. I give you the

9

formula, my notes of the process—I give you everything. You can take my harschite and put it to its work. My part is done." '

Janice said quickly, 'Does it make you sad to let it go—like that?'

He smiled at her again.

'A little, perhaps.'

'Let me give you some more tea.'

'You are very kind.'

He watched her, with the kindness in her eyes, as she took his cup and filled it. She was wishing so much she could say something that would make him feel less sad. She hadn't got the words, she didn't know them—not the right ones—and it would be unbearable to blunder. She could only give him his tea. She didn't know that her thoughts spoke for her in eye and lip, rising colour and eager hand.

He said, 'You are very kind to me.'

'Oh, no——'

'I think you are. It has made this time very pleasant.'

He paused, and added without any change in his voice, 'My daughter would have been just about your age—perhaps a little older—I do not know——'

'I'm twenty-two.'

'Yes—she would have been twenty-three. You are like her, you know. She was a little brown thing too—and she had a brave spirit.' He looked up suddenly and directly. 'You must not be sorry, or I cannot talk about her, and to-night I have a great desire to talk. I do not know why, but it is so.' He paused, and then went on again. 'You know, when there has been what you may call a tragedy—when you have lost someone, not in the ordinary way of death but in some way that puts fear into the imagination —it becomes so difficult to talk about the one that you have lost. There is too much sympathy—it makes an awkwardness. You do not like to speak because your friend is afraid to listen. He does not know what to say, and there is nothing that he or anyone else can do. So in the end you do not speak any more at all. And that I find sometimes very lonely. To-night I have a great desire to speak.'

Janice felt her eyes sting, but she kept them steady, and her voice too.

'You can always talk to me, Mr. Harsch.'

He nodded in a friendly way.

'It would be a happiness for me, because, you see, it is the happy things that I would like to speak about. She had a happy life, you know. There was her mother and I, and the young man

10

she would have married, and many friends. She had much love given to her, and if at the end there was pain, I do not believe that it could blot out the happiness, or that she remembers it now any more than you remember a bad dream you had a year ago. And so I have trained myself to think only of the happy times.'

Janice said what she hadn't meant to say.

'Can you do it?'

There was a little pause before he answered her.

'Not quite always, but I try. At first I could not. They were both gone, you see—my wife, and my daughter. I had no one to keep up for. When you have someone else to support, it makes you very strong, but I had no one. There was a dreadful poison of hatred and revenge. I will not speak of it. I worked like a man in a fever, because I saw before me the way by which I could take a terrible vengeance. But now it is not like that. Even the other day, the last time I saw Sir George, there was something of this poison. It had been there so long, and though there were things that were driving it out, yet in the dark corners there was still some of that other darkness. It is very primitive, and we are not really civilized. If we are struck, we wish to strike back again. If we are injured, we do not care how much we hurt ourselves so long as we can hurt the one who has injured us.' He shook his head slowly. 'Not at all civilized, you see—and foolish with the folly that is poisoning the world.' His voice changed to a homely confidential note. 'Do you know that there, in Sir George's office, I had an outburst like a savage, and I enjoyed it. But afterwards I was very much ashamed—because that sort of thing, it is like getting drunk, only of course much worse, so I did well to be ashamed. But now there is a change. I do not know whether it is because I was ashamed, or because since my work is done I cannot hide any longer in dark corners. I must have light to see what it is that I am doing—I do not know. I only know that I do not wish for vengeance any more. I wish only to set at liberty those who have been made slaves, and to do this the prison doors must be broken. That is why I give my harschite to the government. When the prisons are all broken and men can live again, I shall be glad to feel that I have helped. I do not think you can help when you are poisoned with hate.'

She said with a soft rush of words,

'I'm so glad you told me. I think you're wonderful. But—oh, Mr. Harsch, you're not going away!''

He looked startled.

'Why did you think of that?'

'I don't know—it sounded—like saying good-bye.'

She was to remember that, and to wish that she had not said it.

'Perhaps it was, my dear—good-bye to my work.'

'But not to us—you wouldn't be going away from here? I wouldn't stay without you.'

'Not to help my good friend Madoc?'

She made a little face and shook her head.

'Not to help me, if I stay on here to work with him?'

She said eagerly, 'Are you going to do that?'

'I don't know. Here I am, at an end. Somewhere I have read that every end is a new beginning. At this moment I am at a corner. If there is a beginning on the other side of it, I cannot see what it is. Perhaps I shall stay here and work with Madoc.' His smile became faintly ironical. 'It will be restful to make the synthetic milk and the synthetic egg, the concentrate of beef—and perhaps without any hen or any cow. There have been times when I have envied Madoc—and how much pleasure it will give him to feel that he had converted me! He is a zealot, our good Madoc.'

Janice jumped up.

'He's a very cross, tiresome man,' she said.

He laughed.

'What—you have been in trouble?'

'Oh, not more than usual. He called me dolt three times, and idiot twice, and miserable atomy once—that's a new one, and he was awfully pleased about it. You know, I used to wonder why he had a girl instead of a man, and why he picked me when there are lots of women with proper science degrees. I happen to know that Ethel Gardner applied for the job and didn't get it. She was considered awfully good at college. She got a first, and I didn't get anything because of having to come down and nurse my father. And I couldn't make it out, but now I know. No man would have stood it for half a minute, and no qualified woman would either, but I'm a little bit of a thing and I haven't any qualifications, so he thinks he can stamp on me. I wouldn't stay a minute if you went.'

He patted her shoulder.

'It is just a way of speaking—it has no meaning. He does not think those things.'

'He says them.' Janice tilted her chin. 'And if I were five-foot-ten and looked like Britannia, he wouldn't dare! And that's why he picked me—just to have someone to squash. I really do only bear it because of the times you let me help you. If you go away——'

His hand dropped from her shoulder. Rather abruptly he went

over to the farther window-seat and took up the table telephone which stood there.

'I have not said that I am going away. And now I must ring up Sir George.'

CHAPTER THREE

Sir George Rendal leaned forward.

"Your part of the world, isn't it?'

Major Garth Albany said, 'Yes, sir—I used to spend my holidays there. My grandfather was the Rector. He's dead now—he was pretty old then.'

Sir George nodded.

'One of the daughters still lives in Bourne, doesn't she? She'd be your aunt?'

'Well, a kind of a step. The old man got married three times, and two of them were widows. My Aunt Sophy isn't really any relation, because she's the first widow's daughter by her first marriage. Her name's Fell—Sophy Fell. My father was the youngest of the third family——'' He broke off, laughed, and said, 'I'm not awfully firm on the family history really, but I did spend my holidays at Bourne until my grandfather died.'

Sir George nodded again.

'You'd know pretty well everyone in the village and round about.'

'I used to. I expect there are a good many changes.'

'How long is it since you were there?'

'My grandfather died when I was twenty-two. I'm twenty-seven. I've been down two or three times to see Aunt Sophy—only once since the war.'

'Villages don't change very much,' said Sir George. 'The boys and girls will be off in the Services and the factories, but it's the old people who are the village. They'll remember you, and they'll talk because they remember you. They won't talk to a stranger.'

He sat back a little in his writing-chair and sent a very direct glance across the plain, solid table—a man in his fifties, smart and well set-up, with dark hair grey on the temples. He held a pencil between the second and third fingers of his right hand and set it twirling.

Garth Albany said quickly,

'What do you want them to talk about?'

The direct glance dwelt on him.

'Ever hear of a man called Michael Harsch?'

'I don't think so——' Then, with a quick frown, 'I don't know —I seem to have seen the name somewhere—'

Sir George's pencil twirled.

'There's going to be an inquest on him at Bourne to-morrow.'

'Yes—I remember. I saw the name in the papers, but I didn't connect it with Bourne. I'd have taken more notice if I had. Who was he?'

'The inventor of harschite.'

'Harschite—that's why I didn't connect him with Bourne. I didn't know he was dead. There was a paragraph about this stuff harschite—about a fortnight ago. Yes, that was it—harschite— some sort of explosive.'

Sir George nodded.

'If we'd any sense or logic we'd take the man who wrote that paragraph and the editor who passed it and shoot them out of hand. Here we've been going on like cats on hot bricks about the damned stuff, and out comes a footling penny-a-lining paragraph and gives the show away.'

'It was pretty vague, sir—I can't say I got much out of it.'

'Because you didn't know enough to put two and two together. But someone did, and so there's an inquest on Michael Harsch. You see, we had been in touch with him for some time. He was a refugee—Austrian-Jewish extraction. I don't know how much Jew, but enough to queer his pitch in Germany. He got away about five years ago. His wife and daughter weren't so lucky. The daughter was sent to a concentration camp, where she died. The wife was turned out of her house in the middle of a winter's night and never got over it. He got away with his brains and practically nothing else. I saw him because he had an introduction from old Baer. He talked to me about this stuff of his. He swore it would knock spots out of anything we'd got. Frankly, I thought it was a fairy tale, but I liked the man, and I wanted to oblige old Baer, so I told him to come back. That was four years ago. He used to come back once a year and report progress. I began to believe in the stuff. I went down, and he showed me what it could do. It was terrific. But there was a snag. The stuff was unstable—too easily affected by weather conditions—impossible to store or transport in any quantity. Then he turned up again. He said he had over-come the instability. He walked up and down this very room in a

14

tremendous state of excitement, waving his arms and saying, "Harschite—that is what I have called it! It is my message that I send back to those who have let the devil loose to serve him, and it is such a message that he will hear it and go back to the hell where he belongs!" Then he calmed down a little and said, "There is only the one step more—the small, small step—and I take it now any day. It is the last experiment, and it will not fail. I am so sure of it that I can give you my word. In a week I shall ring you up and tell you that all is well—that the experiment has succeeded." Well, he did ring me up to say just that. That was on the Tuesday. I was to go down next day, but on Wednesday morning I was rung up to say that Harsch was dead.'

'How?'

'Found shot—in the church of all places in the world. It seems he used to go down and play the organ—had a key, and used to go in just when he liked. He was living out at a house called Prior's End with Madoc, the concentrated food man. It was he who rang me up. He said Harsch had supper with them—there's a sister, Miss Madoc, and a girl secretary—and after that he went out. Madoc said he always did unless the weather was too bad—he liked walking at night. Odd taste, but I daresay it helped him to sleep, poor chap. When he wasn't back by half-past ten, they didn't do anything. Of course it's easy to say that they should have, but—well, they didn't. Madoc and his sister went to bed. They said Harsch had a key, and they never thought of anything having happened to him.'

'Well, sir, you don't, do you?'

'I suppose not. Anyhow they went to bed. But the girl sat up. By half-past eleven she was really frightened. She took a torch and walked down into the village. No sign of Harsch. She knocked up the verger and made him come along to the church with her. She said she thought Harsch might have been taken ill. Well, they found him fallen down by the organ, shot through the head—pistol just where it might have fallen from his hand. I went down and found everyone quite sure he'd shot himself. I am quite sure he didn't.'

Garth Albany said, 'Why?'

Sir George stopped twirling the pencil and put it down.

'Because I don't think he would. He'd made an appointment with me, and he was always very punctilious about keeping his appointments. He was going to hand over the formula and his notes. I wasn't going down alone either—I was taking Burlton and Wing. He wouldn't have walked out on us like that.'

Garth Albany nodded.

'He might have had a come-over. You know how it is—people do.'

' "Suicide while the balance of his mind was disturbed"!' Sir George quoted the words with irony. 'That's what the verdict at the inquest will be.' He brought his fist down suddenly on the table. 'It's damnably probable, quite irrefutable, and damnably untrue. Harsch was murdered. I want to find out who murdered him and see that he doesn't get away with it. And that's not just the natural reaction to murder. It goes a lot deeper. If Harsch was murdered, it was because someone had a motive for getting him out of the way at just this time. Not six months ago when harschite was still in the unstable stage, not a month ago when he was in good hope that he had overcome the instability and still had to put his hopes to the proof, but a few hours after the proof had been achieved, and within a few hours of his demonstrating it to me. Is that a likely time for a man to commit suicide? Isn't it a likely time for a man to be murdered? Some strong interest was engaged to prevent the transfer of harschite.'

Major Albany looked up.

'I don't know. He'd been working on the stuff a long time, you know. I expect it kept him going. Then when he'd finished he might have felt there was nothing to go on for. And as to his being murdered to stop your getting the formula—well, it doesn't stop it, does it?'

Sir George picked up the pencil again.

'That, my dear Garth, is exactly what it does do. Because three years ago Michael Harsch made a will which named Madoc his sole executor and sole legatee. He hadn't anything to leave except his notes, his papers, the results of any discoveries or inventions he might make. It's a pretty big exception, you see.'

'But surely Madoc——'

Sir George laughed without amusement.

'It's evident that you don't know Madoc. He's a crank with an infinite capacity for going to the stake for his opinions—he asks nothing better. If no one will oblige him with a stake, he will find one for himself, pile up the faggots, and hold his right hand in the fire in the best traditions of martyrdom. He is one of the most belligerent pacifists in England. I wouldn't mind backing him for the world's championship myself. He naturally won't have anything to do with the war effort, and only pursues his very valuable researches into Food Concentrates because he feels it is a duty to be prepared for a period of post-war starvation on the Continent. Now do you see him handing over the formula of harschite?'

'Do you mean he won't?'

'I mean he'll see us all at Jericho first.'

CHAPTER FOUR

Garth Albany went back to his hotel and rang up Miss Sophy Fell. That is to say, he asked for her number, but the voice which answered him was a deep contralto.

'Miss Brown speaking—Miss Fell's companion.'

This wasn't the companion he remembered. Her name wasn't Brown, and she twittered. Miss Brown and her voice suggested a marble hall with a catafalque and wreaths. Sombre music off. Not awfully cheerful for Aunt Sophy. He said,

'Can I speak to Miss Fell?'

'She is resting. Can I take a message?'

'Well, if she isn't asleep perhaps you could switch me through. I am her nephew Garth Albany, and I want to come down and see her.'

There was a pause which he felt to be a disapproving one, and then a little click, and Aunt Sophy saying 'Who is it?'

'It's Garth. How are you? I've got some leave, and I thought I might run down. Can you put me up?'

'My dear boy, of course! But when?'

'Well, leave doesn't last for ever, so the sooner the better. I could get down in time for dinner—or do you sup?'

'Well, we *call* it dinner, but it's only soup and an economy dish like buttered eggs without the eggs, or mock fish——''

''What's on earth's mock fish?'

'Well, I believe it's rice with a little anchovy sauce. Florence is really very clever.'

'It sounds marvellous. I'll bring my bacon ration and the other doings, and you can cash in on my meat ration when I get down—I draw the line at steak in the pocket. So long, Aunt Sophy.'

Bourne has no station of its own. You get out at Perry's Halt and walk two and a half miles by the road if you don't know the short cut, and a mile and a quarter across the fields if you do. The only thing that had changed since he was a boy was that, step for step with him across the fields, there ran the tall pylons and stretched cables of the Electric Grid, hideous but undeniably useful. Bourne itself had not changed at all. The stream still ran down one side of the village street, bridged at each gateway by a flat stone lifted from the Priory ruins. The cottages, low-roofed, small-windowed, were inconvenient and picturesque, as they had always been—front gardens ablaze with dahlia, nasturtium, phlox, sunflower, and hollyhock; back gardens neatly stocked with carrot, onion, turnip, beet, and all the cabbage family, and guarded by ancient fruit trees heavy with apples, pears, and plums. A good fruit year, he noted.

There were not many people about—one or two who looked and smiled, one or two who nodded and spoke, and old Ezra Pincott, the disgrace of the large Pincott clan, sidling out of the Church Cut on his way to the Black Bull, where he would spend the rest of the evening. Garth reflected that Ezra at least hadn't changed by a hair. There was, of course, not a great deal of room for change, except in the direction of reform, a direction in which he had never been known to cast even a fleeting glance. Dirtier and more disreputable he could hardly become—but a genial rascal and tolerably well pleased with life and his own reputation as the leeriest poacher in the county. No one had ever caught Ezra poaching, but he had been heard to say that their old meat ration didn't bother him, and Lord Marfield, the Chairman of the Bench, once gave it as his opinion that Ezra had pheasant for dinner a good deal more often than he did himself.

Garth called out, 'Hullo, Ezra!' and received a roll of the eye and a wink in reply. After which Ezra came shuffling over and accosted him.

'Bad times, Mr. Garth.'

Garth said, 'Oh, I don't know——''

'Bad beer,'' said Ezra bitterly. 'Costs twice as much, and takes three times as long to get drunk on. That's what I call bad times. I give you my word I can't get properly drunk nohow these days.' He went sidling on as Garth prepared to cross over, but turned his head to wink again and say, 'It's same like the old Rector used to say, "If at first you don't succeed, try, try, try again." But it takes a deal of doing.'

The church was on the opposite side of the street facing the cottages, with its square grey tower and the old slanting tombstones in the churchyard. Just beyond opened the village green, with the cottages continuing on one side of it, while on the other there stood, in its own walled grounds, first the Rectory, and then, lesser in size and in consequence, two or three more houses, inhabited in his time by Dr. Meade and a selection of old ladies.

Dr. Meade was dead. Somebody else would be in Meadowcroft. He wondered what Janice was doing. Funny little kid—used to tag after him and sit as still as a mouse while he fished——

He struck away to the right by the church and went in through the Rectory gate, thinking how horrified his grandfather would have been to see weed and moss in the gravel, and an unpruned growth of years narrowing the drive. Ridiculous of Aunt Sophy to stay on. If the place was too big for the new Rector it was certainly too big for her, only he couldn't imagine her anywhere else.

He walked in at the front door as he had always done, and set down his suit-case, calling cheerfully,

'Aunt Sophy—I've come!'

Miss Sophy Fell came waddling out of the drawing-room—a billowy old lady in a grey dress flowered with white and lavender. In spite of the size of her figure her head appeared to be disproportionately large. A round face like a full moon was surmounted by a mass of white curls which looked as if they were made of cotton-wool. She had round pink cheeks, round blue eyes, a ridiculous rosebud mouth, and at least three chins. As he bent to embrace her Garth felt as if he was coming home from school again. The holidays always started like this—you kissed Aunt Sophy in the hall, and it was exactly like kissing a featherbed which smelled of lavender.

And then, instead of his grandfather's voice from the study, there came through the open drawing-room door the quite alien presence of Miss Brown, whom he felt he would have recognized anywhere. He remembered her voice to a most improbable extent—a kind of female Spanish Inquisitor with hollow cheeks and hollow eyes, and a fine commanding figure gone away to bone. She wore a plain black dress, but it was admirably cut. She had beautiful hands and feet, and under the sallow skin her features were undeniable. He thought, 'Medusa in her forties,' and wondered where on earth Aunt Sophy had picked her up.

Miss Fell supplied the answer without delay.

'My friend Miss Brown. We met in that delightful hydropathic where I stayed last year. You know, I did not mean to go away at all, but my dear friend Mrs. Holford was so pressing, and I had not seen her for so long, that I made the effort. And I was rewarded, for besides having a delightful time, I met Miss Brown and was able to persuade her to come back and keep me company here.'

In her deep, mournful contralto, Miss Brown said,

'Miss Fell is far too kind.' Then, still in the same tone, she observed that dinner was at half-past seven, and that perhaps he would like to go to his room.

He was surprised at his own strong resentment at being shepherded by a stranger. Aunt Sophy said in her fooffly voice, 'You have your old room,' but the irritation persisted long enough to make him feel ashamed of it.

Miss Fell had maligned the dinner, or else he was being treated as the prodigal son, for they had a very good soup, an excellent mixed stew, green peas from the garden, and a coffee ice. Afterwards she walked him down the herbaceous border to admire late phloxes and early Michaelmas daisies. He was glad to get her to himself.

'I didn't know Miss Johnson had gone. How long have you had Miss Brown?'

She beamed.

'Oh, my dear—it was last year. I thought I had told you—I feel sure I wrote. I really was quite distracted at the time, but it has all turned out for the best—things so often do. Though of course it was all very sad, because Miss Johnson's sister died and she had to go and keep house for her brother-in-law—three children in their teens, and he was quite inconsolable. But now she has married him, so it *has* all turned out for the best.' She beamed again.

'And Miss Brown?'

'My dear boy, I told you about that—the hydropathic and Mrs. Holford—I met her there. She had a temporary post, and I was able to persuade her to return with me.' She laid a hand upon his arm and looked up at him in a confiding manner, her eyes quite round and blue. 'You know, my dear, it really was a *leading*. I was missing Miss Johnson so much, and wondering who I could get to live with me. I asked Janice Meade, but of course it would be very dull for a young girl, and I quite understood her preferring to go to Mr. Madoc, although he is an exceptionally disagreeable man.'

So it was Janice who was the girl secretary. That was a stroke of luck. He wondered vaguely how she had turned out, but before the vagueness had time to clear Aunt Sophy was off again about Miss Brown.

'It really was rather wonderful, you know. Mrs. Holford had a friend—well, perhaps not exactly a friend, but they had become very friendly—they had been a month at the hydro before I got there. Miss Perry, her name was, and she could do all sorts of entertaining things—telling fortunes from cards, and writing with planchette. All great nonsense of course, or I used to think it was, but really *very* entertaining. You know, you do get tired of knitting, and the libraries always seem to have so many books that no one can possibly want to read. So it made a change.'

Garth gave an inward groan. What had the old dear been up to, and what had she let herself in for?

Miss Sophy patted his arm.

'Dear boy, you looked so like your grandfather then. And I don't suppose he would have approved, but it has all turned out so well. The very first time I met Miss Perry she was telling all our fortunes with coffee grounds, and she said I had just had a great break in my life. Not that there was anything very surprising about that, because of course Mrs. Holford knew all about Miss Johnson having to leave me, and I daresay she had mentioned it.'

Garth burst out laughing. Aunt Sophy had a shrewd streak which sometimes showed quite unexpectedly. He said,

'I daresay she had. Well, what happened next?'

'The next evening she had the cards out. She told Mrs. Holford that she would be in some anxiety about a relation before long. And that came true, because a cousin's son was missing for three weeks—but he turned up again all right, I am glad to say.'

'And what did she tell you?'

'That is the marvellous part. She told me I was going to meet someone who would make the greatest difference in my life, and within twenty-four hours I had met Miss Brown.'

'How?' said Garth.

'*How?*'

'How did you meet her?'

'I think Miss Perry introduced us,' said Miss Fell. 'And oh, my dear boy, you can't think what a difference she has made! She is so efficient—such a wonderful manager. And so musical. You know how devoted I am to music. She plays the church organ for us, and she is a very fine pianist. She sings delightfully too.'

'You don't find her gloomy?'

Miss Fell had a startled look.

'Oh, *no*. Oh, I know what you mean, but we have all had a very severe shock. You may have seen something about it in the papers. Mr. Harsch—such a nice man, and very musical too—was found dead in the church only the day before yesterday. I am afraid—well, I am afraid that he shot himself. It has upset and distressed us all very much.' She slipped a hand inside his arm and kept it there. 'If anything could make me more glad to see you than I always am, it would be this distressing affair, because the inquest is to-morrow and it would be a great support to have you with me.'

'Do you mean that you are obliged to go?'

The blue eyes were round and troubled.

'Oh, yes, my dear. You see, I heard the shot.'

CHAPTER FIVE

He looked back on the evening afterwards and wondered about it. Just how dense had he been? Just where had he failed in the uptake? To what extent had he been oblivious of that faint current stirring beneath a surface calm? To what extent had he been misled? It was very hard to say. The calm upon the surface was complete. For the time there was no more talk of Michael Harsch. Miss Brown dispensed coffee, and then sat down to the piano to play the classical music upon which Miss Fell's taste had been formed. She played extremely well—Scarlatti, Haydn, Mozart, and Beethoven. Nothing more modern than that.

Aunt Sophy kept up a desultory flow of conversation, interrupting it to listen to a favourite passage and then going on again. She had changed into stiff black satin, with a velvet ribbon tied in a little bow under her third chin, and a diamond brooch catching a piece of Honiton lace across the billowy expanse of her bosom. As long as he could remember she had dressed like that in the evening. There was something very reassuring about it. Europe might go up in flames and the pillars of the world be shaken, but the Rectory drawing-room, the Rectory customs, Aunt Sophy and her fal-lals, were consolingly permanent. The windows stood open to the warm evening air, and the scent of the garden entered with it. Aunt Sophy's voice came and went through the music.

'Dr. Meade is a great loss. Dr. Edwards is very nice, but he cannot be expected to take the same interest. He lives at Oak Cottage, and his wife is an invalid. The new Rector has Miss Jones's house. And you will remember the Miss Doncasters. They are still at Pennycott, but Mary Anne is quite an invalid now—she never goes out. There is a Mrs. Mottram at the Haven, a widow with a little girl of five—very pretty and nice, but not musical. If it were not for that, I really think—but of course we mustn't gossip, must we?'

'Why mustn't we?' said Garth, laughing.

Miss Sophy bridled.

'Well, my dear, these things get about so. But of course I don't mean anything in the least scandalous—far from it. It would, in fact, be a most delightful match for both of them. And so nice to have a lady in Meadowcroft again. One's next-door neighbour always does seem a little nearer than the others.'

He remembered sitting astride the dividing wall under the sweeping branches of a copper beech and pulling Janice Meade up beside him, little and light, to be out of the way when callers came, especially the Miss Doncasters. It seemed a long time ago. He said quickly.

'Who did you say was in Meadowcroft?'

'Oh, Mr. Everton. That is who I was talking about. I think he admires Mrs. Mottram very much, though it is a pity she is not musical. He has a charming baritone voice, and a wife should be able to play her husband's accompaniments—don't you think so?'

'Has he got a wife?'

She leaned forward to tap his arm reprovingly.

'My dear boy, *of course not!* I was just telling you how much he admired Mrs. Mottram. I happen to know for a fact that he has had tea with her three Sundays running. And it would be such a good thing for her—such a nice man, and a delightful neighbour. He often drops in to sing duets with Miss Brown, or to have his accompaniments played. We have quite a musical circle now. And then he is so active in the village. He gives a prize for the best allotment. They have turned all those fields on the other side of the Bourne into allotments. And he is quite a poultry expert. We are registered with him for eggs, and so is the Rector. I believe he was in business, but he had a breakdown and is obliged to lead an open-air life.'

'What is Janice Meade like now she is grown up?'

'Oh, my dear boy, you must meet her.'

'What has she turned out like?'

Miss Sophy considered.

'Well, I'm so fond of her—don't you think it is very difficult to describe people when you are fond of them? I don't suppose you would think she was pretty, but'—she brightened—'she has very fine eyes.'

Miss Brown, unexpectedly graceful in black lace, sat at the piano and swept the keyboard with a series of flashing runs.

Miss Fell nodded approvingly.

'That is what I call brilliant execution,' she said. Then, raising her voice a little, 'Pray go on, Medora.'

The well-shaped hands were lifted from the keyboard for a

moment, then they came down upon it in the full, soft chords of one of Schumann's Night Pieces. The room filled with the sound, deep, mysterious and intense. Night in a black forest, utterly dark, utterly dim, utterly withdrawn. Only so much light as a dead reflecting moon could lend to make the darkness visible.

After a moment Miss Sophy prattled on again.

'She plays so well, does she not? And quite without music. It is the modern way of course. We used never to be allowed to take our eyes from the book.'

Garth said abruptly, 'What did you call her?'

'Oh, Medora. So charmingly uncommon.'

'I never heard it before. Is it English?' And yet the moment he had spoken he knew that if he had never heard the name, he had seen it somewhere. He thought it was a long time ago.

Miss Sophy looked surprised.

'It is unusual of course, but I like it better than Fedora, which I always think has rather an operatic sound. And then there is Eudora, in that delightful book of Miss Yonge's, *The Pillars of the House*. It means a happy gift—and I don't know what Medora means, but I am sure she has been a happy gift to me.'

From where they sat at the far side of the long drawing-room it was impossible that what they said should reach Miss Brown, yet Garth instinctively lowered his voice.

'She doesn't look at all happy.'

Miss Sophy nodded.

'No, my dear boy. But I told you, we have all had a severe shock.'

'Is there any particular reason why it should be a severe shock to her?'

'Oh, dear me—I hope not. But they were great friends—their music, you know, and both playing the organ. He used often to drop in here for a few minutes on his way to the church, and sometimes afterwards.'

'Did you see him the night he—died?' For the life of him he couldn't help that little pause.

Miss Sophy shook her head.

'Oh, no—he went straight to the church. But then he often did that. You know it is really a very fine instrument, and since we have had electricity in the village it is not necessary to have anyone to blow. So tiresome, I used to think. I remember Tommy Entwhistle used to make the most horrible faces over it, and your grandfather put in Rose Stevens instead. It was considered a great innovation, but of course girls are much steadier than boys.'

Garth laughed and said,

'Oh, much! Who is sexton now?'

'Old Bush died a couple of years ago, but he had not really been up to the work for a long time. Frederick used to help him, and of course he got the post.'

'He hasn't been called up?'

'Oh, no—he must be nearly fifty. He was all through the last war, you know. I used to wonder how old Bush felt about it, because though of course the children were born over here, he and his wife were both Germans, and they never thought about being naturalized—people in their position didn't—but they started spelling their name the English way almost at once.'

Something like a mild electric shock set the palms of his hands tingling.

'I'd forgotten,' he said.

'I do not suppose you ever knew, my dear. But the name was Busch, with an sch—Adolf Busch. And of course Adolf sounds terrible now, but there wasn't anything worse about it than any other German name then. Still, your grandfather advised his writing it Adolphus in the English way, and he christened all the children himself with proper English names. The two elder boys were killed in the last war. Frederick was the third, and when he was seventeen he was second footman to Sir James Talbot at Wrestinglea. Well, a very curious thing happened not very long before the war broke out—he was approached by German agents. You know, all sorts of people used to come down to Wrestinglea —soldiers, politicians, newspaper men. And they wanted him to listen to what was said whilst he was waiting at table and write it down for them. They offered him quite a lot of money, but of course he said no. He came and told your grandfather all about it, and your grandfather told me. I remember what impressed him so much was the fact that the German Foreign Office should have kept track of a humble family like this. They must have been in England for quite twenty-five years, but the Wilhelmstrasse knew where to find them, and knew that Frederick was in service in a house where he could pick up just the kind of news they wanted. I remember your grandfather walking up and down the room and saying that it disclosed a very alarming state of affairs.'

'He wasn't far wrong, was he? Well, well—and Frederick is sexton. I must look him up. Let me see—he married one of the Pincott girls, didn't he?'

Miss Sophy began at once to tell him all about the Pincotts. As there were a round dozen of them, it took some time.

At ten o'clock they went to bed, Miss Brown informing him that he could have a bath, but that he must be careful not to take more than five inches of water. Again that absurd resentment flared. But he had the bath, and getting into bed, fell immediately and rather unexpectedly into a dreamless sleep.

He awoke some time later with a start. The moon was up. The two windows, which had been empty and dark when he had drawn the curtains back before getting into bed, now framed a silvered landscape. The night air was so warm as to give the impression that it was the light that was warming it. He got up and stood at the nearer window, looking out. There was nothing that could be called a breeze—only that warm air just moving against his cheek. Below him the lawn and Miss Sophy's border lay under the moon. To the right the churchyard wall rose grey behind the flowers until it melted into the shadow of great trees—copper beech, green beech, and chestnut. The shadow deepened away to the left. More trees, with the moon throwing a black image of each on the blanched grass. Lilacs, a tall red thorn, a cedar nearly as old as the church, a single heavy elm—he could still name every tree, though with the light behind them they showed only in silhouette, all detail lost.

He had stood there for perhaps ten minutes, when he saw that something was moving in the shadows—something, or someone. It moved where the shade was deepest. Only the fact that it moved made it visible. But there was no point at which the shadow extended to the house. The moment was bound to come when there would be an alternative of retreat or emergence. Garth watched with a good deal of interest to see which it would be.

The moment arrived, and he saw Miss Medora Brown cross the barrier and stand quite plainly revealed. She wore the long black dress she had worn at dinner, covering her to the feet, to the wrists. Over her head she had tied a black lace scarf, the ends brought round to cover her to the chin. Only her hands showed white in the drowning light—her hands, and her lifted face.

Instinctively Garth drew back, and then stood wondering whether his own movement might not have given him away as hers had done.

She stood for a moment, and then walked quickly and noiselessly forward until she was lost from view. He had by now no need to watch her. He knew very well that she would come in, as he had so often done himself, by the glass door of his grandfather's study. Only there was a trick with that door. If your hand wasn't perfectly steady, if there was the least interruption in the slow, smooth pressure which opened it, it creaked on you. He knew now that Miss Brown's hand had not been steady, and that it was this creak which had waked him. He listened for it, and heard it again. Wherever she had been, she had been quick about it. She couldn't have been out of the house for more than a quarter of an hour. Well, the show was over and she was back.

He got into bed and lay down. Just as his head touched the pillow, there zigzagged into his mind the recollection of where he had come across the name of Medora.

In a poem—in the title of a poem. One of those long-winded tales in verse which had been the fashion when the nineteenth century was young. He hadn't the slightest idea what it was about, or who it was by, but he could see the title as plainly as he had ever seen anything in his life:

'Conrad and Medora'

He jerked up on an elbow and whistled softly. Whether Medora was English or not, there was no doubt at all about Conrad. Conrad was German.

CHAPTER SIX

At half past six next morning Garth yawned, stretched, and jumped out of bed. There seemed to have been no interval at all. He had remembered about Conrad and Medora, he had looked at his watch and found the time to be half an hour after midnight, and then he had gone to sleep and slept without a break and without a dream. Funny, because sometimes he dreamed like mad.

Well, now he thought he would get up. The maids had no vice of early rising. Mabel had been house-parlour-maid in Aunt Sophy's mother's time, and goodness knew how long ago that was. Florence had cooked the Rectory meals for thirty years. Miss Sophy would get her early morning tea at eight, but very little else would be done before breakfast. He thought he would rather like to walk out into the garden before anyone was up. He felt some curiosity about Miss Brown's nocturnal excursion, and some inclination to prospect.

He emerged from his room upon a well blacked-out passage and switched on the light at the head of the stairs. He had no mind to rouse the household and provide Bourne with another inquest by taking a header into the stone-flagged hall. The light came on, imparting a raffish air to its respectable surroundings. After the early morning sunlight this synthetic product was all wrong, all out of key. It gave the sedate Rectory stair a horrid up-all-night appearance.

He was nearly at the bottom, when something sparkled at him from the heavily patterned carpet. He bent, and pricked his finger on a sliver of glass. As he dropped it into the wastepaper basket in the study he wondered vaguely who had been breaking what. Then he let himself out by the glass door, and was pleased to observe that his hand had lost neither its cunning nor its steadiness. There was no creak of the hinge for him. He stepped on to the dew-drenched lawn and looked down the garden, as he had looked from his bedroom window in the night. It was the same scene, but whereas then everything had been dreaming under the moon, now it was all enchantingly awake, the border jewel bright, the old wall behind it warm and mossy in the early sunshine. Away to the left the shadows lay across the grass, but now it was the sun that laid them there, and the trees themselves were full of colour and light—the cedar with its cones like a flock of little owls sitting all in rows on the great layered branches, the thorn almost as red with berries as in its blooming time. That was where he had first caught sight of Miss Brown last night—not as Miss Brown, but as something that moved in the shadow of the thorn.

He crossed the garden until he came to the place, and stood there frowning. Perhaps Miss Brown had been unable to sleep—perhaps she had come out to take the air. The answer to that was that he didn't think so. They had gone to their rooms at ten o'clock. If Miss Brown had made any effort to sleep, she would not still have been wearing a black lace dinner-dress at half-past twelve.

Two or three yards beyond the thorn tree the grey wall at the foot of the garden broke into an arch filled by a door of weathered oak. He lifted the latch, swung the door inwards, and walked out into the narrow Cut which ran at the back of all these houses facing on to the green. It had on one side of it a long, continuous wall which joined one wall of the churchyard at right angles about twenty feet farther on, and on the other a tall mixed hedge. Between wall and hedge there was just room for two people to walk abreast, or for a boy to ride a bicycle. It was in fact chiefly used by errand boys, who found it a short cut. On the right it skirted the churchyard and came out in the middle of the village. On the left it followed the wall until it ended, and then wandered out to join the road which bordered the Green. Five houses shared the wall. Each had a door which gave upon the Cut.

Perhaps Miss Brown had gone out at one door and in at another. Perhaps she had been to call upon one of her neighbours. Thanks to Miss Sophy's flow of conversation he could name them all—Mr. Everton, the retired business man and poultry expert, in Meadowcroft; the new Rector, in The Lilacs vice Miss Jones; the Miss Doncasters next door in Pennycott; Mrs. Mottram in The Haven; and Dr. Edwards and his wife at Oak Cottage. Not at all a probable lot, with the exception of Mr. Everton, who might for all he knew be in the habit of sitting up till midnight and making assignations with gloomy ladies in evening dress. Hang it all, you couldn't have much of an assignation inside of ten minutes, which was really all you could give it, allowing for crossing the garden twice. There certainly wasn't more than a quarter of an hour between the creak that had waked him up and the creak that had signalled Miss Brown's return.

He moved a step or two, and for the second time his eye was caught by something glinting under the light. This time he had no need to prick his finger. The sun slanted across the hedge and dazzled upon broken glass—quite a lot of it. Nothing in the least mysterious about how it came there. Quite obviously the milk boy had been careless and let a bottle fall. The base had rolled under the hedge and was still sticky with milk.

Garth looked at the splinters on the ground, and thought about the splinter on the Rectory stair. He thought Miss Brown had picked it up on the hem of her black lace skirt and dropped it again as the lace dipped and brushed the carpet on her way upstairs.

Well, it wasn't really his business—or wouldn't have been if it were not for Aunt Sophy. As it was, it gave him a feeling of insecurity. He didn't like the way in which the old dear had come by Miss Medora Brown. Coffee grounds and cards are not really a substitute for first-class references. He wondered to what extent Aunt Sophy had been carried away, and whether she had considered the question of references at all.

He walked slowly past the back door into Meadowcroft, and wondered whether Miss Brown had passed through it last night. When he reached the boundary wall of The Lilacs he turned back again.

He was within a couple of yards of the open Rectory door, and had paused for another look at the litter of glass, when without any warning a voice went off in his ear.

"Coo! That's a smash!' it said. 'Not 'arf!'

Swinging round, he found himself looking down at a leggy boy of twelve, his grey flannel shorts half way up his thighs, and his sleeves half way up to the elbow. He might have been stretched, or the clothes might have shrunk. How much longer they would hold together was conjectural.

'Hullo!' said Garth. "Who are you?'

'Cyril Bond. I'm a 'vacuee. That's my billet.' He jerked an elbow in the direction of Meadowcroft, and added, 'Got hens in there, we have. They don't 'arf lay. I get a negg for my breakfast twice a week, I do.'

'And you made this horrible mess?'

'Naow!' The shrill tone was scornful. 'That's a milk bottle, that is. I don't tike the milk round. That's Tommy Pincott's doing, that is. He done it yesterdye. He's fourteen and left school. He works for his uncle, and I reckon he'll cop it from him.'

Garth stepped over the glass and went in through the Rectory door. The shrill voice followed him.

'You're stying in there? Your nyme's Albany? Come last night, didn't you?'

'You seem to know all about it.'

'Course I do!'

The boy's face brightened. He had fair hair, grey eyes, a fresh colour, and a deceptive appearance of cleanliness. He jerked a thumb in the direction of the church.

'There was a man shot in there a coupler days ago—right in the church. There's going to be a ninquest todye and none of us boys won't be let go to it. Coo—I'd like to go to a ninquest!'

'Why?'

The boy scuffed with his feet among the broken bits of glass.

'I dunno. Miss Marsden, our teacher, she said any boy that went on talking about this gentleman that was shot, she'd keep him in. That's what comes of having wimmen brought in to teach you. My dad doesn't hold with it. He says they'll all be too big for their boots after the war. D'you reckon that's right?'

'I shouldn't wonder,' said Garth, laughing.

He prepared to shut the door, but the boy came edging over the threshold.

'Do you reckon the gentleman shot himself?' he said.

'I don't know.'

'I reckon it's a funny place to shoot yourself, don't you—right in a church?'

Garth nodded.

Cyril kicked at a stone with the toe of a disintegrating shoe. His voice was shriller than ever.

'Fancy going right into a dark church to shoot yourself, when you might do it comfortable at 'ome! It don't seem likely—that's wot I sye.'

'Does anyone else say it?'

Cyril kicked again. The stone went into the ditch.

'I dunno. What do you reckon about it, mister?'

'It's out of my reckoning,' said Garth in rather an odd tone of voice. Then he said, 'Cut along now!' and shut the door.

CHAPTER SEVEN

He strolled into the churchyard after breakfast, and found Bush digging the grave which would be wanted to-morrow for Michael Harsch. Frederick wore his usual air of conscientious gloom. He was a fine broad-shouldered man, and must have cut a personable figure in his footman days, but very few people had ever seen him smile. Some said it was just his gravedigger's pride—'And say what you like, none of us wouldn't fancy having jokes cracked over our coffins.' Others said that if they had to live with Susannah Pincott and eat her cooking, maybe they wouldn't smile either.

Garth said, 'Hullo, Bush!' and got a 'Morning, Mr. Garth,' after which the digging proceeded.

'You're all well, I hope?'

Bush lifted a heavy spadeful.

'As well as anyone's got the right to expect.'

'I suppose this is for Mr. Harsch?' Garth indicated the grave. This time he only got a nod.

'Did you know him? I suppose you did. Was he the sort of chap to commit suicide? Seems an odd place to do it in, the church.'

Bush nodded again and threw out another spadeful. Then he said soberly,

'I doubt there's two kinds of chaps—anyone might do it if they was to be pushed hard enough.'

'What makes you think that Mr. Harsch was being pushed?'

Bush straightened up.

'Begging your pardon, I never said no such thing. Anyone might get pushed so as they couldn't keep a hold of themselves. I seen a car run away down Penny Hill when I was a boy—something gone wrong with the brakes, they said—come an almighty smash against a big ellum in the hedge. I reckon that's just about what happens when a chap takes his own life—brakes don't work and he gets out of control same as a car.' He bent to his digging again. There was no more to be got from him.

The inquest was set for half past eleven in the village hall. Garth walked down between Miss Sophy and Miss Brown, both wearing black. Miss Brown was silent, Miss Sophy tremulously conversational. She kept a hand on his arm, and clutched him hard as they entered.

Rows of wooden chairs, a narrow aisle up the middle, a platform at the far end, an all-pervading smell of varnish. Memories of village concerts, private theatricals, and jumble sales crowded in upon Garth. To the right of that platform he had sat at the upright piano presented by Miss Doncaster and played his first solo, *The Merry Peasant*, with leaden fingers and a growing conviction that he was going to be sick. Behind the very table which occupied the centre of the stage his grandfather's impressive figure had towered as he presented prizes to the more virtuous of the village youth. Where the narrow lane between the chairs now stretched tables groaning with buns had been set for the Christmas Sunday school treat. There was something rather horrid about revisiting the scene for an inquest. One thing there was in common between those past occasions and this gloomy one, the hall was full. Only the two front rows remained unoccupied, but they were farther removed from the platform than they would have been at a concert, and on the right-hand side of the space thus left clear a dozen chairs placed sideways in two rows accommodated nine embarrassed-looking men and three women.

The Coroner, who might have sat alone, had chosen to call a jury—half a dozen farmers; Mr. Simmonds the butcher; the landlord of the Black Bull; the baker; Mrs. Cripps of the general shop; Mrs. Mottram, a pretty fair-haired woman with a rolling blue eye; and the elder of the two Miss Doncasters, Miss Lucy Ellen, very thin, upright and grey, with an air of considering that her gentility was being contaminated.

On the left a couple of reporters and a small, efficient elderly man whose face Garth found familiar without being able to place it, until it came to him that he had seen it bent over papers in Sir George's office. Obviously Sir George was not leaving the reporting of the evidence to chance.

Miss Sophy had led the way to the second row of chairs upon the right. At the far end of the corresponding row on the left there sat a middle-aged gentleman in tweeds which would have looked better if they had not looked quite so new; for the rest a very genial gentleman, not so stout as to be called fat, but a well rounded testimonial to the efficiency of Lord Woolton's food control. He had a bald patch on the top of his head, a pair of ruddy cheeks, and a roving eye. It lighted upon Miss Sophy, and he immediately beamed and bowed.

Miss Sophy's grip upon Garth's arm tightened. She said 'Mr. Everton!' in a fooffly whisper, and returned the bow with a hint of discreet reproof. She had never been to an inquest before, but it felt a good deal like being in church, and though it might be permissible to recognize your friends, she did not feel that it was at all the thing to smile at them. Mrs. Mottram now—she really shouldn't be looking about her like that. To be on a jury was a most responsible and sobering position, and she was wearing that rather bright blue dress which she had bought when she went out of mourning. And turquoise ear-rings—really most unsuitable, though no doubt very becoming. Lucy Ellen Doncaster looked most disapproving, and no wonder. She was wearing the coat and skirt in which she always attended funerals. It must be quite twenty years old, but it was *suitable.* Unfortunately her hat, of approximately the same date, had tipped sideways in spite of the two long jet-headed pins with which it was transfixed. But hatpins are of very little use unless you have plenty of hair, and Lucy Ellen, who had never had much, was now decidedly thin on the top. Even at this solemn moment Miss Sophy heaved a sight of thankfulness at the thought of her own thick, snowy curls. 'After all, there is nothing like a good head of hair,' she concluded.

The room, except for the two front rows, was now packed. All at once a party of three came up the central aisle—a man with an angry crooked face and black untidy hair, a woman in whom the same odd features were blurred by plumpness and timidity, and Janice Meade. Garth would have known her anywhere. She really hadn't altered a bit, and she didn't look very much older—the little pointed face, the way her hair grew, the very bright eyes. She followed the Madocs up to the second row on the left. Mr. Madoc stood aside. Miss Madoc went forward in a hesitating manner and sat down by Mr. Everton. Janice followed her. The Professor jerked the outside chair as far as possible away from them, threw himself into it, and crossed his legs, right over left. After which he dragged a horrid-looking handkerchief from his pocket and mopped a brow which had every appearance of being heated by some inner conflagration.

Garth got all this as an impression. He wasn't really looking at

Madoc. His eyes were on Janice, and he was thinking how nice and cool she looked in a white tennis frock and a sort of garden hat with a black ribbon round it, whilst Miss Madoc weltered in a heavy grey coat and skirt which dipped and bulged, and Madoc wore his aged flannel trousers, his open-necked shirt, and disreputable green jacket as if they had been forced upon him by the Gestapo.

Garth's attention came to him and remained. The man's whole being was a protest. Waves of angry resentment spread out all round him in the most disconcerting manner. He appeared to Garth to be one of those unhappy persons to whom civilization is at once abhorrent and necessary. As a scientist he required its order. As a man he rebelled, and detested its restraints.

The Coroner came in and took his seat to the ancient formula of 'Oh yes—oh yes—oh yes!' Immemorial ritual, immemorial routine, and the little grey man with ruffled hair and a lagging step. But the eyes behind his tortoise-shell-rimmed glasses were steady and sharp. He called the medical evidence first. A hollow-cheeked elderly man recited it in a rapid undertone. Garth gathered that the bullet had entered the right temple, that death must have been instantaneous, that everything pointed to the weapon having been actually in contact with the head.

Janice wreathed her hands together in her lap and tried not to listen. She kept telling herself that these things had nothing to do with Mr. Harsch. He had been here, and he had been her friend, but now he wasn't here, and she hoped he was with his daughter and his wife. All this about bullets, and weapons, and the violence that went with them had nothing to do with him at all.

The police surgeon stood down, and a police inspector took his place. He had been called to Bourne church at 12.20 a.m. on Wednesday 9th September. The call was put through by the sexton, Frederick Bush. He found Bush and Miss Janice Meade in the church when he arrived. He also found the body of Mr. Harsch, lying on the floor in front of the organ. The weapon lay close to his right hand. The attitude of the body was compatible with the shot having been fired whilst Mr. Harsch was sitting at the keyboard. There was no disturbance, and no sign of a struggle. The organist's bench had not been moved. The body appeared to have slipped from it to the ground.

The moment which Janice had been dreading had arrived. She heard her name—'Call Janice Meade!' She had to squeeze past Evan Madoc, who merely scowled and slewed himself a little sideways without uncrossing his legs. The thought that he was the rudest man in the world passed automatically through her mind.

She went up the two steps on to the platform. When she had been sworn, someone gave her a chair and she sat down.

'Now, Miss Meade—will you tell us in your own words just what happened on Tuesday evening. I believe you were Mr. Harsch's secretary?'

'I am Mr. Madoc's secretary. I was very pleased to do anything I could for Mr. Harsch.'

'You have been an inmate of the same household—for how long?'

'For a year.'

'You were on friendly terms with Mr. Harsch?'

Her colour flew up, her eyes dazzled. She said, 'Oh, yes——' on a soft, unsteady breath.

'Well, Miss Meade, will you tell us about Tuesday evening.'

Garth, watching her, saw her right hand take hold of her left and hold it tightly. When she spoke her voice was low and clear.

'Mr. Harsch came in from his laboratory at a little before six. He had finished something that he had been working at for a long time. I gave him some tea, and we sat talking for a little. He put through a telephone call to London, and then we talked again.'

'Was this call in connection with the work which he had finished?'

'Yes. He made an appointment with someone to come down next day.'

'It was a business appointment?'

'Yes.'

'What happened after that?'

'We went on talking.'

'Will you tell us what you were talking about.'

'About his work—and about his daughter. He had a daughter of about my age. She—died in Germany. We talked until nearly supper time. After supper he said he would go out. He always took a walk in the evening unless it was pouring with rain.'

'Did he speak of going to the church?'

'Yes—he said he would go down and play the organ and blow the clouds away.'

'What did you understand him to mean by that?'

She faltered a little as she said,

'We had been talking about his daughter.'

'Her death was a tragic one?'

'I think so. But he never spoke of that—only about how pretty she was, and how gay, and how much everyone loved her.'

'Go on, Miss Meade. When did you become anxious about Mr. Harsch?'

35

'He was usually back by ten o'clock, but I didn't get worried until much later than that, because he sometimes dropped in to see Miss Fell or Mr. Everton. But when he wasn't home by half past eleven I was really frightened. Mr. and Miss Madoc had gone to bed, so I took a torch and went down to the church. The door was locked and everything was dark. I went to Mr. Bush's house and woke him up. He brought his key and opened the door—and we found Mr. Harsch.' The last words were very low. She tried to keep them steady.

The Coroner said,

'I see. Very distressing for you, Miss Meade. Did you touch anything—move anything?'

Still in that very low voice she said,

'I took his hand. Mr. Bush held the torch, and we saw that he was dead.'

'His hand was cold?'

'Yes, quite cold.'

'Did you see the pistol?'

'Yes.'

'How was it lying?'

'About six inches from his right hand.'

'Did either of you touch it?'

'Oh, no.'

'Miss Meade—you said at the beginning of your evidence that you had a long talk with Mr. Harsch. Did he seem depressed?'

She hesitated for a moment, and then said,

'No—I don't think so.'

'You said that he had just finished some work upon which he had been engaged for a long time. Did he say anything to the effect that his work was done—anything that could bear that construction?'

'No—not like that. He said it was like having a child—you brought it into the world, and then you had to let other people bring it up.'

'He did say that?'

'Yes.'

'And then you talked about his daughter who had died in tragic circumstances?'

Janice lifted her head.

'Yes. But he didn't talk about the sad part. He said that was all gone and not to be remembered any more.'

The slightly foreign turn of the sentence gave it the effect of a quotation.

The Coroner leaned forward.

'Did it occur to you at the time, or has it occured to you since, that Mr. Harsch had any thought of taking his own life?'

A bright colour came into Janice's face. She said very clearly indeed,

'Oh, *no*—he wouldn't!'

'Have you any reason for saying that?'

'Yes. He talked of working with Mr. Madoc—he asked me if I would help him if he decided to do that. And he rang up to make an appointment for next day with a very busy man. He was very punctilious, and considerate for other people's time and—and feelings. He would never have made that appointment if he hadn't been meaning to keep it.'

The Coroner looked at her for a moment. Then he said.

'The pistol you found lying beside Mr. Harsch—had you ever seen it before?'

'Oh, no.'

'Did you know that he possessed a pistol?'

'No.'

'You never saw one in his possession?'

'No.'

'Or in the house?'

'Oh, no.'

'Thank you, Miss Meade.' He sat back in his chair and said, 'Call Mr. Madoc!'

Janice went back to her seat. This time she did not have to brush past the Professor, because he was already striding up the aisle. By the time she was once more facing the platform Mr. Madoc was refusing to be sworn. The Coroner was looking at him in a detached manner but with a certain interest, and the village was frankly agog.

'You are an agnostic?'

No question could have led more perfectly into Mr. Madoc's hand. In his best lecturing voice he replied,

'Certainly not. I read my Bible. If you were to read yours you would be aware that the taking of an oath is forbidden—"Let your communication be yea, yea, and nay, nay. Whatsoever is more cometh of evil"—Matthew, v. 37.'

There was one of those pauses. The Coroner coughed, and said rather drily,

'You may affirm, if you wish it.'

Evan Madoc's chin went up.

'I have no desire to participate in any of these perfectly meaningless forms. Do you suppose they would prevent me from perjuring myself if I had made up my mind to do so?'

The Coroner straightened up.

'Am I to understand that you have some objection to answering truthfully the questions which will be put to you?'

'Certainly not. I am a truthful man—my yea is yea, and my nay nay. They will be neither more nor less so because I have or have not recited any of this gabble.'

'Mr. Madoc, I must ask you to respect the court.'

'I respect what is worthy of respect. I respect justice. Honour to whom honour if due. I have made my protest, and am now willing to affirm.'

The village listened spellbound whilst he did so. Gwen Madoc said 'Oh, dear!' under her breath.

Having completed the meaningless form, Mr. Madoc flung himself into the chair set for Janice, thrust his hands into his pockets, and leaned back. This attitude presented him in profile to the hall—black hair, nobby brow, jutting chin, and one light baleful eye. To questions as to Mr. Harsch's position in the household he replied briefly that he had lodged at Priot's End for four years. He was on the footing of a friend, but he paid his way. They met at meals, and occasionally spent the evening together. Their work was widely different, and each had his own laboratory.

This information was flung out in short, abrupt sentences, and with an air of complete indifference. He was then asked whether there had been any change in Mr. Harsch's manner on the Tuesday evening, to which he replied with the utmost brevity,

'No.'

'He was just as usual?'

'Certainly.'

'He was in the habit of going for a walk after supper?'

'He was.'

'Did he say in your hearing that he was going to play the organ?'

'I believe he mentioned it.'

'He was in the habit of playing the organ?'

'I don't know what you call a habit. He liked playing. He was a musician. He played when he had time.'

The Coroner took up one of the papers before him.

'Did Mr. Harsch possess a pistol?'

Evan Madoc took his right hand out of his pocket and hitched the arm over the back of his chair. He said with a kind of angry force,

'I haven't the slightest idea!'

'You never saw one in his possession?'

'Certainly not!'

'He might easily have had one without your knowing it?'

There was an offensive edge on Madoc's voice as he replied.

'He might have had a dozen. I am not in the habit of rummaging in other people's boxes.'

A constable laid something down upon the table and removed a paper wrapper.

'This is the pistol, Mr. Madoc. Have you ever seen it before?'

'I have not.'

'Do you know what make it is?'

'German, I should say.'

'You know something about firearms?'

'I disapprove of them. I am a pacifist. I spent some time in Germany a few years ago. I have seen pistols of this make there.'

'Mr. Harsch might have possessed such a pistol?'

'Anyone who had been in Germany might have possessed one. As to whether Michael Harsch did or did not, your guess is as good as mine.'

He was again called to order, and appeared to consider himself dismissed. His chair made a rasping noise as he pushed it back and got to his feet. The Coroner stopped him.

'I have not finished with you, Mr. Madoc. What were your relations with Mr. Harsch?'

A curious flicker passed over the crooked face. It might have been a nervous twitch, it might have been a smile. He said jerkily but without anger,

'Host and guest—fellow scientists.'

'You were on friendly terms?'

Evan Madoc straightened up. He said,

'Friendship is a big word. I do not use it lightly.'

The Coroner rapped sharply on the table.

'You are begging the question, sir. I must ask you to answer it. Was there any quarrel between you and Mr. Harsch?'

''There was no quarrel.' The words dropped slowly, almost mournfully into the silence.

'You were on friendly terms?'

Again that curious flicker, as swift and elusive as a shadow passing over water. It came, and it was gone again. Evan Madoc said,

'He was my friend.'

Mr. Madoc was dismissed. He came striding to his seat and flung himself down upon it with a complete disregard for the fact that in so doing he had driven the chair forcibly against Mrs. Thomas Pincott's knees. Her muffled exclamation of offence and pain produced no visible effect. He scowled, thrust his hands into his pockets, and once more proceeded to cross his legs, only this time it was left over right, left ankle well hitched up over right knee.

At the grating sound of the chair Garth looked sideways, and found himself presented with an excellent view of the sole of Mr. Madoc's left shoe, a well worn surface to which a Phillips rubber sole had been affixed. This too bore signs of wear. Some of the rubber had broken away. Glistening against this broken surface, a sizable splinter of glass took the light, and Garth Albany's eye. He could have jumped, and was thankful that Aunt Sophy had removed her hand from his arm in order to apply a handkerchief to her eyes.

After an interval cold reaction followed. Broken glass may be picked up anywhere. It is no good saying you don't believe in coincidences, because they happen. On the other hand even complete scepticism would have to admit that a man might walk through the Church Cut and pick up a piece of glass on his show without its having any particular significance. Against that stood the undoubted fact that the Church Cut did not lie between Prior's End and the village. It was difficult to conceive of any reason why Mr. Madoc should have passed that way. If, for instance, he had business at one of the houses served by the Cut, the more natural approach would be by the road which bordered the Green.

He had got as far as this, when he became aware that Bush was giving his evidence, sitting very upright with a hand on either knee, his natural air of melancholy intensified to the point of gloom.

It was Janice's name that had caught Garth's attention.

'Miss Janice, she came knocking at the door. I come down, and she said she was afraid of Mr. Harsch being taken ill in the church, and would I bring my key and come along over. So I come. And there he was, poor gentleman, fallen down and dead, and the pistol lying a matter of six inches from his hand like as if it had dropped when he fell. And Miss Janice, she said, "Oh, Mr. Harsch!" and took him by the hand. And I took hold of the torch and held it up, and I said, "It's no good, miss—he's dead." '

'You did not touch the pistol or move it in any way?'

'There wasn't anything touched, sir, except that Miss Janice she had hold of his hand and she put her other hand on his wrist to feel for the pulse.'

'You are sure that the pistol wasn't moved at all?'

'Yes, sir.'

The Coroner put up a hand and smoothed back his hair. Then he looked down at his notes.

'You have a key to the church?'

'Yes, sir. I'm sexton and verger.'

'What other keys are there?'

'The old Rector, he had three. The one I've got is the one my father had before me.'

'That would be one of the three?'

'No, sir. There was four keys in all. The Rector had three of them—the old Rector that was. Miss Fell, she kept one of them after the Rector died—she used to go in and do the flowers. Miss Brown that lives with her and plays the organ for the services, that's the key she uses. Mr. Harsch's key, that was the one that did use to belong to the organist, but when he was called up the Rector had it back and loaned it out to Mr. Harsch.'

'I'd just like to be sure I've got that right. There are four keys. The Rector has one, you have one, Miss Fell has one which is used by Miss Brown, and Mr. Harsch had one. Is that correct?'

'Yes, sir.'

'There is no other key?'

'No, sir.'

The Coroner leaned forward and wrote. Then he looked up again.

'Where do you keep your key, Mr. Bush?'

'Hanging on the dresser, sir.'

'It was in its place when Miss Meade came for you?'

'Yes, sir.'

'When had you last seen it before that?'

'At a quarter after ten o'clock, when I locked up for the night.'

'You saw it then?'

'Yes, sir.'

'The church door was locked when you went there with Miss Meade?'

'Yes, sir.'

'Do you know whether Mr. Harsch was in the habit of locking the door?'

'Oh, no, sir—he wasn't.'

'You know this for a fact?'

'Yes, sir. I've often been in when he was playing and stood there to listen.'

'Have you ever known him to lock the door?'

'Bush took time to think. Then he said,

'Well, sir—once or twice—if he was there late. But you wouldn't call it a habit.'

The Police Inspector was then called to testify that Mr. Harsch's key had been found in his left-hand jacket pocket. There was a very much smudged fingerprint on it. This print closely resembled the forefinger print on the pistol, which was similarly blurred, the print of the thumb and of the other three fingers being clearly those of the deceased.

'You mean that there was only the one blurred print on the key, and one blurred but four clear prints on the pistol?'

The Inspector said, 'Yes, sir,' and gave place to the spare, ascetic figure of the Rector.

'I would just like to ask you about your key to the church, Mr. Cavendish. It was in your possession on the evening of Mr. Harsch's death?'

'Certainly.'

'May I ask where you keep it?'

The Rector delved into a trouser pocket and produced a bunch of keys depending from a chain. From these he separated an ordinary-looking door-key and held it out.

The Coroner observed it.

'This is the key?'

'Yes. As you see, it is neither really old, nor exactly up-to-date. The church is an old one. The original keys were found too cumbrous to be convenient, and my predecessor had a new lock fitted to this side door. The two main doors are bolted on the inside. The old keys are no longer used.'

'So that access to the church must be by means of one of the four keys of which the sexton spoke?'

'Yes.

'Did you go down to the church at all yourself on Tuesday evening?'

'No.'

'But have you on other occasions visited the church whilst Mr. Harsch was playing the organ?'

'Oh, yes. He played very well. I have gone in to listen to him.'

'Did you ever find the door locked?'

Like Bush, the Rector paused.

'I don't think so. I cannot recall any such occasion.'

'Thank you, Mr. Cavendish, that will be all.'

As the Rector returned to his seat, the Coroner inclined his head in Miss Fell's direction, and spoke her name.

Garth took her up to the platform. She pinched his arm very hard indeed, and looked a good deal as she might have looked if she had been ascending the scaffold. Much to her relief, she was first asked about the key. The Coroner heard her answers, because he wrote them down, and Garth could hear them in the second row, so presumably the jury heard them too, but as far as the rest of the hall was concerned there was merely a fooffle.

What the Coroner wrote down was that Miss Fell kept her key in the unlocked left-hand top drawer of the bureau in the drawing-room, and that Miss Brown, who had very kindly been acting as organist, took it whenever she had occasion.

'Are you sure that your key was in the drawer on the night in question?'

Miss Fell was understood to say that it was always there unless Miss Brown had taken it.'

'When had you actually last seen it?'

Miss Fell had no idea. She had had to give up doing the flowers in the church—she really never used the key now.

She had begun to feel more at home. She remembered meeting the Coroner a good many years ago when he was a young solicitor. Ingleside. . . . Yes, that was the name—Ingleside. Her colour came back, and her voice became much more audible.

'Now, Miss Fell—you have made a statement to the effect that you heard a shot fired on this Tuesday evening. Your house is next to the church? It is in fact the Rectory?'

'Yes.'

'Where were you when you heard this shot?'

'Well, I was in the drawing-room, but I had opened the glass door into the garden and gone down the steps. There are three steps——''

''Why did you do this?'

'I wanted to smell the night-flowering stock, and I wanted to know whether Mr. Harsch was still playing the organ.'

Something like a faint rustle went over the hall. Garth thought that everyone within hearing must have moved a little.

The Coroner went on with his questions.

'You knew that Mr. Harsch was playing the organ in the church?'

'Oh, yes. It was a warm night, and the window was open behind the curtains. I can always hear the organ when the window is open—not the soft bits of course, but when anyone is using the swell.'

'How did you know that it was Mr. Harsch who was playing?'
Miss Sophy looked surprised.

'Miss Brown is the only other person who plays the organ, and she was in the drawing-room with me.'

'And was she with you when you heard the shot?'

'No—I don't think so—I think she had gone to bed. . . . Oh, yes, I know she had, because I remember putting out the light in the hall.'

'What time was it when you heard the shot? Do you remember?'

'Oh, I remember perfectly. It was a quarter to ten—because I had just looked at my watch and thought it was rather early to go to bed, but since Miss Brown had gone up I had better go too.'

'Miss Fell—when you heard this shot, did you think it came from the church?'

'Oh, no—indeed I didn't!'

'What did you think?'

Miss Sophy put her head on one side, as she always did when she was considering anything. Then she said quite briskly,

'I thought it was Mr. Giles. His fields run right down to the church on the other side of the Cut. I knew that he had been losing some of his fowls—the foxes are terrible now that there is no hunting.'

From his seat in the fourth row on the left of the hall Mr. Giles, a rubicund elderly farmer, was seen to nod emphatically, and heard to ejaculate, 'That's right!'

Miss Fell having been released, he was called to the table and asked whether he had in fact been out with his gun on Tuesday night, to which he replied that he had been up until midnight with a sick cow and much too busy to trouble his head about foxes.

Miss Brown was the last witness. She was so pale in her deep black that she might have been the chief mourner. It passed through Garth's mind to wonder whether she was. If he had ever seen a figure of tragedy in his life, he thought he saw one now. And Aunt Sophy talking about happy gifts, and how much 'My dear friend Miss Brown' had brightened her life! There seemed to have been a slip-up somewhere. Of course she might have been in love with Harsch—he supposed middle-aged people did fall in love. Somehow he didn't find the idea convincing.

He listened to the deep voice taking the oath in a kind of husky whisper. Then the Coroner was aaking her about Aunt Sophy's key.

'You were in the habit of using it?'

Still in that husky whisper, Miss Brown said,

'Yes.'

The hall had plain windows set rather high up on both sides. Through the second window on the left, the sun came slanting in, to touch the edge of Miss Brown's hat, her shoulder, the hand which hung at her side. Garth, watching attentively, saw the hand clench upon itself. There was no glove upon it. The knuckles were as white as bone. Under the brim of the black felt hat the cheek muscles were tense, the skin was bloodless. Between the heavy black hair and the curving arc of the eyebrow there was a gleam of sweat. In some apprehension he thought, 'Good lord—she's going to faint!'

The Coroner put his next question.

'Had you occasion to use this key on the day of Mr. Harsch's death?'

Miss Brown did not faint. She said,

'I used it in the morning. I went to the church to practise between eleven and twelve. I put the key back in the drawer. I did not go to the church again.'

'Thank you, Miss Brown.'

The words dismissed her. Garth saw the tense muscles relax, the clenched hand fall limp. She got up, came through the shaft of sunlight to the steps, and back to her seat. She had to pass him on the outside of the row, and Miss Sophy next to him. Unlike Mr. Madoc, Garth stood up to make way for her, stepping out into the aisle between the rows. As she went by, he heard her take a low sighing breath. To his mind, there was no doubt at all that Miss Brown was very much relieved. He thought her emotion at her release a good deal overdone—much ado about nothing in fact. She had only to answer a couple of harmless questions about Aunt Sophy's key, and she had been within an ace of passing out. Odd, because she hadn't struck him as a swooner.

He began very carefully to consider those two harmless questions, both about the key. 'You were in the habit of using it?'—Had you occasion to use it on the day of Mr. Harsch's death?'

Nothing in question number one. Everyone in the village knew she was in the habit of using Aunt Sophy's key. Yet it was immediately after this question that she began to look as if she was going to faint. Quite obviously, she had the wind up. Why? Again quite obviously, she didn't know what was coming next. She was waiting for question number two exactly as a man might wait for a bullet. But when it came it wasn't a bullet after all—just a harmless blank cartridge. So far from swooning when it hit her, she was able to get quite a lot of unsolicited information off her chest and depart heaving sighs of relief. Yet this second question in one form or another was just the one question which was bound to be put—inevitable, unescapable. He came back on the words in his own mind—'*in one form or another.*' She had known—she *must* have known—that she would be asked whether she had used the key. That was why she had the wind up. There couldn't be any other reason.

Suppose the second question had been, 'Did you take the key out of Miss Fell's drawer on that Tuesday evening?' Would her hand have unclenched and those tense muscles relaxed? He wondered. But the Coroner had asked, 'Had you occasion to use this key on the day of Mr. Harsch's death?' and Miss Brown had replied, 'I used it in the morning. I went to the church to practise between eleven and twelve. I put the key back in the drawer. I did not go to the church again.' A very comprehensive answer for a lady who looked as if she was going to swoon.

He cast his mind back to the previous evening and thought furiously—Miss Brown at the grand piano with her back to them, a Beethoven thunderstorm going on up and down the keyboard, and Aunt Sophy telling him that Eliza Pincott who married a young Braybury from Ledstow had had triplets—'So very inconvenient, but she's as proud as a peacock. But then the Pincotts are like that—everything that happens to them is just what they wanted and quite all right, except that old Ezra turned up drunk at the christening and they didn't like that. And she sent me a snapshot—just behind you there, dear boy, in the left-hand top drawer of my bureau——' Well, the snapshot was there all right, but he was prepared to stand up in any court, at any time, and take oath that the key was not. Of course that was Thursday evening and not Tuesday. Mr. Harsch had been shot on Tuesday evening. Aunt Sophy might have removed the key. Miss Brown had only sworn that she had put it back in the drawer after practising in the church between eleven and twelve on Tuesday morning.

He went on wondering furiously.

CHAPTER NINE

On the other side of the narrow aisle Janice Meade was thinking too. Her hands were folded in her lap, her head a little bent. The chairs were set so close together in the row that if she had not been so slim and lightly built, Miss Madoc's lumpy grey shoulder would have touched her on the one side and Mr. Madoc's bony one on the other. She sat between them, quite still and withdrawn. After she had given her evidence she had slipped into the quite place she kept among her thoughts. It was a place which very few people entered. She locked it against everyone except the people whom she really loved. Her father was there. Not the tired, failing man whom she had nursed so devotedly, but the father of her nursery days incomparably strong and omniscient. There was nothing he couldn't do, nothing he didn't know. When she could think of him like that, life didn't feel so lonely. She couldn't remember her mother at all, but she was there too, a lovely shadow, rather felt than seen, never any older than the miniature which had been painted when she was twenty. A few months ago she had opened the door to Mr. Harsch. He came and went. He had been sad, and now he wasn't sad any more.

There was one other person who was always there—Garth Albany. She had not looked at him yet, beyond the one glance which told her where he was sitting when she entered the hall. She knew, of course, that he was staying with Miss Sophy. Tommy Pincott had delivered the news with the milk at eight o'clock. As long as the milkman delivered and the baker called, you were sure of the village news. It was a long time since she had seen Garth—three years. She had been away each time he came. There is quite a gap between nineteen and twenty-two. Nineteen hasn't really quite put off childish things. And how she had adored him when she was a child. She had enough love to go round a dozen brothers and sisters, but there hadn't been any brothers and sisters, so she had to give it all to Garth. And all her hero-worship, and all the silly romantic dreams which must have a peg to hang on when you are in your teens. Now, of course, everything was quite different. She was twenty-two and quite grown-up. You didn't despise your old romantic dreams, but you kept them in their place. They were no part of the practical everyday life in which you lifted your eyes and looked across at Garth Albany sitting beside Miss Sophy.

Her heart turned over, because he was looking at her. Their eyes met and something happened. She didn't know what it was, because for the moment she couldn't think, she could do nothing but feel.

Afterwards she knew only too well what had happened. Garth wasn't going to be put away with childish things, or shut away in a secret place of dreams. He was most actually alive and there. He wasn't anyone's dream. He was Garth on his own, as he had always been, and if she was fool enough to fall in love with him, her folly would be its own reward—she would get hurt. She had an agonized premonition of just how much it would be possible for Garth to hurt her—and she would only have herself to thank.

Garth's eyes smiled at her for a moment. Then she was looking down again at her folded hands and the Coroner was summing up.

It was some time before she could listen coherently. Words came and went—'services rendered to science . . . deplorable persecution . . . cruel personal bereavements. . . . ' She came out of her own thoughts to take in what he was saying.

'Mr. Harsch had just completed work to which he had given all his time and energies for a number of years. There is some evidence to show that he had the feeling which would be natural in such a case. On that last evening of his life he spoke to Miss Meade of having brought a child into the world and having now to give it over to others to be brought up. He was, of course, referring to his work, which had reached the stage when it must be taken out of his hands in order that it might be usefully developed. He also talked at some length about the daughter he had lost in such a tragic manner. When he went out after supper he spoke of blowing the clouds away. I am not musical, but I understand that though music may in some circumstances have a soothing and consoling effect, it has also admittedly the power of heightening the emotions. We have no direct evidence to show the state of Mr. Harsch's mind during the time that he was in the church. We do know that he was there for a considerable time. He left Prior's End at eight, and according to Miss Fell's evidence the shot was fired at a quarter to ten. Even if he had walked quite slowly he must have reached the church not later than twenty minutes past eight. For the best part of an hour and a half, therefore, he was in the church playing the organ. As the sexton has explained, there were four keys to the church, and the Rector has told us that these keys belonged to a modern lock which had been fitted to the side door of the church, the other two doors being bolted on the inside and their keys no longer in use. Of the four keys to the side door, the Rector and the sexton had one each, Miss Fell had one which was used by Miss Brown, and Mr. Harsch had one. When Miss Meade and the sexton arrived at the church the door was locked. Behind that locked door Mr. Harsch lay dead. When his body was examined by the police the key he had used was found in his left-hand jacket pocket. I am going very fully into this question of the keys, because you will have to decide whether you are satisfied that Mr. Harsch locked himself into the church and afterwards shot himself there, or whether it is possible that some other person entered the building and shot him. The sexton's evidence is to the effect that it was not Mr. Harsch's habit to lock himself in but that he had known him do so. If a man were either in some distress of mind or contemplating suicide, it would, I think, be natural for him to guard against intrusion by locking himself in. As to the possibility that some other person entered the church and shot Mr. Harsch, you have to consider how this entry might have been effected. Either Mr. Harsch must have admitted his assailant, or one of the other three keys must have been used. If Mr. Harsch was engaged in playing the organ, the chance of anyone's attracting his attention and thus gaining admittance is a slender one. Even if it is a possibility, it leaves unanswered the question as to how this suppositious person managed to quit the church, leaving the door locked and the key in Mr. Harsch's pocket. There remains the question as to whether one of the other three keys could have been used. On this point you have the evidence of the sexton Frederick Bush, of Miss Brown, and of the Rector. Bush says his key was hanging upon the kitchen dresser when he locked up for the night at a quarter past ten. The Rector says his key was on his chain, and that he did not go down to the church at all. Miss Brown says she used Miss Fell's key in the morning, put it back in the drawer where it was kept, and did not return to the church. The Police Inspector has told us that Mr. Harsch's key shows only one blurred fingerprint, this print being similar to the blurred print left by the forefinger of a set of fingerprints found upon the pistol. These latter prints are unquestionably Mr. Harsch's own, and in the case of the other three fingers and the thumb they are perfectly clear. The blurring of the print upon the key and the printless condition of the other side of it is, I think, accounted for by the fact that the pocket in which it was found contained also a handkerchief, a matchbox, and several other small objects. In these circumstances there would probably be some friction on the surface of the key, especially when it is considered that Mr. Harsch was playing the organ, an occupation involving a considerable amount of movement. As regards the pistol, there is no evidence as to ownership. It is of a common German make. Anyone who had been in Germany might have acquired it and brought it to this country. Mr. Harsch had no licence to cover this or any other firearm. It is, however, a regrettable fact that there are a great quantity of unlicensed firearms in this country, a large number of which are either service revolvers retained by ex-servicemen after the last war or foreign weapons brought in as souvenirs.'

The Coroner paused.

'Well, ladies and gentlemen, that is the evidence. You will now retire and give it your consideration. I may say that the medical evidence will not admit of accident as a basis for your verdict. You have to decide whether Mr. Harsch shot himself, or whether someone else shot him.'

The jury got up and trooped out. They were away for less than five minutes. They returned with the verdict that Michael Harsch had shot himself while the balance of his mind was disturbed.

CHAPTER TEN

Everybody came out of the hall rather as if they were coming away from a funeral. The ceremony being over, you could recognize your friends and converse with them, but in an appropriately subdued manner. Mrs. Mottram's manner could not, unfortunately, be called subdued even by the least candid friend. She was obviously excited, and the bright blue of her dress did nothing to disarm criticism. She rushed, positively rushed—the expression is Miss Doncaster's—up to Mr. Everton and kept him talking on the steps of the hall, her light high-pitched voice making everything she said plainly audible.

Miss Doncaster's strictures were what might have been expected. She joined Miss Fell's party for the short homeward walk, and she had no hesitation in stating that she considered Mrs. Mottram's behaviour brazen.

'Pursuing—positively pursuing Mr. Everton! Asking him at the top of her voice whether she had "done it nicely"! Exactly as if she had been taking part in a play instead of discharging a solemn and most unpleasant duty! I really cannot say what I think of her behaviour!'

Miss Sophy demurred. She was partial to the young. She liked Mrs. Mottram, and she had no objection to her flirting with Mr. Everton, whom she considered very well able to look after himself. She even liked the bright blue dress, which she thought gay and becoming, though of course not suitable to an inquest. She armed herself for the fracas which always ensued when you disagreed with Lucy Ellen.

'My dear, you really have managed to say a good deal.'

50

Miss Doncaster looked down her long, thin nose.

'If I stated my true opinion——'

Miss Sophy hastened to interrupt.

'My dear, I shouldn't. And do you know, I like Mrs. Mottram. She is always so pleasant.'

Miss Doncaster snorted.

'She hasn't the brain of a hen!'

'Perhaps not—but there are such a lot of clever people, and so few pleasant ones.'

They had arrived at the gate to the village street. Whatever Miss Doncaster might have replied was lost because Miss Sophy turned to put out a hand to Janice whom she had at that moment discovered to be just behind her with Garth.

'Come to tea, my dear,' she said. 'I would ask you to lunch, but you know what it is—Florence would give notice. At least she wouldn't really, because she has been with us for so many years, but she would talk about it, and that is almost as upsetting.' She turned back again. 'You may say what you like, Lucy Ellen, but Mrs. Mottram was the only one of us to say straight away that she would take in an evacuee, though in the end she never got one.'

Irritation passed into cold rage. Miss Doncaster paled and stiffened.

'If you imagine, Sophy——' she began, but Miss Sophy made haste with an olive branch.

'Now, Lucy Ellen, don't let us quarrel. No one expects you to take in a child, with Mary Anne in the state she is. And I won't say I didn't beg Mrs. Pratt not to put one in on me, because I did, and everyone knows it. But by the time the village had taken theirs, and Mr. Everton and the Rector, there really were, quite providentially, none left over, otherwise it would have been my duty, and I hope I should have done it whether Florence and Mabel gave notice or not.'

Garth and Janice walked side by side. They had hardly spoken. The feeling of having been at a funeral hung over them. They walked in silence as far as the corner. Here the road branched off on one side to the houses which faced the Green, and on the other something not much better than a track led through a straggle of cottages and beyond them to Prior's End. They stopped and looked at each other.

'You *will* come to tea?'

'Yes.'

'Look here, come out early and we'll go for a walk. I want to talk to you—not in Aunt Sophy's drawing-room. I'll be at the stile by the Priory field at half past two. Can you make it?'

She nodded.

'I'll ask for the afternoon off.'

They stood for a moment. There was at once too much and too little to say, and none of it could be said within earshot of half the village streaming home. She turned and went quickly away from him up the track.

Garth followed Miss Sophy and Miss Doncaster, who by now were safely discussing the best method of storing onions. Far in front of them, moving with a kind of restive energy, was the tall black figure of Miss Brown. As it turned in at the Rectory gate, Miss Sophy heaved a sigh.

'Medora has felt it all very much.'

Miss Doncaster stiffened.

'I hope we have all felt it, Sophy. But some of us were brought up to control our feelings. Miss Brown makes hers too conspicuous for my taste.'

Miss Sophy's round blue eyes administered the reproach which for prudence sake she refrained from putting into words. Then, with a faint chill upon her voice, she went on talking about onions.

Arrived at the Rectory, and Miss Doncaster safely on her way to her own house and her afflicted sister, Garth grasped Miss Sophy by the arm, took her into the drawing-room, and shut the door.

'Look here,' he said, 'you remember last night?'

'My dear boy——'

He shook the arm a little.

'About the Pincott girl's triplets—which one was it—Minnie?'

'No, dear—Eliza.' She gazed at him out of eyes as blue and bewildered as a baby's.

'Well, it doesn't matter. The point is this. You sent me to get the snapshot of them out of your bureau drawer—the left-hand top drawer.'

'I don't see——'

'You will. Isn't that the drawer where you keep the church key?'

'Oh, yes.'

'Well, it wasn't there last night.'

Miss Sophy's gaze was quite untroubled.

'My dear, it must have been.'

'It wasn't.'

'But my dear—it is always there except when Miss Brown is practising, and last night——'

'She was playing the piano with her back to us—I know. And

the key wasn't in the drawer. There was nothing there except a clip of bills and the snapshot.'

Miss Sophy released herself, walked over to the bureau, and pulled out the small top drawer on the left. The clip of bills was there, the snapshot was there, and right on the top of Eliza and the triplets lay the fourth church key. Garth stared at it over her shoulder.

'It wasn't there last night, Aunt Sophy.'

She said, 'It must have been,' but she looked disturbed.

Garth put his arm round her.

'Aunt Sophy, look! If it had been there last night, I couldn't have helped seeing it. And if it had been there last night it wouldn't be on the top of the snapshot now—the snapshot would be on top. I had it out, and I put it back, and the key wasn't there. Someone has put it back since last night. That's the only way it could be on the top of the photograph. *Don't you see*?'

Something touched the blue of Miss Sophy's eyes. They didn't look blue any more, they looked frightened. She put out a hand which was not quite steady and shut the drawer. Then she said,

'There is some mistake, my dear. I think we won't talk about it any more.'

CHAPTER ELEVEN

Garth sat on the stile at the end of Prior's Wood and whistled, 'Tell it to the soldier, tell it to the sailor, tell it to the lad from the marines.' He sat with his back to the wood through which he had come by way of a green winding path known locally as Lovers' Walk, and his face to the Prior's Field, where the ruins of what had been Bourne Priory lay in picturesque disorder. There was still an arch or two of the cloisters where the monks had paced up and down with the western sunlight slanting in, but for the most part what had once been chapel, refectory, dormitories, and kitchen, was now nothing but heaped masonry with much of its stonework pilfered to make the doorsteps, the well-heads, and the tombstones of Bourne. Beyond the field and the tall hedgerow which bordered it was the lane leading to Prior's End. The roof of the house was visible amongst sheltering trees. The nearer hedge was broken by another stile. Janice would not have far to come.

Garth whistled because he didn't particulary want to think. He wanted to see Janice and hear what she had to say before he set his mind working upon such things as the glass on the Rectory stair, the glass on Evan Madoc's shoe, and the odd behaviour of Aunt Sophy's key. It is much easier to make up your mind not to think than it is to stop thinking. Behind the silly jingling words suggested by the tune he was whistling there came and went a crowd of shadowy, half-conscious speculations. It was a relief when something moved behind the hedge on the far side of the field and a moment later Janice came into view at the stile. He jumped down and went to meet her.

She had hurried a little, and there was colour in her cheeks. She wore the white frock which she had worn at the inquest, but she had taken off the hat with the black ribbon. The sun picked up the gold threads in the short brown curls. He thought again how little she had changed. The very bright eyes of no particular colour—they could look grey, or brown, or green—the little brown pointed face, the short bright curls, and the short white frock belonged as much to Janice at ten years old as to Janice at twenty-two.

He laughed, and said,

'You haven't grown a bit.'

The colour brightened against the brown of her skin. She stuck her chin in the air.

'Why should I have grown? Last time you saw me I was nineteen. People don't grow after they're nineteen.'

His eyes teased her.

'I did—I grew two inches.'

'Well, I call that extravagant! You were six foot already—another two inches was just swank. And everybody doesn't want to be yards high anyhow.'

Garth laughed. It was really very difficult to disentangle her from the little girl who had passionately wanted to be tall, and who had coloured up just like this when he teased her. Then all of a sudden the past shut down. The old safe, easy world was gone—it's rules, its pattern, its way of life. The violence which was shaking the world had reached out and shaken Bourne, for whether Michael Harsch had shot himself or had been murdered, he had most certainly died because an Austrian house-painter aspired to an empire beyond the dreams of the Caesars. He said abruptly,

'I want to talk to you, Janice. Where shall we go—up over the downs?'

'Yes, if you like.'

54

'Or we can stay here, if you don't want to get hot.' Her colour had failed, and he noticed how tired she looked—quite suddenly. 'Lots of good places to sit, if you'd rather do that.'

'Yes—I think so——'

They found a place where tumbled heaps of stone would screen them from the lane. Garth felt again how far away the past had gone. The little girl Janice had tagged about at his heels all day with as little thought of fatigue as a rabbit. He frowned and said,

'You look all in. What's the matter? Is it this Harsch business?'

She said, 'Yes. I don't mean just because he's dead.' She leaned forward, her hands locked about her knees. 'Garth—he didn't shoot himself—I know he didn't.'

He was looking at her hard.

'If you know anything, you ought to have said it at the inquest.'

'But I did——'

'You mean you just think he didn't shoot himself. You don't really know anything at all.'

This was the old superior Garth, talking down over a five years gap. She reacted at once.

'Don't be stupid—facts aren't the only things you can know. You can know people—you can know a person so well that you can be quite sure he wouldn't do that sort of thing.'

'Meaning it would be out of character for Harsch to have committed suicide?'

Her 'Yes' was very emphatic.

'But, Janice, don't you see that when something pushes a man off his balance, that's just what he does do—he acts out of character. It isn't normal for a man to pitch on his head or go down on his hands and knees, but if his physical balance is upset, it may happen. And when it comes to mental balance, well, it's the same thing, isn't it? Normal motives and restraints cease to operate, and he does the last thing he would dream of doing if he were himself.'

Janice looked at him with those very bright eyes.

'He didn't do it, Garth.'

'You're just being obstinate. You've got nothing to go on.'

'But I have. You haven't listened to me yet. I want you to listen.'

'All right—go ahead.'

She set her elbow on her knee and her chin in her hand and went on looking at him.

'Well then—it's five years since Mr. Harsch came over here. That's to say it's more than five years since his wife and daughter —died. That would have been the time to kill himself if he was

55

going to do it. The Nazis had stripped him of everything. He hadn't got anything left except his mind, and they couldn't touch that. If they didn't break it then, why should it break suddenly now? I don't care how dreadful a tragedy has been, it can't be quite the same after five years as it was at first. He told me himself that last day that in the beginning he kept going because he wanted punishment and revenge, and he thought this stuff he was working on would give it to him.'

'Harschite—yes.'

Her face changed.

'You know about that?'

'Yes—that's why I'm here. Don't tell anyone, Jan.'

The colour came brightly to her face. She nodded and went on with what she had been saying.

'But now, he said, all that had gone. He said the desire for revenge wasn't civilized. He only wanted to stop the dreadful things that were being done, and to set people free. And he spoke of working with Mr. Madoc, and asked if I would help him. You see, none of that is like a man who is off his balance. He wasn't like that at all—I lived in the house with him for a year, and I know. He was gentle, and considerate, and very patient. He was always thinking of other people. I know he wouldn't have made that appointment with——' She stopped suddenly.

Garth supplied the name she had bitten off.

'With Sir George Rendal.'

'Oh, you know that too?'

'I'm acting for him—but that's not to be known. Go on.'

'I was going to say that he would never have made that appointment and failed to keep it. I know he wouldn't.'

Garth leaned back and looked at her. No doubt about it at all, she most passionately believed what she had said. Her eyes, her lips, the colour in her cheeks, made up a picture of absolute conviction. He was, if not himself convinced, a good deal impressed. The impression was definite enough to make him give a little more weight to such things as two pieces of glass and a key. He said,

'All right, you've got that on the record. Now it's my turn. I want you to answer some question. Will you?'

'If I can.'

'You think Michael Harsch was murdered?'

She brought her hands together in a way he remembered. Her colour was all gone.

'I didn't say that.'

He gave his old impatient jerk of the shoulder.

'What else? If he didn't commit suicide, he was murdered, wasn't he? What else have you been saying, except that he was murdered?'

She looked down at her hands and said, 'Yes.' And then, in a childish, almost inaudible voice, 'It sounds so dreadful.'

It touched him in an odd kind of way, like a child saying 'I don't like it' in the middle of a thunderstorm or a bombardment. He said in a tone that was grim just because he had been moved,

'Well, murder is dreadful.'

She said, 'I know——'

'And the murderer, if it was murder, is still at large. Now let's go back to my questions. I want to know a lot of things that the Coroner didn't ask about. I want to know whether you suspect anyone.'

She took a long time to answer that. Then she said,

'No.'

He looked at her sharply.

'Tell me about the other people in the house. Tell me about Madoc. That show he put up at the inquest—was that genuine, or was it a stunt? Is he like that all the time?'

'Oh, yes—he really is. He doesn't put it on—he's like that.'

'Gosh!'

She was looking at him again. There was a sparkle behind the brown lashes.

'You'd say so if you worked for him.'

'What does he do?'

'Scolds—calls you names—things like *atomy*——'

Garth burst out laughing.

'My poor child! You can sue him for libel.'

'I shouldn't have stayed if it hadn't been for Mr. Harsch.'

Garth was grave again.

'How did they get on?'

'Oh, you couldn't quarrel with Mr. Harsch—nobody could. He always said Mr. Madoc didn't mean anything, and just went on being nice.'

'There was no quarrel between them, then?'

'Oh, no.'

'Jan, what happened on Tuesday night—after Harsch went out? Do you sit with the Madocs in the evening—were you all together?'

She said slowly, 'Miss Madoc and I were together.'

'And Madoc?'

'He hardly ever sits with us.'

'Where does he sit?'

'In the laboratory. It's really his study too. He's got his writing-table there, and all his books.'

'Did you see him at all on Tuesday evening after Harsch went out?'

'Not till he was going up to bed.'

'When was that?'

'About a quarter past ten.'

'Then you can't say for certain whether he left the house or not. You don't know that he didn't leave it?'

Her eyes changed. She looked down again.

He put a hand on her arm.

'Jan, you've got to tell me! Did he go out—do you know that he went out?'

In a whisper which yet seemed not to have enough breath to carry it, she said,

'He often goes out——'

The hand on her arm felt very strong, very warm, very insistent. She wasn't sure whether she was shaking just of herself, or whether Garth was shaking her. His voice wasn't loud, but it meant to have an answer.

'Did he go out on Tuesday night?'

Janice said, Yes.'

The hand let go, but she was still shaking. The voice went on.

'How do you know?'

'I heard the front door. You can't help hearing it.'

'It couldn't have been anyone else? Who else is there?'

'Only the housekeeper, Mrs. Williams, and she'd die before she went out in the dark. She's a townswoman really, from Cardiff. She only stays because she adores Mr. Madoc.'

So Madoc had gone out. He wondered where he had gone.

'When did he go?'

'It was just before we turned on the nine o'clock news.'

'And when did he get back?'

Her voice went away to a whisper again. She said,

'It was about ten minutes past ten.'

CHAPTER TWELVE

Silence fell between them. The sky was very blue overhead and the sun shone, a little wind went whispering through the wood.

58

Garth tilted his head and watched a small white cloud move very slowly just above the line where the downs cut the sky. All the way between, the land ran upwards in a gentle even slope. A very quiet, peaceful land. Sound of the light wind moving among summer leaves. Sound of the Bourne water slipping idly over its stones. Sound of the wind in its bordering willows. The stream ran down the farther edge of the field and then slid into the wood no more than a dozen yards from the stile.

Janice watched him, and wondered what he was thinking about. She had always liked to watch him when he was thinking, and it was quite safe, because his thoughts took hold of him and made him forget that anyone else was there. She thought he hadn't changed at all, but then of course the three years between twenty-four and twenty-seven don't make such a lot of difference to a man. The long, lightly built figure; the thin, dark face; the rather grave mouth; the marked brows with the upward kink which somehow gave him an impatient look; the eyes grey where you would have expected them to be brown; the hair so dark as to be almost black—all these things were as familiar to her as her own face in the glass. Dear and familiar too the knowledge that the grave lips could take on a most mischievous smile, and that when they did this the slant of the eyebrows no longer spelled impatience, but served to set an accent upon laughing, teasing eyes. She had thought a hundred times, 'He'll fall in love with a fair-haired girl—he's simply bound to. She'll be pink and plump, and she'll have lovely blue eyes and a most frightfully sweet temper, and they'll be very, very happy. And if you're going to be stupid enough to *mind*, you'll get hurt, and it will be your own fault and nobody else's.'

Garth brought his eyes down from the sky, and said abruptly,

'What is going on between Madoc and Miss Medora Brown?'

It was partly because she had been caught looking at him that the startled colour ran right up to the roots of her short brown curls, but he wasn't to know that. She gave a little gasp.

'Miss Brown?'

'Miss Medora Brown.'

'Is anything going on between them?'

'I'm asking you.'

Janice got hold of herself.

'What makes you think there's anything between them?'

'Well, I just do. Don't you really know anything about it?'

'No, I don't.'

'What sort of terms are they on?'

'I don't know—I've never thought about it. I suppose they

59

know each other, but she doesn't come to the house or anything like that.'

'Does he go to Aunt Sophy's?'

'He goes when there's music—sometimes, when he's not busy. He really does love music.'

'And Medora is musical.' There was a note of sarcasm in his voice.

Janice looked distressed.

'What do you mean, Garth? She plays beautifully, and she has a very good voice. There wouldn't be anything wrong if they did like each other. I've never thought about it at all.'

He leaned suddenly forward and took her by the wrist.

'Look here, Jan. Last night Aunt Sophy sent me to her left-hand top bureau drawer for a snapshot of the Pincott girl who had triplets. That's where she keeps her church key, isn't it? Well, it wasn't there. I didn't say anything because I didn't know it ought to be there, and Miss Brown didn't see anything because she was playing the piano with her back to us. Somewhere after midnight I looked out of my window and I saw Miss Brown come up the garden in the black lace dress she had worn at dinner. You can think she was just taking the air, or you can think she had slipped out into the Church Cut to meet someone.'

'But, Garth——'

'Oh, she'd been out into the Cut all right. Tommy Pincott smashed a milk bottle there yesterday. Miss Brown picked up a splinter, and I found it on the stair carpet before anyone was up this morning. I wondered who she'd been meeting, because I don't think you go out into the Cut at midnight just to enjoy your own society. And all in the middle of the inquest I found out, because when your Mr. Madoc crossed his legs I could see the sole of his boot, and he had picked up a splinter too.'

'Garth——'

'Wait a minute. When we got back from the inquest I led Aunt Sophy to her bureau drawer to show her that the key wasn't where Miss Brown had just been swearing she put it. And there it was, spang on top of the triplets. Very careless of Medora, but I expect she was feeling flustered. If she'd had the sense to put the key under the photograph she could have sworn it was there all the time, but the only way it could have got on top was the way it did get there. She put it there sometime between bedtime last night and lunchtime to-day. My own guess is that someone else has had the key since Tuesday, that she's been in a most awful stew about it, and that she went out last night to get it back. I heard the study door creak when she went, and I saw her come back. She wasn't away for more than a quarter of an hour, so she didn't go far. When I saw that Madoc had got a bit of glass stuck in his rubber sole, I thought I knew who it was she had gone to meet, and when I saw that the key was back in Aunt Sophy's drawer, I thought I knew why.'

All the blood was gone from Janice's face. He thought, 'She's like a little sunburned ghost.' A momentary amusement stirred, a momentary compunction.

She stared at him, her eyes quite round with horror, and said,

'Oh, *no*! He couldn't—he wouldn't! Why should he?'

His shoulder jerked.

'Lots of reasons. Take your choice. He had a secret pash for Medora, and he was jealous of Harsch. That's a bit fictional, but you never know, do you? Then there's the stone-cold, cast-iron fact that he is Harsch's sole executor and legatee.'

'Garth, there isn't any money. Mr. Harsch hadn't anything to leave.'

'Who's talking about money? He left Madoc all his notes, his papers, his formulae. *That means harschite*. He left it to Madoc. There might be quite a lot of money in it, or there might be just the kind of case of conscience a crank would revel in. I gather that Madoc is going to revel all right. His conscience won't let him loose what he calls "a devil's agent" upon "an already tormented world". Putting the money on one side—and I believe murder has been done for as little as twopence halfpenny in cash—don't you think the chance of restraining a number-one-size devil's agent like harschite might be too much for Madoc?'

Janice shook her head.

'He wouldn't—he wouldn't!'

'My dear, a crank will do anything. I can see Madoc enjoying martyrdom, holding the right hand in the fire in the best traditional manner. He's got zealot written all over him—you've just said yourself that he's the genuine article. Well then, he'd burn for his convictions, and it's not a very long step from that to burning the other fellow. Don't forget that the same century which produced the martyrs produced the Grand Inquisitors too. I doubt if there was anything to choose in the fanatical temper of their minds between Savonarola and Torquemada.'

'Don't—don't—it's horrible!'

'Of course it is. That's not my business. I'm here to find out whether it's true. There's more at stake than just catching a murderer, Jan. Harsch was shot immediately after he had completed his last experiment, and immediately before he could hand on the results. The margin of time is a very narrow one. He came in about six o'clock on Tuesday. He telephoned to Sir George, who was expecting a message, and made an appointment for Wednesday morning. In less than four hours he was dead. Who knew how near his work was to completion? There had been a paragraph in some of the papers. No one seems to know how it got there, but it was the usual vague gossipy puff—it didn't really give much away. The only people who knew how near he was to success were Sir George and the experts he was bringing down, but they didn't know that the last experiment had succeeded until Harsch rang up at half past six. Anyone else who knew must have been someone directly in touch with Harsch himself and deeply in his confidence. It comes back to Madoc again—a fellow scientist living in the same house, a trusted friend.'

'No—no!'

'Who else could have known?'

She beat her hands together.

'You've forgotten about the telephone.'

'You mean someone might have listened in. Well, who was there? The housekeeper—Miss Madoc—Madoc himself—you. By the way, what's the sister like? She looks harmless.'

'She is. Kind—woolly—devoted to her brother—dreadfully afraid of offending him.'

'And the housekeeper?'

'Oh, no. She's a lamb.'

'Then we're back at Madoc—unless you did it yourself. There wasn't anyone else to listen in, was there?' Then quite suddenly his jaw dropped. 'Gosh—I'd forgotten!'

There was a touch of defiant malice about the tilt of Janice's chin and the sparkle in her eyes.

'Yes, I thought you had. We've still got the old party line, and *any* one of the subscribers could have taken up its receiver and heard what Mr. Harsch was saying to Sir George Rendal.'

'That's torn it! Do you mean to say there's still only the one line, and everybody who has a telephone can tap it?'

She nodded.

'Miss Mary Anne Doncaster listens in all the time, like some people do with their wireless. She always took a passionate interest, and now she doesn't go out it's the one thing she lives for. Perhaps you think she shot Mr. Harsch.'

He said quickly, 'She doesn't go out—but do people come in?'

'Oh, yes. What do you mean?'

He said slowly,

'I think I would like to find out who saw Miss Doncaster between half past six and a quarter to ten.'

CHAPTER THIRTEEN

As he and Janice came into the hall at exactly half past four, a buzz of voices proceeding from the drawing-room informed them that Miss Sophy was having a tea-party. She had, in fact, been quite busy asking people to tea before Janice got her invitation.

They entered upon an early Edwardian tea. The table decked with an embroidered cloth, supported a massive tray and full panoply of silver. In a three-tiered metal cake stand to the right of the table plates of Royal Worcester china offered microscopic sandwiches of fish paste, lettuce, and nasturtium leaves. On the left a similar cake-basket carried out in wicker-work supported gingerbread biscuits, Marie biscuits, and rock buns—a wartime product made with egg powder. Behind the table in a large upright chair, Miss Sophy beamed upon her guests and poured out a great many cups of very weak tea. She received Garth and Janice with enthusiasm.

'There you are, my dears! And just in time for tea—though it's so weak it wouldn't matter if it did stand. Florence says we are using a great deal more than our ration, but with tea you can always put in more water and make it go round like that. I only wish you could do that with eggs—such a convenience. Garth, I don't think you've met Mr. Everton. He has the most delightful hens—they really never stop laying.'

Mr. Everton, round-cheeked and ruddy, bowed an acknowledgement and said,

'That is because I know how to manage them.'

On his other side Mrs. Mottram said plaintively,

'I wish you'd tell me how you do it.'

Before he could answer, Miss Sophy struck in.

'Mrs. Mottram—my nephew, Major Albany.'

Garth got a full roll of the blue eyes.

'Oh, I've heard so *much* about you! You will find us very stupid down here—always talking about food—but it's so difficult, isn't it? I've got six hens, but we haven't had an egg for a fortnight. Now Mr. Everton——'

Mr. Everton beamed upon her.

'You have no method. Everyone thinks that method is not necessary with the hen, and then you are surprised that the hen also is unmethodical. But I tell you it is your own fault. She is careless because you are careless. You must set her a good example. Hot mash not later than eight o'clock in the morning. Do you do that?'

Mrs. Mottram gazed at him in a soulful manner.

'Oh, *no*.'

'Then you should.'

'Should I?'

'Certainly you should. Look, I will write you out a diet-sheet, and you shall keep to it. After a fortnight you shall tell me whether you are still getting no eggs.'

They moved off together. Garth took a cup of tea and a cake-stand to Miss Doncaster, who helped herself to a nasturtium sandwich and said she disapproved of tea-parties in wartime. He sat down beside her and prepared to make himself agreeable.

'I'm so sorry to hear that Miss Mary Anne is such an invalid.'

Miss Lucy Ellen helped herself to another sandwich.

'She has every attention,' she said. 'If you ask me, I think I am the one to be pitied. If I go up and down stairs once I go up and down half a dozen times in an hour. We have turned the front bedroom into a sitting-room, and she is wheeled in there from her room. She can see everyone who is passing, and we have a great many visitors—too many, if you ask me—tracking up and down the stairs and bringing a lot of dirt into the house. Well, with only one maid, I'm the one that has to clear it up. I'm sure I never sit down. Are you here for long? I shouldn't have thought you could be spared from your duties. If you ask me, I should say that everyone was getting too much leave. There's Frederich Bush— his son was home for seven days last week.'

'And now it's me. I know—we ought to be working day and night with wet towels round our heads. We really do sometimes.'

'I don't believe it. Things would get done if you did. If you ask me, there's too much idling and sloppy talk.'

They weren't getting anywhere. He had been dragged away from Miss Mary Anne. He made a determined attempt to get back.

'You say your sister sees a lot of people. I suppose she knew Mr. Harsch?'

Miss Doncaster sniffed.

'If you could call it knowing. He was wrapped up in his experiments. I always said he'd blow himself up some day.'

Garth permitted himself a faint tinge of malice.

'But he didn't, did he?'

Miss Doncaster eyed him with the dislike which her features were so well qualified to express. She had the long, sharp nose and reddish eyes of a ferret, and the thinnest lips that Garth had ever seen. The fact that she never opened them far enough to allow anyone to see her teeth had given rise to a legend which had terrified his infancy. It was said, and was possibly still believed amongst the young of Bourne, that she had real ferret's teeth, and that if she caught you alone after dark almost anything might happen.

'I can't say I see much difference between being blown up and being shot,' she said tartly.

Garth went on trying to find out whether Miss Mary Anne could have been listening in on the party line at half past six on Tuesday and who, if anyone, had visited her that evening, but the going was too hard, he got nowhere. Miss Doncaster appeared to disapprove of him even more strongly than she had done when he was in his teens. He gave it up, and being unable to go away and leave her stranded, he found this disapproval, as it were, radiating out to embrace the entire population of Bourne. The only person for whom she had a good word was Mr. Everton, whom she conceded to be good-natured, though she immediately qualified this by remarking that the dividing line between good nature and folly was a fine one, and, 'If men knew how very foolish they appear when they allow a silly young woman to twist them round her little finger, it would at any rate preserve them from exposing themselves to ridicule in company'—the remark being concluded by one of her most pronounced sniffs.

'I expect you find Sophy very much aged,' was her next remark.

Garth was astonished at his own anger. Some of it seemed to come back with him out of that past in which he had been a frightened little boy and Aunt Sophy one of the bulwarks of his world. He said with careful politeness.

"Do you know, I don't think she's changed a bit for as long as I can remember.'

The ferret nose twitched and sniffed.

'Not very observant, are you? Breaking up—that's what Sophy is.'

After which she passed rapidly by way of the Rector's Extreme Views to the incompetence of Dr. Edwards—'His own wife being a complete invalid is hardly a recommendation'; the decline of manners and morals amongst the young, exemplified by pointed references to Mrs. Mottram; and the generally unsatisfactory condition of everybody and everything. He heard about the triplets all over again—'Most improvident.' He heard about the intransigent behaviour of young Podlington, who had married Lucy Pincott and had obtained the Military Medal, by what means Miss Doncaster was unable to say, but it had had a most unhappy effect. Returning on leave, he had accosted her in the churchyard with an unseemly 'Hullo, Miss Doncaster, how are you getting along?' And Lucy, hanging on his arm, goggling her eyes right out of her head, as if no one had ever had a medal before—'And now, if you please, he is to get a commission! I really cannot think what the world is coming to!'

At this point Miss Sophy saved his life by calling him over to be introduced to Dr. Edwards. Out of the tail of his eye he saw Janice handing Marie biscuits to Miss Doncaster and being pinned down.

When the tea-party broke up he walked home with her.

'I'd forgotten what a terror she was,' he said. 'What do you suppose she's saying about us?'

Janice, having been warned against attributing serious intentions to idle young men whose only idea was to amuse themselves, had a pretty fair idea. She blushed slightly and becomingly, and said,

'I am a village maiden whose head is being turned, and you are a gay deceiver.'

There was something about the way she said it that tickled him—a delicately dry inflection, a faint, demure sparkle. He burst out laughing and said,

'She didn't warn you!'

'She did.'

He went on laughing.

'She's a museum piece, you know.'

Rather to his surprise, Janice flared up.

'Then I wish someone would lock her up in a museum.' Her foot tapped the ground and she faced round upon him. 'It's all very well for you to laugh! You don't happen to live here—I do!' Then, before he could speak, 'Did you find out anything about Tuesday? You were talking to her for simply ages.'

'You mean she was talking to me. And I didn't find out a thing. What about you?'

Janice looked doubtful.

'I didn't like to ask questions, because they might have been the same as yours, and once she thought we were up to anything everyone in Bourne would know it too. But I did find out one person who was there on Tuesday evening, only——'

'Who was it?'

'Bush.'

'Frederick Bush?'

She nodded.

'He came in to move some shelves out of the attic and put them up in the sitting-room—you know he does all that sort of odd job. Miss Mary Anne wanted to have her Spode tea-cups where she could look at them instead of being put away in the dining-room cupboard. Miss Doncaster told me all about it because she's feeling very angry with all the Pincotts just now on account of Ernest Podlington. And as Mrs. Bush is a Pincott, of course Bush can't do anything right. She said he had taken twice as long as he need over the shelves and didn't get done until half past seven, which was very inconvenient because of supper. And Miss Mary Anne had talked too much, which was very selfish and inconsiderate of her, because she knows quite well that it gives her a bad night, and when she has a bad night, Lucy Ellen has one too. And it was all Bush's fault.'

Garth said, 'Gosh!'

CHAPTER FOURTEEN

Garth came slowly back. When he reached the village he took the shorter way and came to the bottom of the Rectory garden by way of the Church Cut. Someone had cleared away the broken glass. As he was wondering who it might have been, Cyril Bond emerged crab-like from Meadowcroft.

'I made a good job of it, I reckon. I'm a Scout, so I thought, "Suppose someone was to cut himself," and I picked it all up and put it in the ditch. I reckon that was a good deed all right.'

Garth laughed. There was something artless about the creature.

'I reckon it was.'

Cyril edged nearer.

'Was you at the inquest?'

Garth nodded.

'What did they say?' His a's were all i's, his London twang pure Stepney.

'They said it was suicide.'

'Why?'

'Because he was found in the church with the door locked and his key in his pocket.'

Cyril gave a scornful laugh.

'I reckon there was another key all right, mister.'

'Oh, yes—there are three other keys. The Rector has one, Mr. Bush the sexton has one, and Miss Brown who plays the organ has the third. They were all accounted for.'

Cyril said 'Coo!' And then, 'They don't 'arf believe things, those blokes at inquests. I could tell them something if I liked. And would they believe me? Not 'arf, they wouldn't! I'm not a clergyman, nor a sexton, nor Miss Brown.'

Garth was leaning against the wall with his hands in his pockets. He eyed the flushed cheeks and bright blue eyes and enquired,

'What could you tell them?

Cyril came closer.

'Something about a key.'

'Look here—do you mean that?'

'Coo—I don't tell lies! Scouts don't. It isn't 'arf inconvenient sometimes, but it's better in the long run, because people believe you. See?'

Garth saw.

'All right—what do you know about a key?'

The boy shuffled with his feet.

'I dunno as I'd better say.'

'If you really know anything——'

'O—w, I know all right.'

'Then I think you ought to say.'

Cyril appeared to consider this. He had obviously spent a happy hour and a half since tea-time in getting as much mud on to his person as possible. His knees were plastered, his hands and arms bedaubed, and his face well smeared. In spite of this he contrived a serious, even a dependable look.

'If I was to say it, I couldn't take it back afterwards?'

'No.'

'If anyone was to get into trouble along of what I said, and it come to a trial, I'd have to get up and say it in front of a judge?'

'Yes.'

'And have my picture in the papers? Coo! That wouldn't 'arf be something to write home about!' His face lit up with bright anticipation and then was overcast again. 'I reckon I'd get into trouble though.'

'Why?'

Cyril edged up another six inches or so.

'Well, it's like this. I'm supposed to be in by half past seven. I gets my supper and a wash, and I'm supposed to be in bed by eight. There was a heavy accent on the 'supposed'.

'But you don't always go—is that it?'

'Well, it's like this. I have my wash and I go to my room——'

'But you don't always get into bed?'

Cyril scuffed with his feet. Garth laughed again.

'All right—I see. And Tuesday was one of the nights you didn't go to bed?'

He got a look, at first deprecating but which changed to something uncommonly like a wink.

'What did you do?' said Garth.

Cyril kicked so hard as to endanger the toe of his shoe.

'I reckon I'll get into trouble,' he said.

'Probably. But I think you'd better tell me all the same. What did you do?'

There was another of those sidelong glances, and then,

'I got out of the window.'

'How did you manage that?'

Having taken the plunge, Cyril became extremely animated.

'See that window there on the side of the house? That's my room, and if you get out on the sill and hang with your hands, it ain't so far to drop on to that bit of roof that sticks out over the libery. There's a big branch of a tree comes over, and you can get a good holt of it and come along hand over hand and climb down. I've done it ever so many times and I haven't never been caught once.'

Garth considered it a very sporting effort. He knew the tree, the window, and the distance. He wasn't at all sure that he could have pulled it off at Cyril's age. He nodded and said,

'Well, you climbed down the tree. What happened after that?'

'I larked about a bit, playing Red Indians, crawling up to the house like it was a stockade and surrounding it. Coo—it wasn't 'arf exciting!'

'What sort of time was it?'

'Well, it wasn't far off a quarter to nine when I got out of the window. You can hear the church clock strike, and it had gone the quarter to.'

'All right—go on.'

'Well, after a bit it stopped being dark because of the moon coming up, so I couldn't go on playing Indians near the house in case of anyone looking out of a window and seeing me, so I thought I'd come out here and make a ambush, and if anyone come by I could play I'd scalped them.'

'And did anyone come?'

'Oh, boy—didn't they just! The lady come first—out of this door.' He laid his hand on the jamb against which Garth had been leaning.

'What lady?' He tried not to speak too quickly.

'The lady that lives with the old lady at your house—Miss Brown. You know—the lady that plays the organ in church on a Sunday. I was down in the ditch there right opposite, lying down flat, and I reckon if I'd had a bow-an-arrow I could have shot her dead. Well, she stays there with the door half open—that's when I reckon I could have shot her—and then she comes right out. And then the gentleman comes, and he says, "Where are you going?" and he says her name. It sounded awfully funny to me—something like suet.'

'Suet?'

Cyril nodded.

'You know—in a packet—Atora, like my auntie used to send me for to the grocer's.'

Garth restrained himself.

'Medora?'

'That's right! It isn't 'arf a funny kind of name. "Where are you going, Medora?" he says. I reckon I could have shot him too.'

'Yes—go on. What did she say?'

'She says it hasn't got anything to do with him, and he says oh, yes it has, and what's that she's got in her hand. And she says, "Nothing". And he says, "Oh, yes, you have, and you'll 'and it over to me! You're not using any keys to let yourself into the church to-night. If you want to listen to him playing you can stand out here, and if you want to talk to him you can do it in the day time. 'And over that there key!" '

'And did she?'

'I'll say she did! He'd got her by the arm, twisting it like, and the key fell down. And she says "Oh!" like she was going to cry and pulls her 'and away and back into your garden and shuts the door, and the gentleman he picks up the key and puts it in his pocket and goes off.'

'Which way did he go?'

An extremely dirty finger pointed in the direction of the church.

'Sure?'

'Ow, yes!'

'Who was it?' said Garth. 'Do you know?'

Cyril looked surprised.

'Course I do!'

'Who was it?'

'The one as they call the Professor.'

Here was something with a vengeance. Garth said,

'Are you sure?'

Cyril nodded emphatically.

'Coo—I wouldn't say a thing like that if I wasn't! It was him all right. Ever so angry he was—put me in mind of Boris Banks in Murder at Midnight. It was a smashing picture—he didn't 'arf carry on. You see, he'd murdered a lady——'

Garth recalled him firmly.

'Cut all that and get back to Tuesday! What makes you sure who it was you saw?'

Cyril looked obstinate and a little dashed.

'Well, mister, I seen him. I told you as how the moon was up— bright as bright it was. It was him all right. Lives in the house up at the top of the lane where the field is with the ruings. The gentleman that was shot, he lived there too.'

Garth whistled.

'Well, if you're sure, you're sure. But you mustn't say you are if you're not. It's—very important.'

Cyril nodded again.

'Coo—I know that! It was him all right—name of Madoc.'

Garth stood there a moment. Then he put a hand on Cyril's shoulder.

'While he was there—while he was talking to Miss Brown, could you hear anything else—anything from the church?'

'Only the other gentleman playing the organ.'

'You did hear that?'

'Ow, yes!'

'All right—go on. What happened after that?'

Cyril stared.

'Nothing. I went back in.'

'How do you get back?'

'Up the tree, mister, and a bit higher up—then if you crawl along, there's a branch you can get holt of that brings you down where you can swing on to the window ledge.'

Garth thought of his Aunt Sophy's feelings. He remembered performances of his own which included sliding down the outer slope of the roof and finishing up with his heels in the guttering, yet the human boy survived. He laughed and said,

'Sounds quite a stunt. Then you went to bed, I suppose?'

'Yes.'

'You didn't hear anything after that?'

Cyril shook his head regretfully.

'I went to sleep. If I hadn't I might have heard the shot. I don't 'arf want to kick myself when I think about it. I didn't hear nothing. Oh boy—I wish I had!'

CHAPTER FIFTEEN

The next few hours saw a good deal of activity on the part of a number of people. Garth walked to Perry's Halt and from there took the train to Marbury, from which sizable town he judged that he could without indiscretion ring up Sir George Rendal. As a result of this conversation strings were pulled, a Chief Constable was tactfully approached and prevailed upon to request that the Harsch case should be taken over by Scotland Yard.

Garth, having finished with the telephone, partook of a horrible and very expensive meal at the Station Hotel and made his way back by the late slow local, wondering what hotel crooks did to food to make it so repulsive.

As he walked across the dark fields from Perry's Halt he was wondering about other things. Madoc—why should Madoc have murdered Harsch? Jealousy over Medora Brown? A good stock answer out of all the melodramas that had ever been written. It did seem extraordinarily unlikely. But then people did do very unlikely things, and melodrama was a most constant factor in human affairs. Every day the snappier papers produced the most lunatic stories of human behaviour. Medora wasn't his cup of tea, but she might be Madoc's. She might even have been Michael Harsch's. She was quite a handsome woman in her way. She could have sat or stood for almost any one of the darker heroines of Greek tragedy. A little old perhaps for Cassandra, but quite a possible Electra, who could never have been young, and a very credible Clytemnestra. Or Medusa. Yes, Medusa had it—a Medusa who had seen something which had turned her to stone. The legend in reverse.

Well, Madoc was bound to be arrested unless he had a very good explanation to hand about the key. He found himself wondering how Madoc would take arrest. These men who got angry about trifles sometimes found control in an emergency. He wondered, and wondered again, why Madoc should have shot Michael Harsch. There was the obvious melodramatic motive of jealousy. There was the impossible-possible twisted motive of the pacifist who sees himself rescuing the world from the latest perversion of science. It might be either of these, or a tangled mixture of both. He thought the police might have their work cut out to get a case that would hold water. A jury wasn't going to like hanging a man on the unsupported evidence of a boy of twelve. He was glad the thing was off his shoulders anyway. He had made the report he was bound to make, and that finished it as far as he was concerned.

It felt like the middle of the night, but it was actually no more than eleven o'clock when he got back to the Rectory, where he discovered Miss Sophy in a woollen dressing-gown sitting up for him with hot coffee and sandwiches, over which she became very chatty but most admirably abstained from asking any questions. In her generation the men of the family came and went, and you never dreamed of asking them where they had been. It simply wasn't done.

She talked instead about Miss Brown.

'I am afraid Mr. Harsch's death has been a very severe shock. I would not let her sit up—she is really not at all herself—but I hope perhaps in the morning, with the inquest behind her, she will be feeling better.'

Garth had his doubts. He felt concerned and embarrassed, and made haste to talk about Miss Doncaster. He had heard Aunt Sophy become quite animated on the subject before now, but to-night she merely sighed and said,

'You know, my dear, I am sorry for her. She and Mary Anne had a very difficult time when they were young. Their father was a most peculiar man. He didn't like people coming to the house, and they never had any opportunities even when they went abroad. I think they would have liked to marry, but they never met anyone. Mr. Doncaster was really so very reserved, and he lived till they were both past middle age. And now Mary Anne is a complete invalid, so I feel sorry for Lucy Ellen, though sometimes she does make me lose my temper.'

Garth felt very warmly towards his Aunt Sophy as he said good-night.

At a little after ten o'clock next morning the very empty train which was then approaching Perry's Halt contained two officers sent down from Scotland Yard. They were Chief Detective Inspector Lamb, a large imperturbable person with a sanguine complexion and strong black hair wearing a little thin upon the top, and Detective Sergeant Abbott, than whom no greater contrast could be imagined. They might, in fact, have furnished material for a cartoon entitled 'The Police Officer, Old and New' —Abbott being an extremely elegant young man who had arrived at his present position by way of a public school and the Police College. His fair hair was slicked back from rather a high brow. His clothes were of the most admirable cut. His expression as he sat opposite his superior officer was one of boredom verging on gloom. He had, as a matter of fact, just had his fourth application to be allowed to join the R.A.F. refused, and refused with what could only be described as an official raspberry. To his Chief Inspector's well meant recommendation to look upon the bright side he replied bitterly that there wasn't one.

Lamb looked at him reprovingly.

'No call to say things like that, Frank. I can feel for you all right, because the same thing happened to me in nineteen-fifteen. Downright put out about it I was, but I've come to see things different, and so will you.'

There was a faint insubordinate gleam in Sergeant Abbott's pale blue eyes as he passed in review the shoulders, the girth, the very considerable avoirdupos of his superior, the reproof of whose glance became intensified.

'Now you listen to me! I don't mind betting—not that I'm a betting man or ever have been, but that's just a manner of speaking—well, I don't mind betting that you've been thinking, "What's it matter whether an odd professor gets murdered, when there's thousands blowing each other to bits all over the world?" '

Abbott's lips framed inaudibly the words, 'Archibald the All-right', and then passed rapidly to a bowdlerized version.

'You're always right, sir. That is exactly what I was thinking.'

'Then you stop it and listen to me! What's at the bottom of this and every other war that's ever started? Contempt for the law, just the same as any other crime. Someone wants something, and he goes to grab it. If anyone gets in his way they get hurt, and he doesn't care. Pity of it is, when it's nations there isn't anything strong enough to stop them. But when it's what you might call private crime there's the law and there's us. Every time we lay a criminal by the heels we're making people see that the law is there to protect them and to be respected. That's the way you get a law-abiding people. And when you've got that, you've got people with a respect for other people's law—what you might call International Law. You can't keep things like that for yourself unless you're willing for other people to have 'em too—not when it's law anyway. That's what's gone wrong with the Germans—they've stopped respecting the law—other people's first, and then their own. Well, that's not going to happen over here. But the law's got to be served, and that's where we come in. Servants of the law—that's you and me, and it don't matter whether we're flying, or driving a tank, or hunting a murderer, we've got to do our job. Well, here we are. There's the local man on the platform, and I hope he's got a car.'

He had, and they were driven in it to the police station at Bourne, where they interviewed a cocksure and uplifted Cyril

Bond and took his statement. Questioned upon it, he gave definite and very clear replies, and was dismissed with an injunction to keep his mouth shut. After which Lamb announced that they would walk to the Rectory if someone would show them the way, but they would like to see the church first.

CHAPTER SIXTEEN

Miss Brown faced them across the table in the old Rector's study. She was of such a pallor as to rouse some apprehension lest she should bring the interview to a sudden close by fainting. She wore a black dress. She sat stiffly upright. She kept her eyes upon the Chief Inspector's face—haunted eyes with dilated pupils.

Sergeant Abbott sat at one end of the table with a notebook. He had seen a good many frightened people in the course of his professional duties, but he thought Miss Brown had it as badly as any of them.

After an impressive pause old Lamb was leading off.

'You are Miss Medora Brown?'

'Yes.'

'You gave evidence yesterday at the inquest on Mr. Michael Harsch, during which you stated that, having used your church key on Tuesday morning, you put it back in the top left-hand drawer of Miss Fell's bureau, and that you did not go to the church again.'

'Yes.'

'Would you like to modify that statement at all, or to add to it?'

Her lips hardly moved, but they said, 'No.'

Lamb made a show of unfolding a paper. He did not hurry over it.

'I have here the statement of a witness who says he was in a lane known as the Church Cut somewhere between nine and a quarter to ten p.m. on the night of Mr. Harsch's death. He states that you came through the garden door into the lane, and that Professor Madoc met you, and asked you whether you were going to the church to see Mr. Harsch, who was playing the organ there. He said that you should not go, and that you should hand him over the key. When you refused, he twisted your arm and the key fell.

The witness declares that Mr. Madoc picked it up and went off in the direction of the church, whilst you went back into the garden and shut the door. Have you any comment to make?'

Miss Brown stared with those dilated eyes. She moistened her pale lips and said,

'No.'

Lamb leaned forward.

'It is only fair to tell you that Major Albany says that your key was not in the drawer on Thursday evening, but that by the time you all returned from the inquest on Friday morning it had been replaced. There is further evidence to show that you left the house at midnight on Thursday for a quarter of an hour, and that you went into the lane. There was some broken glass there, and you brought a bit of it in on your dress. Mr. Madoc also picked up a bit of broken glass. From which we infer that you met him again on Thursday night, and that he then gave you back the key which he had taken from you on Tuesday.'

There was a somewhat prolonged pause. Lifting his eyes from his notebook, Sergeant Abbott surveyed Miss Brown. She was not looking at him but at the Chief Inspector. He at once became aware that the quality of this look had changed. It was as if, having heard the worst, she was assembling her courage. At least that is how it struck him. Certainly something had happened since he had looked at her last. She was, for instance, no longer so rigid. The extreme pallor was gone. You couldn't say that her colour had come back. That thick, smooth skin of hers probably never had any, and when she wasn't paralysed with fright it would appear very much as it did now.

As the thought went through his mind, she made a slight movement and said quick and low,

'Will you let me explain?'

Lamb said, 'Certainly. I shall be glad to hear anything you have to say.'

She moved again, leaning a little towards him.

'Of course I don't know who your witness is, but he is quite mistaken in what he saw. I can tell you exactly what happened. I could hear that Mr. Harsch was playing the organ in the church. He is——' she paused and corrected herself—'he was a very fine musician. I have often gone into the church to listen when he was playing. I meant to do so on Tuesday evening. I took my key because sometimes he has locked the door. I went down through the garden and opened the door into the lane. There is a similar door into the churchyard a little farther along.'

'Yes—we have been over the ground.'

'Then you will understand. I was just going into the lane, when I heard footsteps and saw someone coming from the direction of the village. It was a man, but I didn't recognize him. It certainly wasn't Mr. Madoc. The man called out something, I don't know what, and I went back into the garden and shut the door as your witness says. I thought the man was intoxicated, and I gave up the idea of going to the church. Afterwards when I got up to my room I found that I had dropped my key.'

Lamb gazed at her with solid gravity.

'Did you go back to look for it?'

She shook her head.

'No.'

'Why not?'

'It was getting late—the man had startled me—I thought Miss Fell would be coming up to bed—I didn't want to make explanations—I thought I would leave it till the morning.'

Frank Abbot thought, 'One reason would have been enough—and she's given us five. Five explanations means that something wants a lot of explaining away. Women always overdo things. In fact, "methinks the lady doth protest too much." '

He wrote what she had said, and heard Lamb ask,

'How do you know that it wasn't Mr. Madoc who came along the lane?'

'It wasn't anyone as tall as Mr. Madoc.'

'Did you see his face?'

'No.'

'Why not? It was bright moonlight, wasn't it?'

'There are trees overhanging the wall. His face was in shadow.'

'You are sure that you didn't recognize him?'

She sat easily now, her hands lying loosely in her lap. She said,

'Quite sure.'

'Then how do you account for the fact that he addressed you as Medora? That is your name, isn't it?'

The hands took hold of one another. Frank watched them. They strained and tightened.

'I told you he called out. I couldn't hear what he said. He may have mistaken me for someone else. The cook next door is called Dora.'

Bent over his notebook again, Frank Abbott permitted himself a slight sarcastic smile. Lamb said,

'You deny having had any conversation with this man? The statement I spoke of says that words passed between you on the subject of Mr. Harsch.'

'There was no conversation. I went back into the garden.'

'Yes—leaving your key. When did you get it back again, Miss Brown?'

It appeared she was quite easy about that. She took it in her stride.

'I went to look for it on Wednesday morning. I am afraid I didn't look very carefully. We had had the news of Mr. Harsch's death, and I was terribly upset—I couldn't think about anything else. I didn't think about the key being important until someone —I think it was Miss Doncaster—said that of course the police would ask a lot of questions about the other church keys. That was on Thursday. So that evening I waited for the moon and went out into the lane to see if I could find my key.'

'Why did you have to wait for the moon? Wouldn't it have been a good deal simpler by daylight?'

She threw him an odd protesting glance.

'I hadn't time—I couldn't get away. I am Miss Fell's companion. Major Albany was coming to stay—there was a great deal to do.'

The same multiplicity of reasons.

Lamb said, 'I see. Go on, Miss Brown.'

Protest changed to something like defiance.

'There isn't anything more. I found the key. There was some broken glass there, as you said. I suppose I must have brought a bit in. I naturally didn't imagine that anyone would be spying on me.'

There was just a spark of temper there. Lamb took no notice of it.

He said gravely, 'Where did you find the key?' and at once she was relaxed again The answer came readily.

'It was lying up against the wall under a dandelion plant.'

'Which side of the door.'

'On the right. It was close up against the wall.'

Lamb got up, went to the window, and stood there looking out. He could see the wall, and the shape of the door breaking it. Without turning round he said,

'The handle's on the left. Those doors open inwards, don't they?'

'Yes.'

He came back to his seat. Miss Brown went on speaking.

'The key must have fallen out of my hand when the man startled me. It was right up against the wall, quite close to the jamb. The moon happened to shine on it, or I might not have seen it.'

'And did Mr. Madoc come there to help you look for your key?'

She drew back. The effect was that she flinched.

'How could he help me? He wasn't there. Nobody helped me.'

'You deny that you met Mr. Madoc in the lane on Thursday night.'

'Of course I deny it. He wasn't there. I went out, and found the key, and put it back in the bureau drawer.'

Lamb took a frowning glance at the paper he had handled before, and then looked up and asked with an effect of suddenness,

'Just how well did you know Mr. Harsch?'

Miss Brown was not at all discomposed.

'I knew him—we were on friendly terms. Miss Fell is fond of music—she often invited him.'

'You were friendly?'

'Yes.'

'Were you more than friendly?'

She lifted her eyebrows and said coldly,

'Certainly not.'

'And Mr. Madoc?'

There was a pause before she said,

'I don't know—what you mean.'

Her tone was very nearly the same, but not quite. It was still cold, but Frank Abbott thought that it had changed. He thought she was afraid.

Lamb said, 'I am asking you how well you know Mr. Madoc.'

This time her answer came quickly in a tumble of words.

'I know him—we all know each other here—it's a small place. Is there anything wrong about that?'

'Does he call you by your Christian name?'

'Certainly not! Why should he?'

'That is not for me to say, Miss Brown.'

The Chief Inspector pushed back his chair and got up.

CHAPTER SEVENTEEN

When Miss Brown had left the room Frank Abbott met his Inspector's eye and smiled faintly.

Lamb said, 'Well?'

'Oh, she's lying—quite strenuously, I think, but not all the

79

time. Some of it came easy, and some of it came hard. There's an eel under the stone, as they say in France.'

Lamb looked suspicious.

'This isn't France, and you'd do better to keep your mind on your job. Or if you want to play at proverbs, here's a good old English one—"Fine words butter no parsnips". We'll be getting along to Prior's End to see what Madoc's got to say. Of course they may have fixed up their tale so that it will hang together, but there's quite a chance they haven't. What with the inquest going off as smooth as butter, and the verdict what it was, they wouldn't know they'd been seen in the lane, and they wouldn't risk meeting or telephoning till it had blown over a bit.'

'How are you going to stop her telephoning now?'

Lamb chuckled.

'Mr. Madoc's line is going to be out of order, just in case anyone wants to ring him up before we get there. I doubt if she'd risk it though. It's one of those party lines, they tell me, where anyone can take a turn at listening in. Anyhow, she won't get the chance. But the girl at the Exchange will let us know if she has a try at it.'

Frank Abbott slipped an elastic band round his notebook and put it in his pocket. His gloom had departed, his pale blue eyes were alert.

'She's a clever woman,' he said. 'It was pretty good, the way she pulled herself together. A bit of a knockout blow, our coming in with that evidence just as she must have been thinking they'd got away with it.'

Lamb nodded.

'She didn't put up a bad story. Counsel for the defence could make quite a good thing of it, if it ever comes to that. By the way, just check up on that cook next door. Ask one of the maids here—they'll know. I'll have a word with Major Albany, and then we'll be going.'

He had his word, and was out by the gate, when Frank came after him.

'The name is Doris, sir. What you might call a near miss. Bright of her to think of it though.'

Lamb grunted.

'Well, we'd better be getting off.'

It was close on twelve o'clock when they came up the track to Prior's End. Mrs. Williams opened the door, elderly and neat, with her grey hair in a bun and her hands damp and steaming.

'As sure as you've got your hands in the flour or the water, there'll be someone come to the door,' she told Janice a minute or two later. 'Two strangers, and wanting Mr. Madoc, so I told them he wasn't to be disturbed, and I showed them in on Miss Madoc.'

Miss Madoc had been very much surprised. She was engaged in the homely occupation of darning socks, and what with her size, her loose untidy dress—serge of the colour of boiled spinach, with dibs and dabs of embroidery here and there—and a green scarf that belonged to the dress, and a rust-coloured one she had put on in a fit of absent-mindedness, and her mending-basket, and a scatteration of socks, she pretty well filled the old-fashioned sofa. When she got up, first removing the glasses she wore for needlework, she managed to upset the basket, and was evidently in two minds whether to retrieve it or to greet her unexpected guests. On being informed that they were police officers from Scotland Yard she sat down again rather heavily and forgot everything else.

'Oh, then it will be about poor Mr. Harsch. But I am afraid you can't see my brother—we never disturb him when he is working. He is doing very important work for the Government—at least everyone says it is very important. But I don't think I shall like it at all if it comes to living on tabloids, but he says that we all eat a great deal too much, and——'

Lamb interrupted her in his most solid voice.

'I'm afraid that we shall have to see Mr. Madoc. Will you kindly let him know that we are here.'

Frank Abbott was thinking that never in his fondest dreams had he expected to meet anyone so exactly like the White Queen. The greyish sandy hair in a confused tangle on her neck, the crumpled pallor of her face, the vague protuberant eyes, the general air of not knowing quite where anything was or what to do about it—you had only to put her into a crinoline and clap a crown on her head, and she could wander through to the far side of the looking-glass and be more at home there than she had ever been or ever could be on this side of it.

She was shaking her head at Lamb and saying,

'Oh, dear—I don't really see—I don't know—he is so very easily put out—if there is anything that I can do——'

Lamb said heartily, 'Well, that's an idea!' He took a chair and sat down. 'We shall have to see your brother presently, but I daresay there are things that you can tell us just as well as he can.'

Besides the scarves, she wore a very large mosaic brooch depicting the Coliseum at Rome, and three strings of beads, a short one of blue and silver Venetian glass, and two, much longer, of coral and little round gold pierced beads respectively. Every time she moved the coral rubbed the glass and the gold beads clinked.

Lamb felt in a pocket and produced a door-key.

'Now, Miss Madoc, perhaps you can tell me whether you have seen a key like this before.'

She inspected it diffidently, and then brightened.

'Oh, yes—it is like the one Mr. Harsch had—the key of the church. There was something about it at the inquest, but I really didn't take it all in. I find that sort of thing very confusing, if you know what I mean.'

'Well, we're trying to get it all quite clear. I hope you can help us. When did you last see any key like this one?'

Miss Madoc appeared to be trying to think. When she spoke she had just the right voice for the White Queen, Abbott thought—high and rather bleating.

'Well, let me see—Mr. Harsch kept his key lying on his dressing-table—but it wasn't there on Tuesday night when I turned down the bed. Mrs. Williams wasn't quite the thing, and I did it for her, but of course he never slept in it, poor man—only I couldn't have known, could I? But then I seem to have seen it later than that—at least I didn't see it then—but if I had it would have been later, if you know what I mean.'

Lamb remained imperturbable.

'You are speaking about the key?'

Miss Madoc twitched a scarf. All the chains jangled.

'Was I? I'm afraid I've forgotten. It was so very sad about Mr. Harsch.'

'Yes. You were telling us about turning down his bed on Tuesday night. But it was later on that you saw the key, wasn't it?'

'Oh, yes—yes—of course—I remember. I couldn't have seen it then, could I, because he had taken it to let himself into the church. But next day when I was brushing my brother's clothes the key fell out of his pocket on to the floor.' She made a bewildered pause. 'But of course it couldn't have been Mr. Harsch's key—could it? Do you know, I never thought about that.'

Lamb was not at all anxious that she should think about it now. He interposed with a direct question.

'These clothes that you were brushing—were they the ones that Mr. Madoc was wearing the night before?'

'Oh, yes.'

'On the Tuesday evening?'

'Oh, yes.'

'And the key that fell out was like this?' He held out Bush's key on the palm of his hand.

'Oh, *yes*!' said Miss Madoc brightly.

'What did you do with it?'

She looked shocked.

'Oh, I put it back. My brother is most particular about nobody touching his things.'

Lamb got up.

'Thank you, Miss Madoc. And now we will see Mr. Madoc.'

She rose in alarm, shedding socks.

'Oh, but I'm afraid you can't—he's working—I really couldn't —I mean, we never interrupt him when he's working.'

The Chief Inspector had a formidable manner when he chose. He evoked it now with so much success that Miss Madoc found herself meekly treading the forbidden path to the laboratory door, knocking upon it and impelled across the threshold with a few faltering words of introduction, after which she departed in a hurry and was thankful for the sound of the closing door.

Evan Madoc, straightening up with a test-tube in his hand, stared haughtily at the intruders. On being informed of their identity he abated nothing of the haughtiness, but enquired what they wanted in very much the same tone which he would have used to Mrs. Williams or his sister. Politeness to strangers or deference to the law had no part in it. He was at work—he had been interrupted. Would they kindly state their business and get out. If not in words, at any rate in tone and manner, nothing could have been plainer.

'Riding high,' was Frank Abbott's mental comment, 'Well, it's one way of playing a bad hand.'

Old Lamb was being quite polite, quite businesslike.

'We have been asked to make some enquiries in connection with the death of Mr. Michael Harsch. I believe you can help us, Mr. Madoc.'

The erratic black eyebrows rose. The eyes beneath them sharpened, hardened. An icy voice said,

'I should think it most improbable. What do you want?'

Lamb let him have it.

'I want to know what you were doing in the Church Cut at a time not very long before a quarter to ten, when the shot which killed Mr. Harsch was fired.'

The black slanting line of the brows came down again, descending until they made an angry line above the frowning eyes. The hand which held the test-tube closed hard and then relaxed.

83

The glass dropped broken to the floor. Evan Madoc did not even look at it. He said,

'Who says that I was there?'

Lamb pulled a paper out of his pocket and unfolded it without hurry.

'You were seen and heard, Mr. Madoc. I have a statement here which says, "Mr. Madoc came along the Cut from the direction of the church. I could see him quite plainly in the moonlight. Miss Brown was just outside the garden door of the Rectory. Mr. Madoc said, 'Where are you going, Medora?' and she said, 'It hasn't got anything to do with you.' " Have you any comment to make on that statement? The witness is prepared to swear to it, and to the conversation which followed. He says, in effect, that you forbade Miss Brown to go to the church, and that you took from her the key which she had in her hand and went off with it. I may say that Miss Brown admits to having gone into the lane.'

Evan Madoc laughed. It was a very angry sound. His face was haggard and his eyes burned.

'Oh, she says she went into the lane? What else does she say?'

'I'm not here to tell you about other people's statements—I'm here to ask you what you have to say. There is evidence to show that you were in possession of one of the church keys at the time that Mr. Harsch was shot. There is evidence that you quarrelled with Miss Brown about him. Have you anything to say on these two points?'

Madoc drew himself up.

'If you have all this evidence, what more do you want?'

'Do you admit that you were in the Church Cut at somewhere round about half past nine on Tuesday evening?'

'Why shouldn't I admit it?'

'Would you care to make a statement as to what took place there?'

He laughed again.

'So that you can check it up with your witness and try and catch me in a lie! That's what you would like to do, isn't it? But that's just what you won't do, because I don't tell lies—I speak the truth. That's one thing you don't reckon on in someone you suspect, is it—that he may tell the truth. That knocks the bottom out of your trap—doesn't it? Write down what I say and you can have your statement, and every word of it will be true!'

Lamb looked round over his shoulder and nodded. The notebook came out of Frank Abbott's pocket. He found himself a chair and wrote upon his knee.

Madoc began to walk up and down, throwing off short, furious sentences, his hands plunged deep in his pockets, every jerky stride, every abrupt turn, full of angry energy.

'Tuesday evening. I didn't look at the time. I went out and walked. When I came to the Church Cut I saw Miss Brown. I thought she was going to the church. I thought she was making a fool of herself. I could see she had got something in her hand. Harsch was playing in the church. I told her she could listen to him from where she was. I told her to hand over the key. When she wouldn't, I twisted her arm. The key fell down. I picked it up and went away. That's all—make anything you like of it! And get out of here! I'm working!'

No one was in a hurry but Mr. Madoc. Sergeant Abbott wrote. Lamb presented his imperturbable front (Impersonation of a Prize Ox at Grass, as his irreverent subordinate had it).

'Just a moment, Mr. Madoc. This business is important for you as well as for us. It can't be rushed over. I'd like you to take time to think before you speak, and it is my duty to warn you that what you say will be taken down and may be used in evidence against you.'

The words pulled Evan Madoc up short. He checked in the middle of a stride, flung round, and said,

'Good God! What are you suggesting?'

'It is not my place to suggest. I am warning you. I've got my duty to do, and it would be better for yourself as well as for me if you would sit down quietly and think before you say anything. All right, it's just as you like—but I've warned you. I'm asking you whether you used the key you took from Miss Brown. I'm asking you whether you went to the church and saw Mr. Harsch on Tuesday evening.'

Madoc had already made a violent gesture of dissent. He now repeated it, shaking his head with an energy which shook his whole body too. After which he stood, hands in pockets, shoulders hunched forward, glowering, a lock of black hair tossed up like a ruffled feather accentuating the upward twist of the eyebrow.

'You deny that you went to the church?'

Madoc said with the extreme of bitterness,

'If I say no, you'll be sure I lie. If I say yes, you will ask me whether I shot Michael Harsch, and if I say yes to that, you will believe me with greediness. But if I tell you that I loved him like a brother, and that I would give my right hand to have him back, you will again be very sure that I am lying. Because it is not in you to believe good—you can only believe evil.'

Lamb cleared his throat.

'I should like to ask you to clarify those remarks, Mr. Madoc. We don't want any confusion over this. I am not clear whether you are stating that you did go to the church, or that you did not.'

Madoc reduced the volume of his voice, but not the venom.

'I did not go to the church. I did not shoot Michael Harsch. Is that quite clear?'

'Oh, yes, quite. You went home, and you took the key with you. When did you return it to Miss Brown?'

Madoc gave a disagreeable laugh.

'Hasn't she told you that? I'm surprised! I returned it to her on Thursday night. She seemed to want it back, so I brought it down and handed it over.'

'Thank you, Mr. Madoc. Have you any objection to signing the statements you have just made?'

'Not in the least. Why should I? I have nothing to hide.'

There was a pause. Frank Abbott wrote, and afterwards read aloud what he had written. Unlike the majority of statements recorded by the police, the words were recognizably Madoc's own. He listened to them with that black frown dominating his face, snatched the paper, and picking up a pen from his writing-table, drove it deep into the inkpot and scrawled a thick, smudged 'Evan Madoc' across the page.

CHAPTER EIGHTEEN

At four o'clock that afternoon Janice came hurrying down the track from Prior's End. She was not conscious of hurrying. She was not really conscious of her body at all, only of immeasurable disaster and the need she had to find Garth. She was bare-headed, and her white dress was too thin for the day, which had turned suddenly bleak, as days are apt to do in an English September.

She came into the village street, found it alive with children, and remembered with a kind of shock that it was Saturday afternoon. When something violent and abnormal has jolted your world out of focus, it is difficult to realize that life is going on quite normally for other people.

As she crossed the road she almost ran into Mrs. Mottram, who immediately clutched her and said,

'Darling, how dreadful! Don't tell me it's *true*. The baker said so, but I can't believe it? Have they really arrested Mr. Madoc?'

'Yes, it's true.'

Mrs. Mottram's blue eyes rolled.

'Darling, how devastating! Of course you mustn't stay there a single moment. You must come to me. I'm afraid I've only got a most uncomfortable camp bed and no carpet on the floor, because I've never really furnished the room, but you must come down at once. I'll just go straight back and put the sheets to air.'

'It's very kind of you, but I couldn't leave Miss Madoc.'

'Darling, you must! You can't possibly stay there! Do you know I always did think there was something peculiar about Mr. Madoc. You mustn't dream of staying.'

Janice shook her head.

'I can't leave her, Ida. You couldn't yourself, so it's no use asking me. And for goodness sake don't go about saying Mr. Madoc was peculiar, because he didn't do it.'

Mrs. Mottram had quite a pretty mouth except when it fell open. It fell open now, all on one side.

'Don't you think so?'

Janice stamped her foot.

"I *know* he didn't! Why should he? Mr. Harsch was the one person in this world he never quarrelled with. He thought a lot of him—he really cared for him. When you live in the house with people you can't make a mistake about that sort of thing.'

Ida Mottram had the happy faculty of always believing what she was told. It made her very popular with men. She gazed confidingly at Janice and said,

'I suppose you do. But, my dear, how devastating if he's innocent—and how dreadful for Miss Madoc! Are you sure he didn't do it?'

'Of course I'm sure.'

'Darling, I do hope you're right, because it really wouldn't be at all nice to feel you'd been living with a murderer. But if he didn't do it, who did? And how are you going to find out? Because of course the police wouldn't have arrested him unless they were quite, quite sure he'd done it, and it would be too, too dreadful if they were to hang him when he was innocent. I remember Billy saying that innocent people did get hanged—or as good as. Billy Blake—he was a great friend of Robin's and of mine too, and he was a barrister before he went into the R.A.F., so of course he knows. Did you meet him when he was down the other day—because I want you to so much. But he'll be coming again quite soon, and then you simply must. Of course he always says he only wants to see me, but I know you'll adore him. . . .

87

Oh, where was I? I know—I was thinking what we could do to prevent Mr. Madoc being hanged. You're quite, quite sure that he didn't do it? Because of course I quite *loved* Mr. Harsch. He had that sad, noble kind of look like someone in a film—and of course when they look like that you know they're going to die, so I always have a hanky ready—' She broke off suddenly and clutched at Janice with the other hand. A dreamy skyward gaze was replaced by one of considerable animation. 'Darling, I know—*Miss Silver*!'

Janice said, 'You're pinching me!' And then, 'Who is Miss Silver?'

'Darling! She's too marvellous! I can't tell you what she did for me. I daresay you'll think it was only a tiny little thing, but Robin's mother is so *suspicious*. She never liked his marrying me, you know, and she would *never* have believed that I hadn't sold it. But I can't tell you about it, because I simply swore to Robin that I would never tell anyone—in case of his mother getting to know, you know. Anyhow Miss Silver put it all right in the most marvellous way. And you may say it was only a little thing—only of course not for me—but how I heard about Miss Silver was from a girl who was in a perfectly dreadful murder case, and Miss Silver put it all right and found out who had really done it. So don't you see, you must have her down at once and get poor Mr. Madoc out of prison. And then you'll be able to come and stay with me, because Miss Madoc will be quite all right as soon as he gets home. I'm so glad I thought about it, and I shall love to see her again. She's just like a governess, you know, only rather an angel. Darling, I really must rush. I'm going to tea with Mr. Everton, and I shall get into dreadful trouble if I'm late. You won't forget, will you—Miss Maud Silver, 15 Montague Mansions. . . . Oh, yes, London, of course, but I never can remember whether it's S.E. or S.W. But they'll look it up for you at the post office—they always do for me.'

CHAPTER NINETEEN

Janice had rung the bell, when it came over her that it was no good thinking, 'I must go to Garth—I must see Garth', because of course she would simply have to ask for Miss Sophy. And then the door began to move, and there was Garth opening it. She forgot all about everything except how frightfully glad she was to see him, and almost before he had finished saying, 'I saw you out of the window,' she had her hand on his arm with a quick,

'Oh, Garth, they've arrested him!'

He took her into the study and shut the door.

'Aunt Sophy has gone to see Miss Mary Anne, but Miss Brown is somewhere about. I don't think we want her in on this.'

She sat down, looked at him forlornly, and said,

'Oh, Garth, he didn't do it—I know he didn't—but they've arrested him.'

He sat on the edge of the writing-table, quite near, and leaned towards her.

'I don't see what else they could do. He had Miss Brown's key.'

'Oh, Garth!'

'I'm afraid he did. Look here, this is just for you. There's been something going on between them. The evacuee boy next door saw them meet in the Cut. Madoc made a scene about her going to the church to see Harsch, and he took her key and went away with it not more than a quarter of an hour before Aunt Sophy heard the shot. That's why it wasn't in the drawer on Thursday evening. And that's what she was doing in the middle of Thursday night—meeting him again and getting the key back. I don't see what else they could do except arrest him.'

'But he didn't do it,' said Janice, her eyes wide with horror.

'Didn't he?'

'No.'

Garth gave rather a curious laugh.

'Stubborn little thing—aren't you? You always were. Now perhaps you'll tell me why you've got this touching belief in Madoc.'

She flushed brightly and said what she had said to Ida Mottram.

'I've lived in the house with them. He loved Mr. Harsch.'

'He loved Medora, and he was jealous of Harsch. I think he shot him. Having that key would make it so awfully easy.'

'Not if he hadn't planned it beforehand. Don't you see, if it was murder it must have been planned before-hand. You don't carry pistols about with you all ready and loaded. And that's what I can't believe about Mr. Madoc—he's got a simply frightful temper, and he goes off like a bomb and says the most outrageous things, but he wouldn't plot and plan, and load a pistol, and go out to find someone he was fond of and murder him. Garth, you know perfectly well there are things a person could do, and things he couldn't. This is one of the couldn'ts.'

He smiled at her suddenly.

'All right, counsel for the defence, next time I do a crime I'll brief you.'

Her colour deepened.

'You're laughing at me! I can imagine him throwing a chair or a flower-pot at someone—he did fling a vegetable dish full of burnt porridge out of the window not very long ago—but I just can't see him creeping up behind someone with a pistol.'

Garth's brows drew together, whilst his lips still smiled.

'Well, I don't know that the porridge is an awfully sound line of defence. I think I should cut it out if I were you.'

And with that the door was pushed open and Miss Brown stood there looking in. Garth swung round, leaning on his hand. She did not speak for a moment, but stood there, those dark eyes of hers staring from a colourless face. Then she came in and shut the door behind her.

Garth and Janice got up. Neither of them could think of anything to say. It was Miss Brown who spoke.

'What has happened? Tell me!'

'They have arrested Mr. Madoc.'

Miss Brown said, 'Oh!' It was really more of a gasp than a word. She took hold of the writing-chair and stood there gripping it. 'They *can't*!'

Garth said, 'They have.'

She turned on him with a surprising energy.

'They can't prove it—they can't prove anything! I didn't tell them anything—only that I went into the Cut! They'll never make me tell them anything more than that! He wasn't there—I tell you he wasn't there!'

Garth said, 'He was seen.'

She came back at him almost with fury.

'Who saw him? They wouldn't tell me! Whoever it was is lying! I tell you he wasn't there! It was a man I didn't know. I dropped my key! It wasn't Evan! They can't make me say it was!'

Janice looked frightened and sorry. She said in a little voice,

'It isn't any good—he told them he was there.'

'Oh, *no*!' The chair shook under her shaking hands.

Janice went on.

'He told them he took your key. It's no good saying he didn't. I know he didn't shoot Mr. Harsch, but they think he did. Because he had the key.'

Miss Brown let go of the chair and walked round the table,

feeling her way by the edge of it as if she were blind. When she was close to Janice she said in a voice which had lost all its strength,

'How do you know he didn't do it?'

CHAPTER TWENTY

'It is all very extraordinary,' said Miss Sophy.

She sat on the drawing-room sofa, billowing, with Garth on one side of her and Janice on the other. She had been holding a hand of each. She now withdrew what may be called Garth's hand and dabbed her eyes with a fine linen handkerchief which had a large S embroidered on the corner in a perfect bower of forget-me-nots, tulips, and shamrocks, all exactly the same size. After which she patted Janice affectionately and folded both hands in her lap, keeping the handkerchief ready for the next dab.

'Poor dear Medora! And she won't tell me anything—not anything at all. She doesn't even cry. You know, it really does you a great deal of good to cry when you are feeling unhappy.' She turned from one to the other as she spoke, her fat white curls ably supporting the not inconsiderable weight of her best hat, which was trimmed with four yards of black velvet ribbon of pre-war quality, three massive ostrich plumes, and a bunch of violets. Her eyes were very round, very blue, very bewildered. 'I said to her, "Medora, if you can't tell me what it is all about, do for goodness, gracious sake have a comfortable cry", and I brought her a clean folded pocket handkerchief. But she just lay there and looked at me. So I said, "Well, Medora, I can't force your confidence, and I won't try, but if you don't take your tea, I can send for Dr. Edwards, and I will" And I came away.'

'I expect she took it,' said Janice.

Miss Sophy dabbed again.

'And where does that get us?' she said in her soft fooffly voice. 'We were so comfortable, and everything was so pleasant—except of course for the war. Poor Mr. Harsch—such a fine musician—and Mr. Everton and the Madocs—such a musical circle.' She turned to Garth. 'Miss Madoc is quite a good accompanist, and when Mr. Madoc isn't in a temper he has a very agreeable tenor voice—only he never would sing unless he wanted to, and he had to choose the music, which was sometimes a little awkward. But I should never have dreamed that there was anything between him and Medora. I always thought they didn't even like each other.'

'I expect that was the trouble, Aunt Sophy—they didn't like each other, but they fell in love. It's the sort of thing that's likely to make trouble, isn't it?'

Miss Sophy looked more bewildered than ever.

'I don't know, my dear boy. When I was a girl there was no one for me to fall in love with, so I never did—though a Mr. Hoathley did propose to poor Papa for me, but it would have been very unsuitable, and Papa said no at once.'

'Didn't you get a chance of saying anything?'

She bridled.

'My dear, I hardly knew him—he was a veterinary surgeon. I remember he had very nice curly hair, and I believe he afterwards had a very good practice in Brighton. But of course all that has nothing to do with this very distressing affair. Poor Medora! And then there's Miss Madoc—I really can't bear to think about her—so nice, and such a devoted sister! And Mr. Madoc in prison! You know, my dear, I just can't believe he did anything so dreadful. I don't mean to say he hasn't a very bad temper, because everyone knows that he has, but I always did think that he was fond of Mr. Harsch—quite a softening influence, if you know what I mean. And if he is innocent, what a terrible, terrible thing for him to be accused of murdering his friend! I find it terribly upsetting. You know, it all seems quite different when you read about it in the papers, but when it is people you know, it doesn't seem as if it could really be happening. And the dreadful part is that there isn't anything one can do.'

Inside Janice's mind something said, 'Miss Silver.' She began to tell Miss Sophy what Ida Mottram had said, but before she had got very far she was interrupted.

'Miss Maud Silver? My dear, how extraordinary!'

'Oh, Miss Sophy—why? Do you know about her?'

The three black feathers flapped as Miss Sophy nodded. She put up her hands, removed two large jet hatpins, took off the hat, and skewered it to the back of the sofa.

'Handsome, but heavy,' she said with a sigh of relief.

'Mamma's cousin, Oswald Everett, brought her the feathers from South Africa. They have worn extremely well, though not in fashion now. But Mary Anne Doncaster would take offence if I went to see her in anything but my best hat. Now what were we talking about? Oh, yes—Miss Silver.'

'Ida says——'

Miss Sophy waved Ida Mottram away.

'She means well, my dear, but quite between ourselves she's a goose. Now I know all about Miss Silver.'

'Aunt Sophy!'

'Miss Sophy!'

Garth and Janice gazed at her.

She patted a hand of each in a very complacent manner.

'Sophy Ferrars is a distant cousin of mine—through dear Mamma of course. An aunt of hers, Sophronisba Ferrars, married my grandfather's brother. I am called after her, and so was she. And of course I don't suppose you have ever heard of Sophy Ferrars, but her young cousin Laura Fane, a very charming girl, was placed in a most terrible position about eighteen months ago. It didn't all get into the papers, but some of it did. Another cousin, Tanis Lyle, was murdered——'

Garth made a sudden exclamation.

'The Prior's Holt murder!'

Miss Sophy nodded in a pleased sort of way.

'Yes, my dear. And Laura was very nearly murdered too. Sophy Ferrars wrote and told me all about it. If Miss Silver had not been staying in the house, almost anything might have happened. She was staying there just as an ordinary visitor.' Her voice died suddenly away. Her mouth remained open, round and surprised, above three quivering chins. She fetched as deep a breath as she could and said, 'Why shouldn't she come here and stay with me?'

CHAPTER TWENTY ONE

Sunday intervened. Garth accompanied Miss Sophy to church and listened to the new Rector's austere, academic voice with a curious feeling of unreality. Where his grandfather had boomed and thundered—a portly presence with the eagle eye which could detect a napping villager in the farthest pew—this ascetic scholar, whispering the prayers and running through the lesson in a vague, monotonous undertone, sounded unreal.

His thoughts must have communicated themselves to Miss Sophy. She turned and fooffled into his ear.

'So different from poor Papa.'

When they stood up for the psalms he detected Cyril Bond, singing a piercing quarter of a tone sharp against the native choir who were even flatter than he remembered them. Glancing across the church, his eye lighted upon Mrs. Mottram in a flibberty-gibbet hat which matched the very bright blue of her dress. On one side of her a little girl of five with a fuzz of yellow hair and a frilled pink frock. On the other Mr. Everton, who looked as if the choir was hurting him quite a lot. The eye roamed farther, and discovered that Janice wasn't there.

During a dry and practically inaudible sermon Garth searched his mind for reasons why this should be any concern of his. He came to the conclusion that it was not. After which he went on thinking about her until the service was over.

Janice was, and had been for what seemed like a very long time, sitting on the sofa beside Miss Madoc, who passed continuously from self-reproach, through protestations of her brother's high-mindedness and perfect innocence, to the despairing conclusion that everything was against him, and that he would certainly be hanged.

'If only I hadn't said anything to them about the key——'

'But, dear Miss Madoc, he told them about it himself. What you said didn't make the least bit of difference—it didn't, truly.'

Two large tears ran down Miss Madoc's face and dripped miserably upon a peacock-blue scarf which she had put on by accident, and which swore quite horribly at the rather bright purple of her Sunday dress. The skies might fall, Evan might be in prison, she herself far too prostrated to be able to think of going to church, but she had been brought up to wear a different dress on Sunday, and she would have felt quite desperately irreligious in her everyday green serge.

'That's what you say, my dear, and I'm sure it's very kind of you, and I don't like to feel that I'm keeping you back from church, but really when I think that it was only last Sunday that poor Mr. Harsch was with us and the blackberry tart was so particularly good! It isn't everyone who cares for cold pastry, but Evan never will have any cooking done on Sunday, so what can you do? But last Sunday it really was as light as a feather, and poor Mr. Harsch enjoyed it so much, and had a second helping.' Two more tears ran down, and she wiped them away. 'Oh, my dear—do you believe in premonitions?'

'I don't know——' said Janice.

'Nor do I,' said Miss Madoc with a gulp. 'But do you think perhaps Mr. Harsch had one? He said such a curious thing to me on Monday night. He'd been over to Marbury, you remember, to get something he wanted for that last experiment, and he came in late because he missed the bus and had to walk from the Halt. And I thought he looked bad when he came in, so I said to him, "Are you very tired, Mr. Harsch?" and he said, "I don't know—I think I must be. I have just seen a ghost." '

Janice said, 'What!'

Miss Madoc nodded.

'That is what he said, my dear. And I said, "Oh, Mr. Harsch!" and he smiled and said, "Did I frighten you? I wouldn't like to do that. It is nothing for you to be afraid of?" Do you think that he really saw something?'

'I don't know——'

Miss Madoc wiped her eyes upon a folk-weave handkerchief which had rough yellow and green threads running across it. Even at a moment like this Janice couldn't help thinking how uncomfortable it must be.

'I do wonder what he saw,' said Miss Madoc. 'My grandfather knew a man who met himself. He was going out to do something which he ought not to have been doing—I don't know what it was—and he met himself face to face in the bright moonlight. My grandfather said it was like Balaam and the ass, only I don't know why, because Balaam was riding the ass, and this man was quite alone and on foot. And the moon was very bright—he could see himself quite clearly. A most dreadful terror came over him, and he turned round and ran, and never stopped running until he came to the minister's house. And he could hear his own footsteps coming after him all the way. My grandfather said he was a changed man from that day. He had been a terrible one for drink and women, but he became a very sober, god-fearing man. Do you think Mr. Harsch saw anything like that?'

Janice said, 'I don't know——' She was thinking of what Mr. Harsch had said to her.

Miss Madoc covered her face with the folk-weave handkerchief and burst into tears.

'I'm a wicked woman to be telling stories, and Evan in prison waiting to be hanged! If only I hadn't told them about the key!'

It went round like that in circles all the morning. By the time Garth came up after lunch to take her for a walk Janice was feeling as if she had been put through a wringer. The afflicted lady was induced to go and lie down, and Mrs. Williams was left in charge.

As soon as they were well away Garth said,

'I've got it all taped. We catch the nine o'clock bus to-morrow morning and go up to town. I'll go and see Sir George, and you can fix things up with Miss Silver. The sooner she gets here the better—it's a cold scent now. She'd better come down with us and get cracking. By the way, Mrs. Mottram came up after church and poured a bit of cold water—at least I thought it was meant to be cold water.'

'What did she say?'

He laughed.

'Oh, a piece about perhaps the police wouldn't like it if you had Miss Silver down, and most likely she would be away on a case, but of course she really was too marvellous, only if Mr. Madoc had really done it there wasn't anything any one could do, was there? It's rather a pity she's had to come in on it at all, because now everyone in Bourne will know why Miss Silver is here.'

'I expect they'd know anyhow. You can't keep secrets in a village.'

He slipped a hand inside her arm as they walked.

'What will they say when we're seen to go off on the bus together in the morning?'

When her face looked so white and small it did something to his feelings. It pleased him to see her colour rise.

'Perhaps they'll think we're eloping. It will be a dreadful disappointment when we come back in the evening with Miss Silver.'

'It would be rather fun to elope. Shall we?'

Janice met his laughing, teasing look and said,

'There's nowhere left to elope to till after the war.'

On the top of her mind she was rather pleased with this answer, but deep underneath something despaired and said, 'It's no good—I love him frightfully—I always have, and I can't stop.' It was like being caught by an undertow which took your feet off the bottom and carried you out to sea—it was too strong to resist. *She didn't want to resist it.* The colour that had come up into her face died down until it was altogether gone. There was just that little bit of a white face, and the very bright no-coloured eyes that wouldn't look away.

They were standing still on the edge of a tilted field. Nothing but sky, and air, and the green slope of the grass. Garth put an arm round her shoulders. He said in a startled voice,

'What's the matter, Jan?'

'Nothing.'

'Are you all right?'

She nodded. Now she could look away.

'I've had a dreadful morning with Miss Madoc.'

'Hasn't she any relations who could come?'

'I don't think so. If we can make her feel that something is being done, it will help. You see, she's made up her mind that he's going to be hanged. She keeps on talking about it.'

The arm about her shoulders tightened.

'My poor child!'

'Oh, it doesn't matter about me. It's dreadful to see a much older person all gone to pieces like that.'

They walked on in silence for a minute or two. Garth kept his arm where it was. Presently he said,

'Why has she made up her mind that he's going to be hanged?'

She looked up at him. A shadow went across her eyes. She looked away.

'I don't know——'

'Jan—does she think he did it?'

He felt her shake. She began to say, 'I don't know,' but her voice stopped in the middle of a word. Her face quivered and she began to cry, quite quietly but with no more attempt at concealment than if she had still been ten years old.

Garth put his other arm round her.

'Jan—Jan—darling! Don't cry like that—please don't!'

And then he was kissing her—her forehead, the curve of her cheek, the wet weeping eyes.

'Jan, don't—I hate it! It's going to be all right—we'll make it all right. We'll get Miss Silver. Jan, don't cry any more! Here's a handkerchief. I'm sure you haven't got one.'

She stopped crying. How many other girls' tears had he dried? She took the handkerchief and dried her own. Then she said,

'Please let me go.'

He went on holding her. Funny little thing—darling little thing. He wanted to kiss her again, but somehow he couldn't. Her eyes looked up at him with a sort of sorrowful candour.

'I'm sorry about crying—men do hate it so. But it doesn't mean very much—just Miss Madoc, and—and things.'

He put his cheek against hers for a moment. The words that had been in his mind said themselves aloud.

'Funny little thing—darling little thing!'

This time she stepped back resolutely.

'Thank you for being kind. We'd better go on walking.'

'I don't think I want to walk.'

She said in a grave little voice,

'What do you want to do?'

The colour came up in his face.

'I think I want to make love to you.'

Janice felt cold at her heart. She shook her head.

'Oh, no—not really.'

He couldn't help laughing.

'And what do you mean by that?'

She stood and looked at him, very quiet and sad.

'I just mean not really. It's because I cried and you were sorry for me, and because you were fond of me when I was a little girl. I don't want to have it spoiled. I'd rather be friends.'

Something happened when she said that. He didn't quite know what it was. The relationship between them changed. He had the feeling that it had been wrenched, and that the wrench had been quite agonizingly painful, but whether it was Janice who felt it or he himself, he didn't know. For just that one instant they had been so close that he didn't know. He stared at her with troubled eyes and said,

'What happened?' And when she looked at him in surprise, 'Jan—something happened then, but I don't know what it was.'

They finished their walk. Neither of them talked very much. What they said had hardly any connection at all with what they were thinking. When they said good-bye Garth put a hand on her shoulder and looked at her in rather a puzzled way. Then he said, 'The nine o'clock bus. Don't be late,' and she went back to Miss Madoc.

It seemed about a hundred years before she got to bed that night. She was so tired that she thought she would go to sleep at once, but she didn't. As soon as she lay down and put out the light everything that she had said to Garth and everything that he had said to her came crowding into her mind and going round and round there like a gramophone record. 'Shall we elope?' 'There's nowhere to elope to.' 'I want to make love to you.' 'Oh, no—not really.' Over and over again the clear, vivid feeling of his cheek, against hers—not his kisses, but just the feeling of his cheek, hard and a little rough. It was the last thing she remembered before she slipped into a dream in which she was walking from Perry's Halt because she had missed the bus. It was black dark without moon or stars, and somewhere right out in the open fields a clock was striking twelve. When the last stroke died away she could hear a footstep following her. It came into her mind that Mr. Harsch had seen a ghost when he walked this way in the dark. She began to run, and waked up to see the moonlight slanting in across the floor.

CHAPTER TWENTY TWO

Miss Silver was going out to tea. She very often went out to tea on Sundays, and although this was no very special occasion it would be quite pleasant. A friend of her niece Ethel had recently come to live in Putney. Miss Silver had invited her to tea and found her agreeable, and this was a return visit. The afternoon being exceptionally mild, she wore her summer dress, now two years old, a navy blue artificial silk upon which a number of discordant colours were scattered in what looked like an imitation of the Morse-code. In deference to her idea of what was suitable, the skirt displayed no more than three or four inches of grey lisle thread stocking and black Oxford shoe. In case it should be chilly before she got back, she wore over it an old but still serviceable coat of black alpaca, and on her neat mousy hair a black straw hat with a glacé ribbon bow and a kind of trail of purple pansies. The neck of the dress was filled in by a cream net chemisette with a high boned collar and securely fastened by a brooch with a heavy gold border and a centre of plaited hair. Black cotton gloves, rather a shabby handbag, and a neat umbrella completed her toilet.

As she passed through her sitting-room on the way to the door she cast an approving glance about her. It was so comfortable, so cosy. The peacock-blue curtains were wearing so well, and the carpet really hardly looked at all rubbed even when the sun came slanting in. She considered her own prosperous lot with deep thankfulness. The curtains; the carpet; the curly yellow maple chairs upholstered in the same bright shade; the writing-table with its many drawers; the steel engravings of her favourite pictures— The Soul's Awakening, The Black Brunswicker, Bubbles, and The Monarch of the Glen; the row of silver-framed photographs upon the mantelpiece—all spoke to her of the comfortable independence she had, under Providence, achieved by her own intelligent exertions.

She went down in the lift, walked a quarter of a mile, and entered a Tube station. Half a dozen people were queued up for tickets as she took her place at the end of the row and waited whilst a lady whose dyed hair had seen better days argued at length with the harassed elderly man behind the pigeonhole as to whether she could or could not get a connection for some place whose name she appeared to have forgotten. A little grey-haired man in front of Miss Silver put up his hand to his mouth and said

'Balmy!' in a loud stage whisper. Behind her two women were talking about a girl called Janice. One of them had the high fluting voice of Mayfair, the other sounded elderly and rather cross.

Miss Silver listened because there wasn't anything else to do, and because the name Janice was strange to her. She wondered if she had heard it rightly. Perhaps they had said Janet. No, there it was again, and with a surname this time—Janice Meade.

The cross woman said, 'I always thought her a most unreliable girl.'

And the other, 'Rather charming, don't you think?'

'Oh, charm—I suppose so, if you like that sort of thing! Of course everyone in the college knew you couldn't trust a word she said.'

There was a high fluting laugh.

'My dear, how crushing! Poor Janice—she wasn't really a bad little thing. Too much imagination—that's all. Do you know where she is?'

'Still down at Bourne, I believe. I haven't seen her for an age.'

The queue began to move forward. The voices began to talk of something else. Miss Silver made a mental note of a new and rather attractive name and proceeded on her way to tea with Ethel's friend.

CHAPTER TWENTY THREE

Janice rang the bell of 15 Montague Mansions, and was admitted by a stout elderly woman who looked like the comfortable sort of cook of one's dreams. She smiled, and said it was a nice morning in a pleasant country voice, and,

'You'll be the lady Miss Silver was expecting—the one that sent the telegram—Miss Meade. Well then, come along in.'

One door shut and another one opened. The full beauty of Miss Silver's maple furniture, her peacock-blue curtains, her wallpaper, her brightly flowered carpet, her steel engravings, and her silver photograph frames was disclosed. Janice saw them first, and then she saw Miss Silver, very neatly dressed in a most unbecoming shade of drab, with a bog-oak brooch and a quantity of mousy hair in a fringe controlled by a hair-net and primly coiled behind. She rose from the writing-table at which she was sitting, shook hands, and indicated a chair with bow legs, round back, and a very hard seat upholstered in the prevailing peacock-blue.

Janice sat down, and found a pair of small, nondescript eyes surveying her in a manner that took her back to school again. Not that the Head had remotely resembled Miss Silver, but there was the same flavour of kindness and authority, the same expectation that you would come to the point and not waste valuable time. Sitting up as straight as the curly chair would allow, Janice came to the point.

Observing her, Miss Silver saw a girl of twenty-one or twenty-two in a dark blue coat and skirt which was neither new nor very well cut. The plain small hat was tilted at a becoming angle over short gold-brown curls. The face had a good deal of charm, without regularity of feature or beauty of colouring. There were those very bright eyes with their unexpectedly dark lashes. There was the way the ears were set—very prettily shaped ears, in just the right place to emphasize the curve of the cheek. There were the lips, not too much reddened, and taking a serious sweetness in repose. The skin though pale was very smooth and clear. Miss Silver considered the question of this pallor. Her eyes fell to the hands in their rather shabby gloves, and saw how tightly they were clasped.

She smiled that sudden transforming smile which had won her so many confidences and said,

'Pray do not be nervous—there is nothing to be afraid of. And take your time. These things are not to be told in a moment. I am quite at your disposal.'

The smile came in among Janice's thoughts and warmed them. She had had a sense of coldness, of confusion, of the terrible responsibility of being the one to tell this story in such a way that Evan Madoc would be helped and his sister comforted. She went on with a feeling that the weight had lifted, and that it didn't matter so terribly what she said, because Miss Silver would understand.

When she had finished, Miss Silver opened a drawer, took out an exercise-book with a bright green cover, opened it at the first page, and wrote a heading—The Harsch Case. After which she picked up a half-knitted sock of Air Force blue and began to knit in the continental manner, needles clicking, hands held low, eyes fixed upon Janice, who was taking something out of her bag. The something was a long envelope which was filled with typescript.

'This is the evidence which was given at the inquest. It was taken down in shorthand for a government department which was interested in Mr. Harsch's work—but I was to say will you please consider that confidential.'

Miss Silver coughed.

'Certainly. I regard all professional communications as strictly confidential. I shall be interested to read the evidence. Meanwhile——'

A little colour came into Janice's face.

'You'll take the case?' she said in an eager voice.

Miss Silver looked at her kindly.

'Why do you wish me to do so, Miss Meade?'

The cold, confused feeling came back. She had muddled it. Miss Silver hadn't understood—she was going to refuse. She said piteously,

'His sister is so unhappy. He is all she's got. And he didn't do it.'

The kind look persisted. It seemed to go right through her.

'You want me to prove that Mr. Madoc is innocent?'

'Yes—yes—of course I do!'

Miss Silver was knitting briskly, the sock revolved. She said,

'I cannot take any case with such a condition attached to it. It is beyond my province to attempt the proof of either innocence or guilt. I feel obliged to make this perfectly clear. I can only take a case with the object of discovering the truth. Sometimes this truth is at variance with the client's wishes and hopes. As Lord Tennyson so aptly says—"Oh, hard when love and duty clash!" But once I have undertaken a case I can be swayed by duty alone, and that duty must always be the discovery of the facts. They may be unexpected, they may be unwelcome. They may deepen a tragic situation instead of relieving it. I say this to every client.'

Janice's colour rose a little more.

'He didn't do it—he didn't really!'

Miss Silver smiled.

'You are a good friend, Miss Meade. You are attached to Mr. Madoc, and so you believe in him. You think him incapable of a crime.'

'Oh, no, it isn't like that at all—it really isn't. I've worked for him for a year, and if you had asked me before all this happened, I would have said that I detested him. He is the rudest man in the world—he says the most insulting things—he has a simply dreadful temper. But he didn't kill Mr. Harsch. I want you to find out who did. I want you to come down with me this afternoon and stay with Miss Fell. She says you helped her cousin, Laura Fane, when Tanis Lyle was murdered. All the Fanes and the

102

Ferrars are relations of hers. She is an old lady and very kind. Her nephew, Major Albany, has been down there watching the case. He got the copy of the evidence at the inquest for you. Miss Fell wants you to come down and be just an old friend who is staying with her, but I'm afraid that's not much good because of Ida Mottram——'

'Mrs. Mottram? Dear me!' Miss Silver coughed gently.

'She talks such a lot. I'm afraid she'll tell everyone how wonderful you are.'

Miss Silver knitted in silence for a moment. Then she said,

'Gratitude is a virtue, but it is sometimes inconvenient. What train do you wish to catch, Miss Meade?'

CHAPTER TWENTY FOUR

By half past eight that evening Miss Silver might have been residing at the Rectory for years. She had placated Mabel, who did not consider that visitors were at all necessary in wartime, she had shown Miss Sophy a new knitting stitch, and satisfied Garth that she could be trusted to behave with discretion and tact. What impression she had made upon the remaining member of the party, it was impossible to say. Miss Brown, it is true, appeared at dinner and joined occasionally in the conversation, but her look was so lifeless, her voice so mechanical, that it was impossible to feel that she was really there. As soon as they rose from the table she withdrew. Garth, coming last into the hall, watched her slowly mount the stairs, her hand upon the balustrade, her fine eyes fixed, her air that of a woman who walks in a haunted dream.

When he reached the drawing-room Miss Sophy was telling Miss Silver that he had weighed ten and a half pounds when he was born. It was not until the coffee had been brought, partaken of, and cleared way that she could be detached from the saga of his infancy. Aunt Sophy was indeflectable. She supported anecdote by documentary evidence. Photographs showing Garth in a vest, Garth in a bathing-suit, Garth completely *au naturel*, were bandied back and forth. He retired into the *Times,* and thanked heaven that Janice wasn't there.

But when Mabel had carried out the tray and the door was shut, the photographs went back into their drawer and the talk got down to business. Not as crudely as this may suggest, but after a seemly fashion, and by consent of both the ladies, for if Miss Silver desired to hear, Miss Sophy was certainly anxious to talk.

Garth put down his paper, and was edified. It appeared that Miss Silver was now thoroughly conversant with the evidence given at the inquest. She touched upon it here and there, referring to Garth as well as to Miss Sophy for details as to the voice, manner, and general tone of witnesses. He became aware of a thought penetrating and illuminating whatever it touched. The prim, old-maidish manner which was its cloak began by amusing him, but before long the amusement changed to something not unlike discomfort. He felt a little as if he had picked up an old lady's work-bag and found it to contain a bomb.

Aunt Sophy on the contrary was completely happy. It was years since she had had so appreciative an audience. She poured out information about everyone and everything—about Michael Harsch; about the Madocs; about her neighbours on the Green; about the village, about the Pincotts; about the Rector, the sexton, the church, the organ; about poor dear Medora and what a terrible shock it had been to her; about the party telephone and how extremely inconvenient it was—'or might be if I ever had anything to say that I would really mind everybody knowing, because Mary Anne Doncaster—she is the younger of the two Miss Doncasters who live at Pennycott and a shocking invalid, poor thing—she sits and listens in by the hour when she hasn't got anything else to do. And I daresay there are others as well, though I wouldn't put a name to them. But I'm afraid that the only person who has interesting calls is Mrs. Mottram. She is a widow, you know, and very pretty, and young men do ring her up. Mostly friends of her husband's, I expect, but of course Mary Anne and Lucy Ellen make the most of it.'

Miss Silver coughed and said that gossip was usually ill-natured and very often untrue. After which she picked up the ball of wool which had rolled from her lap to the floor and steered the conversation back to the Tuesday night when Mr. Harsch had met his death.

'You were sitting in here with the window open, Miss Fell?'

Miss Sophy nodded. She was feeling pleased and important. If she had been a cat she would have purred.

'Oh, yes—behind the black-out. It was such a mild evening.'

'And you could hear the organ?'

'Oh, yes. Mr. Harsch was playing Purcell's Trumpet Voluntary —only now they say that it wasn't by Purcell at all, but by somebody called—Clark, I think it is. So beautiful.'

'What time would that have been?'

'Well, I don't know that I can say exactly, but I suppose some-where before half past nine, because Medora was still in the drawing-room, and she had gone upstairs before the half hour.'

'You could hear the music quite clearly?'

'Oh, yes, quite.'

Miss Silver stopped knitting for a moment and leaned forward.

'When did you stop hearing it?'

Miss Sophy's blue eyes became quite round with surprise. All her sausage curls wobbled, and so did her chins.

'I don't know. Did I stop hearing it?'

Miss Silver smiled and went on knitting.

'I think you must have done. Before half past nine Miss Brown was in the room with you. Quite probably you were talking.'

'Oh, yes.'

'Yet you heard the music distinctly—you could identify the Trumpet Voluntary. But at a quarter to ten you had opened the glass door and gone down the steps to the garden because—I am quoting your evidence—you wanted to smell the night-flowering stock and to hear whether Mr. Harsch was still playing the organ.'

Miss Sophy nodded again.

'Yes—so I had.'

Miss Silver's needles clicked.

'Will you try and remember when the music stopped. Did you hear anything after the Trumpet Voluntary?'

'Oh, yes, I did. But I don't know what it was. I thought he was improvising.'

'That was after Miss Brown had left the room?'

Miss Sophy took a moment to think about this.

'Oh, yes, I am sure it was, because I remember being sorry she wasn't there. But then it stopped.'

'How long before you opened the glass door?'

Miss Sophy considered.

'I don't know. It might have been ten minutes, because I waited a little, and then I put my patience cards away, and I found a letter from my cousin Sophy Ferrars which had got pushed into that drawer by mistake, and I read it all through again and thought of answering it next day, only I never did because of the dreadful news about Mr. Harsch. Yes, I think it must have been quite ten minutes. And then I thought I would go out and smell the night-scented stock, and see if Mr. Harsch was still playing.'

'Did you hear the organ at all after you opened the glass door?'

Miss Sophy shook her head. The curls wobbled again, and so did the chins.

'Oh, no—only that dreadful shot.'

'So that there was an interval of about ten minutes between the time the organ stopped and a quarter to ten when you heard the shot.'

Miss Sophy said, 'Yes.'

Garth leaned forward and spoke for the first time.

'Ten minutes during which he may have been making up his mind to shoot himself?'

Miss Silver coughed.

'Or talking to the person who shot him, Major Albany.'

'That line of argument isn't going to help Madoc very much—is it?'

Miss Silver looked at him.

'If Mr. Madoc is innocent, every bit of fact which can be uncovered will help him. If he is guilty, no one can help him at all. The facts will always fight for an innocent person. I have explained to Miss Meade that they are my only concern.'

Garth found himself refusing to be snubbed.

'There is no proof that there was anyone except himself in the church, but if anyone did talk to him there, it is more likely to have been Madoc than anyone else. He had the key, he was angry, he was jealous, he is a man of violent temper—I think the case against him is pretty strong. On the other hand, if he did shoot Harsch it must have been planned beforehand. People don't walk about Bourne with revolvers. I don't know the man, so I can't really base any argument on his character. Janice says she can. She swears through thick and thin he didn't do it. But she also swears that Harsch didn't do it himself, and quite frankly, that seems to me to be the only alternative.'

Miss Silver was approaching the heel of her sock. She set the knitting down upon her knee for a moment in order to give her full attention to Major Albany.

'How long have you known Miss Meade?'

Garth frowned, he didn't quite know why.

'I've known her always. Her father was the doctor here. They lived next door.'

Miss Silver smiled.

'Pray do not be offended if I ask you some questions about her. I will give you my reason for doing so presently, and I hope you will agree that it is a good one.'

There was something disarming about voice and manner —authority stepped down to ask instead of demanding. Garth lost his frown, met her look with one as straight, and said,

'What do you want to know?'

She was grave again.

'Miss Meade is young. She has enthusiasm and loyalty—I do not doubt that. But I would like to know your opinion of her judgment. Is it likely to be unduly swayed by feeling?'

'I don't think so. I don't know that I agree with all her arguments, but they are arguments—they represent a point of view. She was fond of Harsch and sorry for him. She doesn't like Madoc particularly—he is an intensely disagreeable person—but she is quite sure he isn't a murderer. Is that what you want? I don't think feelings come into it—at any rate not unduly.'

'Would you agree with that, Miss Fell?'

Miss Sophy started slightly.

'Oh, yes—I suppose so. Poor Mr. Madoc, he really can be very disagreeable indeed.'

Miss Silver coughed.

'To return to Miss Meade. Would you take her account of anything as being accurate?'

Garth said, 'What do you mean by that?'

Miss Silver coughed again.

'I will tell you presently, but just now I should like an answer to my questions.'

'Well then, the answer is yes. I should say she was rather scrupulously accurate.'

'A very sweet girl,' said Miss Sophy. 'And such a good daughter. Her father had a very sad illness, and she was most devoted—so reliable and unselfish.'

'And truthful?' said Miss Silver.

Miss Sophy bridled.

'Oh, yes, indeed!'

'What do you mean, Miss Silver?' said Garth in a low, angry voice.

She took up her knitting again.

'You consider that Miss Meade is most truthful and accurate?'

'Of course I do!'

'Then I am wondering why two total strangers should have been at some pains to give me the opposite impression.'

'What!'

The sock revolved briskly.

'I heard Miss Meade's name for the first time on Sunday afternoon. Two ladies behind me in a Tube booking-office were talking about her. I could not avoid hearing what they said, and I was struck by the Christian name, which I had not heard before. They spoke as if they knew her well. There was a mention of being at college together. They said she was charming but quite unreliable—you could not believe a word she said—that kind of thing. It was very well done, and I thought nothing of it at the time, but when I got Miss Meade's telegram this morning, and later on when I had seen her, I wondered why it had been done at all.'

'What a strange coincidence——' said Miss Sophy in rather a bewildered voice.

Miss Silver's needles clicked sharply. She said in her most governessy tone,

'I am really quite unable to believe that it was a coincidence, Miss Fell.'

CHAPTER TWENTY FIVE

Mrs. Bush, who had been born Susanna Pincott, was the kind of stirring woman whose energies are quite unable to find sufficient scope in the domestic round. As soon as her children could be bundled off to school she embarked upon the contest with a reluctant husband which resulted triumphantly in the addition of a glass bay to their living-room and the stocking of it with picture postcards, bottles of lemonade and other soft drinks, china ornaments, cigarettes, and cheap sweets. She could thus see life, enjoy unlimited opportunities for gossip, and ensure her own control over at least a part of the family finances.

When Miss Silver entered the shop at eleven o'clock, Mrs. Bush was deep in conversation with a little elderly person with a long nose, pale eyes, and a black felt hat tipped sideways over straggling grey hair. Mrs. Bush herself towered mountainous behind her counter, her hair still as black as when she was a girl, her cheeks red and firm, her massive figure upright and controlled in spite of the temptation offered by the prevailing village fashion. Like every other woman in Bourne, she wore a loose flowered overall, but beneath it were the formidable stays of her youth.

In a most deprecating manner Miss Silver enquired if she might look at some postcards.

'I am in no hurry—no hurry at all. Pray do not let me disturb you. I always like plenty of time to make a choice.'

She became immersed in a colourful series depicting the ruined Priory, Bourne village showing the stream running down the side of the street, the church with its old squat tower, the new secondary school at Marbury, and the water-works. As she turned them over she was aware of the two women's voices, hushed to a sibilant undertone. Not for the first time, she felt gratitude for the excellence of her hearing.

'He did ought to be ashamed of himself,' said the little elderly woman.

Mrs. Bush was leaning close. Her voice was deeper.

'Ezra never did have any shame, nor never will. Nothing but a trouble to the family first and last, and no good expecting anything different. I suppose he was drunk as usual.'

Out of the tail of her eye Miss Silver saw the black felt hat shaken.

'Not to say drunk, Tom says—it takes more than what you can get nowadays to make Ezra Pincott drunk, Tom says. Just a bit above his usual, if you know what I mean, and telling everyone that'd listen to him as how he knew something that'd be money in his pocket if some he wouldn't name knew which side their bread was buttered.'

'Gracious, goodness me!' said Mrs. Bush.

'And all of them laughing and egging him on, but he wouldn't say no more than that, only of course everybody knew what he meant.'

'Ssh, Annie!'

There was a nudge across the counter. Two pairs of eyes were turned upon Miss Silver, who gazed with rapt attention at the card which depicted the secondary school, bright yellow against the kind of blue sky which an English summer has seldom been known to achieve. The voices dropped still lower. No more words were discernible until Annie straightened up and said she must be going.

And I'll be taking my sweet ration here same as usual, Susannah, if you'll bear me in mind for the first lot of peppermints as come through. Wonderful partial to peppermints, Tom is.'

She went out, and Mrs. Bush moved down the counter.

'Very interesting views,' said Miss Silver. 'I am staying with Miss Fell at the Rectory. She told me you would have pictures of all the most interesting places in the neighbourhood. So nice, I always think, to be able to send a really interesting card to a friend when one is on a holiday.'

The ice thus broken, conversation flowed. There were reminiscences of the old Rector, of Miss Sophy at the time of the last war.

'They had the sewing-parties up at the Rectory regular, and nothing would serve them but I must do the cutting out. No good at all with the scissors, Miss Sophy wasn't. Oh, well, we didn't think we was going to have it all over again, and worse, did we? That's the church, and a very good likeness, as you can see if you take a look out of the window—and the last one I've got left. You wouldn't believe the run there's been on them this week on account of poor Mr. Harsch shooting himself while he was playing the organ. And I'm sure he played beautifully, though I'm not such a one for music myself. It's Mr. Bush that'll go anywhere for a bit of good playing, and what I say is, it's all very well in its place and a little of it don't hurt anyone, but look at poor Mr. Harsch when all's said and done—it didn't do *him* any good.'

'A dreadful fatality,' said Miss Silver.

'Shocking,' said Mrs. Bush. 'A nice quiet gentleman if ever there was one, in spite of being foreign. And it's my belief he shot himself same as the verdict in the inquest. Rubbidge, I call it, their trying to put it on Mr. Madoc. Isn't that just the police all over? I've got a nephew in them—constable, he is—Jim Pincott, my eldest brother's son—and I said to him only last night, "And what's the good of an inquest, will you tell me, if that's all the notice you take of what the jury says? Didn't they hear all the evidence? Didn't the Coroner put it to them proper? And didn't they bring it in suicide while the balance of his mind was disturbed, same as you see it in the papers? And what call have you got to go bringing down the London police after that?" Let them stay at home and mind their own murders, I say, and not come ferreting and worriting where nobody wants them!'

Miss Silver gazed in timid admiration.

'How well you put it!'

Mrs. Bush smiled complacently.

'Oh, I can hit a nail on the head when it's there to be hit. And I'll say that for Jim, he hadn't got a word to say, only it wasn't none of his doing.'

'Then it is the London police who have arrested Mr. Madoc?'

'Two of them,' said Mrs. Bush. 'You'd think they'd have enough to do at home with all you see in the papers. Come in to see Mr. Bush, the two of them—Chief Detective Inspector Lamb and Sergeant Abbott. Of course Mr. Bush being the one to find the body along with Miss Janice Meade, they couldn't move hand nor foot, as you might say, without his statement. But it wasn't anything they got from him that made them go after Mr. Madoc. It was something one of those 'vacuee boys said, and if he was mine I'd put him across my knee—coming down here and taking people's characters away! I'm sure Mrs. Brewer was in here Saturday evening, the very day poor Mr. Madoc was took. She goes there twice a week to oblige, and she said, "Mrs. Bush, he never done it. Hasty he may be, but what's a hard word to two when you're used to them?—and there's a lot of difference between language and shooting people." '

'Yes, indeed,' said Miss Silver in reverential tones.

Mrs. Bush leaned nearer.

'Of course they do say there was something going on between him and that Miss Brown.' She checked suddenly and drew back. 'Well, there—I shouldn't have said that, with you staying at the Rectory. I hope you won't mention it to Miss Sophy.'

Miss Silver looked shocked.

'Oh, no, indeed. It was quite natural, I'm sure. I don't really know Miss Brown at all, but I have heard that there was some talk about her and Mr. Madoc. She seems to have had a very severe shock, poor thing.'

Mrs. Bush primmed her lips. Even according to her own indulgent standards she had been indiscreet. But what a chance of obtaining inside information. The Rectory maids were as tight as tight—not a word out of either of them. She allowed temptation a foothold, and succumbed.

'Hardly eats a thing, they tell me.'

Miss Silver sighed.

'She seems very low, poor thing.'

Mrs. Bush leaned half across the counter.

'They do say she went out to meet Mr. Madoc in the Cut, but there's such a lot of gossip, you don't know what to believe. Mr. Bush, he's never seen anything—not in that quarter. I won't say as much for other people. I'm sure I don't know what the girls are coming to. There's that Gladys Brewer, no more than turned sixteen—it's not once nor twice Mr. Bush has had to speak to her, up in the churchyard nights with bits of boys that want a good tanning if you ask me. And I'm sure I pity Mrs. Brewer from my heart, for if she hasn't got trouble coming to her, I don't know who has—and her own fault, poor thing, the way she's spoilt the girl. Mr. Bush, he's had to speak to her very severe, and she's not the only one. But as to anything between Mr. Madoc and Miss Brown, he's never seen anything, as I said. And who'd be likely to if it wasn't him? That's what I say. Regular as clockwork round the churchyard every night of his life, and if there were any goings on, well, he'd be the first to know, wouldn't he?'

'Unless they counted on his being so regular and waited till he was gone, Mrs. Bush. People can be sadly deceitful when they are doing wrong.'

Mrs. Bush nodded condescendingly. She had put Miss Silver down in her own mind as one of those humble dependents, neither fish, flesh, fowl, nor good red herring—a governess or some such that Miss Sophy had got down to stay by way of a kindness. That sort was in the way of knowing things, but you didn't have to mind your p's and q's with them.

'That's right,' she said. 'Never five minutes out, Mr. Bush isn't. Ten o'clock he takes his key from the hook on the dresser and out he goes on his round, wet or fine.'

Miss Silver coughed in a deprecating manner.

'Why does he take his key?' she enquired.

Mrs. Bush looked important.

'Because he's responsible for the church as well as for the churchyard—verger and sexton, same as his father before him. And if there was to be a window left open or suchlike, he'd go in and shut it. Of course they're too high up for anyone to get in, but if it was to come on to blow there'd be the rain, and if it was a gale, broken glass on the top of that. It's the Rector opens them—that's just between you and me. Says the church is damp. He's one of those learned gentlemen that can't see past what they've read in a book. Now it stands to reason no place won't keep dry with the windows open to the rain, but he goes on opening them, and Mr. Bush, he has to watch his chance to get them shut. Quite worries him, but as I say, what's none of your doing it's no use worrying after. But you know what men are—it's no good talking, they just go their own way.'

Miss Silver gazed.

'He does his round at ten o'clock every night?'

'Regular as clockwork,' said Mrs. Bush.

CHAPTER TWENTY SIX

Miss Silver came out of the shop with six postcards in her handbag. A hundred yards down the road she was overtaken by Sergeant Abbott. He had hurried to catch her up. He now contemplated her with a mixture of surprise, affection, and awe.

'Miss Silver!'

She had a charming smile for him.

'Dear me, what a pleasant meeting.' She shook hands.

Sergeant Abbott's expression became modified. It took on a shade of sardonic humour. He had met Miss Silver on a case before, and the experience had left him her devoted admirer. He wondered very much what she was doing in Bourne, and whether she would tell him, or leave him to find out for himself.

She was graciously pleased to inform him that she was staying at the Rectory, to which he replied that he was on his way there to see Miss Brown. After a slight pause Miss Silver coughed and came to the point.

Later in the day Sergeant Abbott was reporting to Chief Inspector Lamb. The word report is perhaps too formal an expression. Sergeant Abbott was sometimes informal to an almost impudent degree. He cocked an eyebrow now and said sweetly,

'Maudie has turned up, sir.'

Lamb said, '*What!*'

'Miss Maud Silver, sir—Maudie the Mascot.'

Lamb was a good Methodist. He didn't swear, but he turned purple.

'At Bourne? What's she up to this time?'

Sergeant Lamb declaimed musically, 'Blow, blow, thou winter wind, thou art not so unkind as man's ingratitude.'

'Stop playing the fool and let's have a bit of sense, Frank! We've got our case, haven't we? We've got our man? We could do with a bit more evidence, but you can't expect murders to be done before witnesses. I say it's a good enough case. He had motive and opportunity. And he recognized the weapon—that came out quite clear at the inquest—said he was familiar with the type. Well, I say that's good enough. You'll never get me to believe he put that key in his pocket and went home like he says. He took it because he meant to have things out with Harsch then and there. And he shot him. That's what I say, and I think a jury will say it too. Well then, what does Miss Silver want? Who's called her in?'

'Miss Fell.'

Lamb stared angrily.

'Well, of all the——! Look here, Frank, what does it mean? Miss Fell—she's a nice old lady—what's it got to do with her, unless she's doing it on account of this Miss Brown? Did you see her?'

'Oh, yes, I saw her. And I might just as well have stayed at home. She had nothing to add to her statement, she had no comment to make on what Mr. Madoc might have said, and that was that. All very petrified, very haughty—the Great Ice Age—and what is a policeman that I should tell him anything? In fact, as our Maudie would say, "Icily regular, splendidly null". Quotation from the late Lord Tennyson.'

Lamb growled, 'Quit fooling!' and rapped the table with his knuckles.

'What did she say to you—Miss Silver, not Miss Brown. What has she got in her head?'

'I don't know—she didn't let on. It's clear she is being retained by Madoc's friends. I won't say in Madoc's interest, because, as she's always so careful to point out, she's out for the truth, the whole truth, and nothing but the truth. But she wants to see Madoc.'

'Oh, she does, does she?'

'Alone,' said Abbott with some emphasis.

'Now look here, Frank——'

Abbott's mouth twisted.

'I said I would lay the matter before you, sir.'

Lamb gazed at him with suspicion.

'Very correct—aren't you? When you start saying sir every time you open your mouth, I begin to look out for what you've been up to. And you needn't go out of your way to tell me I'm ungrateful like you did just now, because I'm not saying, and never will, that Miss Silver didn't do us a good turn over the Vandeleur House murders. I don't mind admitting that we were on the wrong line and she put us on the right one, and that we both got some good marks out of it. And I'll admit she's not one to make a fuss of herself, or to get into the papers.'

Frank Abbott had his faint sardonic smile.

'Strange, isn't it?' he said in an easy conversational voice. 'She's known to the police, but not to the Press, and whenever she comes into a case, we come out of it in a blaze of glory. And she just fades away quoting Tennyson and saying "Bless you my children". What about her seeing Madoc, sir?'

Lamb relaxed.

'Oh, she can see him if she's got a mind to. But I'd like to know what she's got up her sleeve.'

Frank Abbott came and sat on the corner of the writing-table.

'Well, here's something she gave me. That man Bush, the sexton—it never came out at the inquest that he makes a round of the church and the churchyard every night at ten o'clock because the Rector goes leaving windows open and he doesn't hold with it.'

Lamb stared.

'There wasn't anything about that. If it's true, why wasn't it brought out. The local constable would know—everyone in the village would know.'

Abbott laughed.

'Village people don't exactly rush to the police with information. Mrs. Bush was a Pincott, and as far as I can make out every other soul in Bourne is either a Pincott or has married one. Very prolific family. The constable is a nephew—Jim Pincott. I suppose he would have said if he'd been asked—I suppose any of them would. But nobody asked them whether Bush went round the church at night, so they held their tongues in the fine old English way. Maudie suggests that we have Bush on the mat and ask him what about it.'

Lamb's face grew slowly purple. His eyes, always rather reminiscent of the old-fashioned peppermint bullseye, showed a tendency to bulge. He smacked the table with his open hand.

'Look here, what are you giving me? She hasn't been there five minutes—how did she get all this? When did she come?'

Frank looked demure.

'By the six-fifty-eight at Perry's Halt last night, with Albany and Janice Meade. I gather that she engaged Mrs. Bush in gossip over the local picture postcards this morning. She has a flair for that sort of thing.'

Lamb said heartily.

'Good thing for her she wasn't born a couple of hundred years ago, or she'd have been ducked for a witch, if it didn't get farther than that.'

Frank laughed.

'Makes you feel that way—doesn't she? Well, here's something else. There's a disreputable old chap called Ezra Pincott—leading light in poaching circles, strong perservering upholder of the local bar—Maudie says he's been shooting off his face to all and sundry in the Bull about knowing something that would put money in his pocket if somebody knew what was what. She takes this to mean he's got a low-down on the Harsch business, and she feels we ought to keep an eye on Ezra in case somebody thinks it would be simpler to do him in than to start paying blackmail.'

Lamb grunted.

'That all? Nothing else she'd like? She's about to say of course. All right, all right—you can see about it to-morrow.'

Miss Silver had a busy afternoon. Lunch was not a comfortable meal. Florence had taken a great deal of trouble and everything was very nice, with good country vegetables, a plum tart, and the best she could do with the meat ration, but however well balanced you are, it is difficult to enjoy a meal with someone sitting opposite who looks as if she had just received a death sentence and has braced herself to endure its instant execution.

Miss Brown was more like Medusa than ever. Her eyes remained fixed upon her plate, but she did not eat. She merely pushed the food about in a jerky, mechanical manner. When it was apparent that the plum tart with its really very nice custard made from egg substitute was to share the same fate as the curried mince, the baked tomatoes, the beans and potatoes of the first course, Miss Sophy could bear it no longer. She said, 'Medora ——' in a pleading voice.

Miss Brown's face remained blank—eyes cast down, heavy black hair shading the marmorial brow, heavy black lashes shading the marmorial cheek. It certainly was exasperating to the last degree. Quite suddenly Miss Sophy lost her temper. Her voice, incapable of being loud, shook with vexation.

'Medora, you'll be ill, and nothing puts Florence out like leaving what she has cooked—and I'm sure I don't wonder when you think about the Navy having to bring everything hundreds of thousands of miles, except the plums and the vegetables which are out of the garden, but it would be all the same if they weren't! And what good you think you do, making yourself ill like this, I don't know, but you are making me very unhappy—very unhappy indeed!' She screwed up her eyes, and two bright little tears popped out.

Miss Brown's black lashes lifted, disclosing sombre eyes. She said in a deep whisper,

'I am sorry—I had better go,' and with that pushed back her chair and went out of the room in an unhurried, sleep-walking sort of way.

Miss Sophy burst into tears.

When she had been consoled, and lunch concluded, Miss Silver betook herself upstairs. Her tap upon Miss Brown's door was so briskly followed up that she was well into the room before her entry was perceived. It occasioned so much surprise as to shake that cold control.

Miss Silver coughed in a deprecating manner.

'I have come to have a little talk with you. Shall we sit down?'

Miss Brown shook her head.

'You are a detective. I have nothing to say.'

Miss Silver surveyed her compassionately.

'You are very unhappy, are you not?'

Miss Brown turned abruptly and walked over to the window. She stood there looking out, but she saw nothing. A sudden rush of tears blinded her. She neither moved nor did anything to wipe them away. They remained a distorting crystal through which the outside world had no form nor meaning.

Miss Silver stood where she was and waited. After a moment she said,

'It will be more comfortable if you will sit down. It does not matter if you are crying, but I think we must talk.'

There was a slow negative movement. Miss Silver said briskly,

'Let us be practical. When something has happened it is no use trying to remain in the past, or to refuse to accept what the present demands of us. I think Mr. Harsch was your friend. He is dead, and you cannot bring him back. Mr. Madoc is not dead— yet. He is alive, but he is in a very serious position. For some reason you have made up your mind that he shot Mr. Harsch. I want you to tell me why you think so.'

Without turning round, without moving at all, Miss Brown repeated what they were all so tired of hearing.

'I have nothing to say.'

Miss Silver sighed.

'That is not at all practical, I am afraid. If Mr. Madoc is guilty, your silence will not prove him innocent. There is a strong case against him. If he is innocent, any fact you can contribute will help to prove him so. One is not always the best judge of what is helpful to a person in whom one is interested. I beg of you to give me the chance of arriving at the truth. There is a good deal about this case which cannot be explained on the supposition of Mr. Madoc's guilt. Be frank with me, and I do not believe that you will regret it.'

Miss Brown continued to stare at a formless world through the distorting crystal of those unfallen tears. She made again the faint movement of the head which said 'No.'

Miss Silver said in her quiet, pleasant voice,

'You are making a grave mistake. Have you considered that the prosecution can call you as a witness, and that you can be compelled to speak? Even if you were prepared to refuse and to incur the penalty for contempt of court, your very refusal would tell most terribly against Mr. Madoc. Prosecuting counsel would be able to put questions which, in the absence of an answer, would strengthen the case for the Crown. You have no means of escaping this. You cannot avoid being called as a witness.'

Miss Brown turned round with a sudden quick movement. The tears which had blinded her fell unregarded. Her eyes blazed with something like triumph. She said in her deep, full voice,

'They can't call me as a witness. I'm his wife.'

Miss Silver said, 'Dear me!' and then, 'Pray let me beg you to sit down. It will be so much more comfortable for us both. I have always noticed when a conversation of any importance is carried on standing that it tends to become dramatic. Let me beg of you to be seated.'

Miss Brown walked over to a chair and sat down. Quite suddenly she was glad to do so. The stiffness had gone from her limbs, she felt relaxed and weak. She became aware that she had had very little food for days. She leaned back and shut her eyes. She heard Miss Silver leave the room, and presently she heard her come back again. A cup of soup was held to her lips. When she had drunk it she was encouraged in a kind, matter-of-fact way to partake of warmed-up mince and vegetables. After which she found Miss Silver looking at her in a friendly manner.

'Now why did you not tell Sergeant Abbott what you have just told me?'

'I don't know.'

Miss Silver coughed.

'It was not very wise. But when one has kept a secret for a long time it tends to become a habit.'

Miss Brown said, 'Yes.'

'Will you tell me when you were married, and where? There must be proof, or you cannot be protected from giving evidence.'

'Five years ago—in London—the Marylebone Register Office—June 16th. We didn't give it out because he was waiting for a job. We couldn't really afford to get married, but we were very much in love. It wasn't anyone's business but our own. He had his sister to support. I went on with my work, and he went on with his. We met when we could. Sometimes there were weekends.' She spoke in short, detached sentences, and in an absent voice as if she were looking back over those five years and remembering bit by bit. What no one could have known was just how much relief it brought her to remember and to speak.

She pushed back her heavy hair and let her hands fall again in her lap.

'We quarrelled of course. We weren't young enough to live that

118

sort of life. When you are not young you want a home, companionship—everything that is normal. We couldn't have it. Somebody else got the job that he was hoping for. He couldn't support me unless he stopped supporting his sister. He couldn't do that. The quarrels got worse. He has a very bad temper, but I could have managed if we had had a normal life. We couldn't have it. It all came to an end about three years ago. He didn't even write. Then I heard he had got this government job. I thought if we could meet again. But I couldn't leave my post—I couldn't afford to do that. Then the old lady I was with died and left me some money—enough to have made all the difference if it had come before. I went on thinking about coming here. A friend of mine helped me to meet Miss Fell, and I came here just over a year ago. At first I thought it was going to be all right. Then we quarrelled again. He began to make scenes about Mr. Harsch.' She pushed back her hair again and looked wretchedly at Miss Silver. 'There wasn't any reason for it—there wasn't indeed. We talked about music, and sometimes about Evan—we both loved him. But he is so difficult. I think he was jealous of both of us. That evening he knew Mr. Harsch had gone to the church to play the organ. He came down to see if I was there, and he took my key just as that boy says he did. And I don't know—I don't know what happened after that.'

'Then we must find out,' said Miss Silver in a brisk, and cheerful voice.

CHAPTER TWENTY EIGHT

'Who is Ezra Pincott?' enquired Miss Silver. She had the mild expectant look of a teacher addressing her class. For the moment this consisted of Miss Fell, Major Albany, and Miss Janice Meade. Miss Brown had been persuaded to go to bed. Her absence was felt to be a relief.

'All three of them said, '*Ezra* Pincott?'

'Dear me,' said Miss Silver, 'there seems to be a great many Pincotts in Bourne.'

There was nothing in her manner to show that she had already acquired a considerable amount of information about the Pincotts in general and about Ezra in particular.

Miss Sophy stopped pouring out tea, but kept the teapot poised.

'Oh, *yes*,' she said. 'Old Jeremiah Pincott had eighteen children. Susannah Bush is one of them, and they have mostly had large families themselves. Not Susannah—she has only two without counting the twins who died. Jeremiah was a well-to-do farmer, but Ezra is the son of his brother Hezekiah who ran away to sea.'

'He's the local bad hat,' said Garth.

Miss Silver accepted a cup of tea, produced her own bottle of saccharine, and dropped in one tablet.

'I see——' she said. And then, 'I should like very much to speak to him.'

Garth laughed.

'Then you'd better let me catch him for you to-morrow before the pubs are open.'

Miss Silver coughed.

'He drinks?'

'As much as he can get. What do you want him for?'

He wondered if he was going to be snubbed, but it appeared that the teacher would answer his question.

'I hear he was boasting last night in the Black Bull that he knew something that would put money in his pocket. No names were mentioned, but I received the impression that the reference was to Mr. Harsch and the manner of his death. You do not think it would be possible for me to see him before to-morrow?'

'I don't think so. You see, he's by way of working for Giles who farms the land on the other side of the Church Cut. The minute he gets off he goes down to the Bull and stays there till it shuts. The only time I could get hold of him for you would be during his dinner hour—that is, if you want him sober.'

Miss Silver looked grave.

'I should prefer it. I should also prefer to see him to-day, but it cannot be helped.' She coughed and continued, 'I should also be glad to have some information about Gladys Brewer.'

Miss Sophy looked mildly shocked. She helped herself to a rock bun and said in a soft, distressed voice,

'Not at all a satisfactory girl, I am afraid. She does daily work up at Giles', and her mother has very little control over her.'

Janice leaned forward with an appealing look.

'I don't really think she's as bad as they make out.' She turned to Miss Silver. 'She's one of those giggling, bouncing girls who get themselves talked about. She likes boys, and she'll do anything for a lark, but she's not bad—really.'

'I would like very much to see her,' said Miss Silver. 'I wonder if it could be managed. When is she likely to be free—about six o'clock?'

'Yes, I should think so.'

'She lives with her mother? . . . Then perhaps we might take a walk in that direction and look in.'

'Oh, yes, but——' Janice hesitated—'I wouldn't like to get her into trouble.'

Miss Silver smiled.

'There is a country proverb which says, "If you don't trouble trouble—trouble won't trouble you." '

Garth Albany gave her a direct look.

'What do you mean by that?'

She turned the smile on him.

'Gladys won't get into trouble—from the law—if she hasn't broken the law. I do not for a moment imagine that she has done so, but if she was in the churchyard on Tuesday night she may have seen or heard something. I should like to know whether she did.'

Janice said, still in that hesitating voice,

'I could take you in to see Mrs. Brewer. I know them quite well.'

At a little before six Miss Silver and Janice turned off the main street into a narrow lane where half a dozen old cottages mouldered. They were of the kind which are called picturesque, with old tiled roofs, minute windows, and a general air of dilapidation. Mrs. Brewer's cottage was the smallest and the most dilapidated. It had sunflowers and hollyhocks in the garden, and a few ragged gooseberry and currant bushes. The doorstep was freshly whitened.

When Mrs. Brewer opened the door Miss Silver thought she looked rather like the cottage, battered, and as if time had been too much for her. She had lost most of her front teeth, the late Mr. Brewer having knocked them out when 'under the influence'. She had told Janice all about it whilst obliging at Prior's End. She seemed to feel a kind of gloomy pride in her husband's prowess—'Life and soul of a party he was, and no harm in him as long as he wasn't crossed. And Gladys is as like him as two peas, but a bit tiring, if you know what I mean, miss.'

She invited them into her spotless kitchen. The door opened directly upon it, and disclosed very old uneven flagstones on the floor, and very old sagging beams not very far overhead. In the corner a narrow ladder-like stair led up to the bedroom. With the exception of a lean-to at the back to hold fuel and store vegetables, there were only these two rooms. Bathrooms and indoor sanitation were unguessed at when these cottages were built, and the petrifying dictum that what was good enough in the past was good enough for the present had never been disputed.

Mrs. Brewer pulled forward a couple of chairs and invited her visitors to be seated.

'Was it about me coming up to Prior's End, miss? If there was anything extra, I'd be very pleased——'

But even as she spoke, the horrid fear took hold of her that Miss Madoc might have sent to say that she needn't come any more, and then she'd be two days short, and nowhere to fill them unless she went back to the Miss Doncasters that never stopped telling you what do to and what not to do until you didn't know one from the other. And as like as not some of the china got broken. There was a cup with a blue border and little bunches of flowers the last time she was there, and such an upset as never was.

But Miss Janice wasn't saying anything like that. It was just, 'Miss Silver is staying with Miss Sophy, and I was showing her the village. She was saying your cottage must be very old.'

Mrs. Brewer looked relieved.

'Mr. Brewer's grandfather lived here,' she said, as if imagination could go no farther back. She turned to Janice. 'Oh, miss, what a dreadful thing about Mr. Madoc! I'm sure I never slept a wink after I heard. Oh, miss, he never done it!'

Janice said, 'No, we don't think he did.'

And with that the door swung in with a clatter and Gladys Brewer bounced into the room—a large plump girl with a bright colour and a fine head of chestnut hair piled up in front and hanging in a bush behind. She had bright blue eyes, very good teeth, and an exuberant air of health and jollity.

She said, 'Hullo, Mum!' and then caught sight of the visitors and giggled, voice and laugh at full stretch. 'Hullo, Miss Janice!' She giggled again.

Miss Silver said, 'How do you do?' and then went on talking to Mrs. Brewer about the cottage.

'So picturesque—but sadly inconvenient.'

Gladys let off another loud giggle.

'I'm sure you'd say so if you'd bumped your head as often as I have going upstairs! Well, I'll go up and change. I'm going out. You can expect me when you see me. We're going into Marbury to the pictures.'

Miss Silver addressed her directly.

122

'It must be rather dull for you in Bourne. What do you do in the evenings when you do not go to the pictures?'

Gladys giggled twice as loudly as before.

'What does any girl do if she gets the chance?'

Miss Silver smiled affably.

'You have a boy friend, I expect—or perhaps more than one, which is quite the best way when you are young. You will not want to settle down until you are older, and meanwhile, I expect, there are lots of boys of your own age to go about with?'

Mrs. Brewer fidgetted with her fingers, twisting them in and out. She looked from Gladys to Miss Silver.

'Oh, miss—she don't want any encouragement with the boys!'

Gladys seemed to take this as a compliment.

'Oh, get on with you, Mum!'

Miss Silver continued to smile indulgently.

'I am afraid you have spoiled her, Mrs. Brewer.'

By this time Gladys was in high good humour.

She felt herself the centre of attention, and was duly flattered. She thought Miss Silver ever such a kind old lady. Most of them expected a girl to behave as if she was dead and buried. That there Miss Doncaster with her 'Does your mother know you're out, Gladys?'—she never had no boy friends in her life. You could tell that as easy as easy—looked as if she'd been brought up on vinegar and never got rid of the taste of it.

Miss Silver's voice came in amongst these meditations. Quite a low voice it was, but something about it you couldn't help taking notice of.

'When you were in the churchyard on Tuesday evening, Gladys——'

'Who says I was in the churchyard?'

The interruption came so quickly as to suggest practice.

'There would be no harm in it if you were—I am sure of that. You are not that sort of girl, are you? But you do sometimes go in there with a friend on a fine night, don't you? I expect there are places where you can sit and talk.'

Gladys giggled.

'And I think you were there on Tuesday night. You were, were you not?'

Mrs. Brewer fairly wrung her hands.

'Oh, no, miss—she wouldn't do a thing like that! She's a good girl.'

'I am sure she is,' said Miss Silver. 'I am quite sure that there was no harm in it. Come Gladys—you were there, were you not?'

The blue eyes met Miss Silver's and found that they could not

123

look away. She made you feel like a kid at school again, when you were called out in front of the class and you dursn't hold your tongue, no matter how much you wanted to, or what you were asked.

'What if I was?' Her voice was half defiant, half afraid.

Miss Silver said equably, 'Well, then, my dear, I would like you to tell me just what you saw or heard.'

'I didn't hear nothing.'

'But you saw something, didn't you?'

'Who says I did? There wasn't nothing to see!'

Miss Silver's smile was gone. Her look was steady and grave.

'Have you ever done a jigsaw puzzle, Gladys?'

The girl's shoulder jerked. She stood where the stair came down, holding to the old newel-post, dark and smooth from all the hands which had touched it, lightly, lingeringly, heavily, for more than three hundred years.

'Course I have! My Auntie Brewer, she's nuts on them.'

'Well then, you will know how all the little bits fit in to make the picture. You may have a piece which does not look as if it was important at all, but if you get it in its right place you are able to see your way.'

Gladys stared, then brightened.

'She'd one like that last time I was there. A little bit of red it was, and when we got it down you could see where the next bit 'ud got to come.'

Miss Silver inclined her head.

'That is very well put. Now what you saw in the churchyard on Tuesday is just like one of those pieces in a jigsaw puzzle. It may be a very little bit and you may not think that it matters, but it may be just the piece which is needed to save a man's life. What would you feel like if an innocent man was hanged because you kept back something that would save him?'

Gladys stared with all her might.

'You have seen pictures about an innocent man being suspected. What would you feel about a girl who did not speak when she might save him?'

Gladys shifted from one foot to the other.

'It wasn't nothing like that.'

'You might not know.'

'Well then, it wasn't. It wasn't nothing. Only Mum goes on so. I suppose she never went for a walk with a boy!'

Mrs. Brewer said, 'Oh, Glad!'

Gladys let go of the newel and sat down on the third step from the bottom.

'All right, all right—it wasn't nothing to make such a fuss about!' She looked angrily at her mother. 'I went up to Mrs. Bowlby's like I told you I was going to, and we listened to the wireless for a bit, and then Sam and me went for a walk.'

'Oh, Glad!'

'Come off it, Mum! A girl can't sit indoors all the time, nor a boy neither. What's the good of saying, "Oh, Glad!"? It was ever such a lovely night, and we went for a walk. And when we come back we went into the churchyard and sat down for a bit, but we didn't see nothing nor nobody but Mr. Bush, and he didn't see us—not that time, though he's always on the look-out. He was in a hurry and went off quick. So what's all the fuss about?'

Janice had been sitting quite still. She moved now. Bush—yes, of course Bush would have done his usual round on that Tuesday night. She hadn't thought of it before. She supposed nobody had. Bush going round the churchyard every evening at ten o'clock was as much a part of the day's routine as moonrise and sunset, and as little to be considered. She heard Miss Silver say,

'You saw Mr. Bush. What was he doing?'

Gladys stared.

'Going his round.'

Miss Silver coughed.

'Oh, yes. But what exactly was he doing when you first caught sight of him?'

'He was coming out of the church.'

Janice had a choking sensation. There was no air. She took a quick, shallow breath. Miss Silver's even voice went on without any change.

'I see. It was bright moonlight, was it not?'

'Oh, yes, it was ever so bright.'

'And where were you sitting with your friend?'

Gladys giggled.

'Right up against the Rectory wall. There's a tree comes over. We were sitting on Mr. Doncaster's grave. It's got a nice flat stone on it.'

'So you could see the church door quite plainly, but Mr. Bush couldn't see you?'

'That's right.'

'And Mr. Bush was coming out of the church?'

'That's right. He come out and he locked up, and he went off quick—didn't come spying round like he does.'

Miss Silver coughed.

'What time was this?'

'I dunno.'

'But the church clock strikes, does it not? Did you not hear it strike whilst you were in the churchyard?'

Gladys nodded.

'That's right—it struck ten.'

'Before Mr. Bush came out, or afterwards?'

'Oh, afterwards.'

'How long after?'

'It wouldn't be more than a minute or two. He went off round the church, and then the clock struck.'

'There are three gates to the churchyard, I believe—one leading to the Green, one to the Church Cut, and one to the village street. Which way did Mr. Bush go?'

'Right out to the street. That's his way home.' She got up. 'I'm going to be late for the pictures. I'm going to change.'

Miss Silver got up too.

'Just a moment, Gladys. Where did you go for your walk?'

'Oh, just round the Green.'

'How long had you been in the churchyard before you saw Mr. Bush?'

'Oh, I dunno—about five minutes.'

'Did you hear a shot at any time during your walk?'

'I dunno. Mr. Giles, he shoots at the foxes—there's often shots—I didn't take any notice.' She went up a step or two, then turned. 'I told you it wasn't nothing—any of it. And I'm going to be late.' She giggled with a return of her easy good nature. 'Do Sam good to keep him waiting, but I don't want to miss the picture.'

CHAPTER TWENTY NINE

Garth Albany came knocking on Miss Silver's door before she was dressed next morning. She opened it in a warm red flannel dressing-gown trimmed with hand-made crochet, her hair rather flat but perfectly neat in spite of the absence of a net. He slipped inside, shut the door behind him, and said,

'Ezra Pincott has been found dead. The milk boy brought the news—Mabel has just told me. I thought you ought to know at once.'

'Yes—yes, indeed.' She stood quite still for a moment. 'I felt very apprehensive. I had asked that he should have police protection.'

'Well,'' said Garth, 'at any rate they can't say Madoc did it—can they?'

Miss Silver said, 'No——' in rather an absent voice. And then, 'Pray give me any particulars you may have learned.'

'I didn't see the boy myself. He's about sixteen—Tommy Pincott, a cousin of Ezra's and quite a bright lad. Mabel says he told her Ezra was found face down in the stream just beyond the last house in the village. It's no depth there—not more than about a foot—but if he was drunk and tumbled in, there would be enough water to drown him.'

Miss Silver coughed.

'You think it may have been an accident?'

Garth said bluntly, 'No, I don't. Drunk or sober, Ezra knew his way home, and got there. He'd been at it for too many years to drown himself a good quarter of a mile out of his way. I think somebody did him in and hoped it would be taken for an accident —and if he had been trying his hand at a spot of blackmail, there's your motive.'

She said, 'Yes.' And then, 'I must dress. Inspector Lamb must know of this at once. He will be coming down.'

But it was half past three in the afternoon before the Chief Inspector and Sergeant Abbott rang the Rectory bell. Miss Silver received them in the study. Even at a moment like this she could not dispense with the personal side of a valued friendship. She shook hands with a smile. She enquired by name for each of the three daughters who were the pride of old Lamb's heart.

'The one in the A.T.'s has her commission? How very nice. Such a pretty girl—I remember you showed me her photograph. Lily—such a sweet name, and so appropriate for a fair girl. And Violet—in the Wrens, was she not? . . . Engaged to a Naval officer? How very, very interesting. And your youngest daughter Myrtle—I think she was a W.A.A.F.? Such important work. I am sure she is enjoying it. And I hope Mrs. Lamb is well, and does not miss her girls too much.'

Frank Abbott controlled a humorous twist of his lips. There had been a time when he suspected Miss Silver of diplomacy, but it was all as serious on her side as old Lamb's. She really wanted to know about his daughters, and whether his wife was enjoying good health. He took the opportunity of sharpening a pencil and waited for them to emerge from domesticity.

Lamb led the way.

'Well, well, we must get down to business. I hear you want to see Mr. Madoc.'

'I should like to do so, if you will be so very kind as to make it possible.'

He nodded.

'Eleven o'clock to-morrow. He's in Marbury jail, as I expect you know. There isn't very much you don't know—is there? And whilst you are there, see if you can get him to talk. Not about the crime of course—that wouldn't be proper now he's been charged—but the War Office is pestering us about this invention of Mr. Harsch's in which they were interested. Harsch made a will leaving everything to Madoc, and that includes all the notes about his experiments, and this invention, whatever it is. They say the whole thing was practically completed and they want it badly. Madoc won't play because he's a pacifist. They don't know whether they can get the will set aside or not, but meanwhile they are in a regular stew about Harsch's papers, because if he *was* murdered for them, they won't just be left kicking about. Mind you, I'm not saying that's why he was murdered. Our case was against Meade, and the motive there would have been jealousy, but this Sir George Rendal is very hot on its being the work of an enemy agent, and he's like a cat on hot bricks about those papers. Madoc, he won't play—just says they were left to him and they're his affair.'

'So I understand from Major Albany.'

'Well, you try and get Madoc to say what he's done with them. Between ourselves, we've put on two men from the Special Branch just to see there isn't a convenient burglary up at Prior's End.'

Miss Silver coughed.

'You said just now that your case *was* against Mr. Madoc. Did you use the past tense advisedly?'

Lamb had seated himself in the Rector's old chair, which was of very comfortable proportions for a man of his size and weight. There was a shade of reluctance in his expression as he looked across at Miss Silver busily knitting a khaki sock for her second cousin Ellen Brownlee's son in the Buffs. The Air Force pair, duly completed, now reposed upstairs in the left-hand top drawer of Miss Fell's spare bedroom, waiting for the address which she had asked her niece Ethel to send on to her as soon as possible. The needles clicked, the ball of khaki wool revolved. Miss Silver sustained that reluctant look with a pleasant, deprecating smile.

Lamb cleared his throat.

'As a matter of fact, this man Ezra Pincott's death—well, it's a complication, there's no doubt about that. I'll give you what we've got. If you can see where it fits in, I can't.'

Miss Silver coughed.

'You mean, Inspector, that it does not fit in with your case against Mr. Madoc?'

Frank Abbott, sitting up at the writing-table with his notebook ready, chose this moment to lean upon his elbow and slide a hand across his mouth. Behind this screen he relaxed into an appreciative smile. Lamb said stolidly.

'I'm not saying that one way or the other. I'm giving you the facts.'

Miss Silver said brightly, 'Unfaith in aught is want of faith in all. It is the little rift within the lute That by and bye will make the music mute And ever widening, slowly silence all.' She coughed and added, 'Dear Lord Tennyson—and how true!'

Sergeant Abbott gave himself up to reverent enjoyment. His Chief Inspector's response was all that he could have hoped.

'If that's poetry, I'm not much of a hand at it. And as to being true, it sounds to me like throwing away an apple because it's got a speck on it.'

Miss Silver smiled.

'What a good illustration! I fear I interrupted you. You were going to tell me about Ezra Pincott. Pray continue.'

'Well, there it is. The police surgeon's done the post mortem, and the man was drowned.'

Miss Silver knitted.

'I think there was something more than that.'

Lamb gave a grunt.

'He was found face down in a foot of water. He was drowned. What more do you want?'

'A shocking fatality. But there is something more, or you would not be concerned about it.'

Lamb shifted in his chair.

'Well, if you must know, he'd been hit. Bruise behind the ear. He didn't get that falling on his face into water.'

Miss Silver said, 'Dear me!'

'He went in alive, but he'd been hit first. He'd had a good deal of liquor—some of it was brandy. Now he didn't get brandy at the Bull. Beer was what he drank there, and by all accounts he could put away more than most before he was what you could call drunk. One of your steady day in day out topers, but they tell me nobody's ever seen him incapable or in any way unable to get himself home. And he didn't have that brandy at the Bull.'

'Where did he have it?'

'I'd be glad if someone would tell me that. Well, there you are. You sent me a message yesterday to say he was boasting that he knew something that would put money in his pocket, and you thought someone ought to keep an eye on him. I'm sorry I didn't take you at your word and put a man on to him then and there. I didn't think there was all that hurry. Abbott was coming down here today, and I left it over till then. Seems I was wrong, but it's no good crying over spilt milk. The man's dead, and I'm going to find out how he died, whether it knocks the case against Madoc endways or not.'

Miss Silver gazed at him approvingly.

'That is just what I would expect from you, Inspector.'

He said rather gruffly, 'It sounds as if he was planning to blackmail someone. I've had a word with the landlord of the Bull, and he says Ezra always talked big when he'd had a few, but he'd been talking bigger than usual. I asked him if Mr. Harsch's name was mentioned, and he said it was. Just that—and he'd got something that would put money in his pocket if someone knew which side their bread was buttered. The landlord said he didn't take it at all seriously. But there you have it—the man boasted of what he knew. Now after that somebody gave him brandy, somebody hit him, and he drowned in a foot of water. No evidence to say how he got there, but he may have been put. The place he was found was out of his way if he was going home. There's one thing more—the sort of thing that mayn't mean much, or then again it may—I haven't had time to think it out. Frank there can tell you about it—it's his pigeon.'

Abbott took his hand away from his mouth and sat up.

'It's just that I had a look at his boots,' he said, 'There was a speck or two of dry gravel on them.'

Miss Silver looked at him with extreme interest.

'Dear me!'

Rightly considering this to be a tribute, he continued.

'You know how sloppy the village street is. Even in the warm, dry weather we've been having it's damp, and between the Bull and the place where this fellow was found there's a dip in the road which is more or less of a quagmire. The only gravel anywhere about is on the drives of the houses round the Green and on the paths in the churchyard. If Ezra got gravel on his boots from any of those places, it couldn't possibly have been dry and clean by the time he got to the place where he was drowned—if he walked there.'

'That is very interesting indeed,' said Miss Silver.

'His boots were muddy all right—that's how the gravel stuck.

But once it got there it stayed clean. It wasn't walked on—not to that miry place where he was found. I say he was given a tot of brandy and knocked out. Then he was taken down to the stream and put into it. It could have been done with a hand-cart or a wheel-barrow. Unfortunately the place has been so trampled over that there isn't much to go by. I should think everybody in the village has been out to have a look. Anyhow all the traffic there is goes along that road, so there isn't much chance of picking out a single track.'

'The churchyard——' said Miss Silver slowly. 'That is very interesting. Yes—of course—there are gravel paths in the churchyard. And that reminds me that I have some information for you. The first item takes us a little away from our present subject, but it is so important that I feel you should have it without delay. You will, I am afraid, be unable to call Miss Brown as a witness in any possible case against Mr. Madoc.'

Lamb stared.

'Indeed?'

The needles clicked, the khaki sock revolved.

'I had a conversation with her this afternoon, and she informed me that she married Mr. Madoc on June 17th five years ago, at Marylebone Register Office.'

Frank Abbot said, 'That's torn it!'

His Chief Inspector turned a deep plum colour.

'Well, if that doesn't beat the band!' he said in an exasperated tone.

Miss Silver coughed.

'I felt that you should be informed immediately. But let us return to Ezra Pincott. Without wishing to link my second item of information with his death, I cannot but feel that it has a certain relevance in view of the fact that the churchyard paths are gravelled. I have discovered a witness, a young girl by the name of Gladys Brewer, who was in the churchyard round about ten o'clock on the night of Mr. Harsch's death. Her companion was a lad of the name of Sam Bowlby. I have not interrogated him, but Gladys says they saw the sexton, Bush, come out of the church at a little before ten.'

The Chief Inspector's eyes bolted.

'She saw him come *out of the church*?'

Miss Silver inclined her head.

'She says he came out, locked the door behind him, and went off in a hurry round the building in the direction of the gate which opens upon the village street.'

'Miss Silver!'

She inclined her head again.

'Yes, I know. It makes a very considerable difference, does it not?'

'Bush came out of the church before ten o'clock?'

'A few minutes before the clock struck. We must allow time for him to lock the door, skirt the church, and be out of sight before the clock struck. Gladys and her friend were sitting on the flat stone of Mr. Doncaster's grave right up against the Rectory wall. They were immediately opposite the side door of the church, and it was bright moonlight. They could see perfectly, but were screened themselves by the branches of a copper beech which overhangs the wall at this spot.'

Lamb was leaning forward, his big body tilted, his eyes more like bulleyes than ever.

'You think she's reliable, this girl? She's not having us on—or working off a grudge against Bush? If she's in the way of going into the churchyard with her boy friend at night she might have had the rough side of his tongue—see?'

Miss Silver coughed.

'I do not think so. I believe that she was telling the truth. I arrived at the point in a somewhat oblique manner, and it was only when pressed for every detail of what she had seen on Tuesday night that the facts emerged. She was impatient to be gone to the pictures with Sam Bowlby, and she had, I am sure, no idea that what she told me was of any importance whatever. She said at the end, "I told you it wasn't nothing, any of it," and went off without a thought in her head except about her boy and the film they were going to see.'

Lamb took a deep breath and exhaled it slowly.

'Well, I'll take your word for that. But what a mix-up! Bush came out of the church before ten. He was in it not so very long after the shot was fired. If he hasn't got an alibi to cover the time, there's nothing to say he didn't fire that shot himself. He was seen coming out. If he wasn't seen going in, well. . . . And there's another thing. If that girl's telling the truth and she saw him lock the door, then all that business about the key goes west—there's nothing to show that the door was locked at all before Bush locked it. The fact that Madoc had a key isn't nearly so important as it was.'

Miss Silver said, 'Exactly. The theory that Mr. Harsch committed suicide was based on the fact that he was found behind locked doors with his own key in his pocket. The case against Mr. Madoc was based upon the discovery that he had come into possession of Miss Brown's key after a jealous scene with her, and about a quarter of an hour before the shot was fired. But since it now appears that the door behind which Mr. Harsch's body was found was neither locked by his own key nor by the one in Mr. Madoc's possession, but by Bush, it seems to me that the case against Mr. Madoc is very much weakened. When it is further considered that there is evidence that Ezra Pincott was murdered last night, the case would seem to be very weak indeed, since Mr. Madoc could have had no hand in this murder.'

Lamb hoisted himself out of his chair.

'Well,' he said, 'I won't say yes, and I won't say no. But this man Bush has certainly got something to explain. We'll have to see him and ask him what about it.'

Half way to the door he turned back.

'You haven't got a motive to hand us, I suppose? Respectable sextons don't go about murdering organists as a rule. You've got to have a motive, you know. Juries are funny that way.'

Miss Silver drew herself up. It was the slightest, most ladylike of gestures, but it certainly conveyed to Sergeant Abbott, if not to his superior officer, that the Chief-Inspector had allowed a perhaps natural exasperation to impair the courtesy due to a gentlewoman. There was a faint chill upon her voice as she said,

'There is a possible motive, and I feel it my duty to acquaint you with it. Bush, though born a British subject, is of German origin. His parents settled in this country. The name was Busch, spelt in the German manner with an sch, the English spelling being adopted during the last war. Miss Fell informs me that a short time previously this man Frederick Bush, who was then about seventeen years of age, was approached by enemy agents who endeavoured to persuade him to obtain information for them. He was at that time under footman in a house where the conversation at the dinner table might have been of considerable value. I must hasten to add that he immediately refused, and that he acquainted Miss Fell's step-father, who was then Rector of Bourne, with the particulars.'

Lamb pursed up his mouth and whistled.

'*Well*!' he said. Then with an abrupt movement he turned to the door again. 'Oh, come along, Frank—come along before she tells us anything more! I've got as much as I can get through with for today.'

Whilst this conversation was going on Miss Sophy had slipped into a gentle refreshing sleep in the drawing-room. Though she never admitted to an afternoon nap, and would not on any account have put up her feet, she had no objection to supporting them on a footstool, or to leaning back against a number of comfortably piled cushions and closing her eyes. Garth Albany on one side of her and Janice upon the other became aware that they no longer had her attention. Her white woolly curls rested becomingly against a blue silk cushion, her breath came evenly and without sound from the slightly parted lips, her plump hands were folded in a purple lap. To all intents and purposes they were alone.

If Janice could have been anywhere else she would have been glad. Or would she? She didn't know. Ever since that walk on Sunday she didn't know what she wanted. Down deep in a hidden corner something wept and refused to be comforted. Because Garth had been going to make love to her and she had stopped him, and now she wouldn't have anything to remember. He would go away, and it might be years before he came back again. He might go abroad, he might be killed, and she would have nothing, nothing to remember. He might have said, 'I love you,' he would certainly have kissed her. Even if it had meant nothing to him, it would have been something to treasure up and remember when he was gone. But she had chosen her pride instead. She was finding it icy comfort.

She looked at him across Miss Sophy's plump bolster of a shoulder, tightly upholstered in plum-coloured cashmere, and found him unbearably dear. The way his hair grew, the line of cheek and jaw, and the way his eyes crinkled at the corners when he smiled——

They crinkled now. He said in a laughing voice,

'Stock situation from a farce! The chaperone is asleep. What do we do about it?'

Her heart gave a little jerk. Her lips trembled into a smile. She said,

'Ssh!'

Garth laughed again.

'Oh, no—I don't think so. My stage direction says, "Crosses R." ' Getting up as he spoke, he came round the sofa and sat down on the arm of her chair. 'You needn't worry, you know—she won't wake. Family trait—once I'm off, I'm off—it takes a bomb to wake me.'

'But you're not any relation—she's a step. You can't inherit something from your grandfather's step-daughter.'

His arm stretched lazily across the back of the chair behind her shoulders.

'I didn't say it was inherited. There are such things as acquired characteristics. Anyhow the point is, she's good for at least half an hour, and—wilful waste makes woeful want. I suppose you wouldn't like to be kissed?'

He saw the colour leap like a flame in either cheek and flicker out. When she slowly turned her head and looked at him she was so pale that he was startled. She moved colourless lips to say 'Yes.' Instead he put his hand upon her shoulder.

'What's the matter?'

'Nothing.'

He gave her a little shake.

'My child, this was a farce. You're playing tragedy—"Unhand me villain—I have taken poison". What's the matter?'

'I'm not very good at farce.'

He looked at her with laughing eyes.

'I'm not at all set on it myself. Let's make it drawing-room comedy—the great proposal scene. I come of rich but honest parents. I know all about you, and you know more than any other girl does about me. Life's highly uncertain for both of us. As someone once wrote, "Gather ye roses while ye may". What about it?'

Her lips were stiff. She forced them to a smile.

'I don't know my part, Garth.'

His hand came up on the far side, taking her by the elbow, turning her a little.

'There's always the prompter. If it's a very modern play, you say casually, "All right, I don't mind if I do." But if it's one of those romantic period pieces, it would be, "Oh, Garth—this is so sudden!"'

She managed to go on smiling.

'It is rather, isn't it?'

'I suppose it is. It's funny the way things are. I've always been fond of you. You were such an odd little thing—I was very fond of you. And then I went away and forgot all about you, but when I saw you come in at the inquest I felt just as if I hadn't ever been away at all. It's difficult to explain, but it felt good—it felt quite extraordinarily good. I—Jan, I'm really trying to tell you something.'

'Yes——'

'It's just as if you were part of me—part of the boy I was. You can't ever get away from what you've been, and you really are a part of that. I found that out when I came back, and now I keep finding out that you're still a part of me. It goes deep down as far as I can get. If it's been like that and it's like that now, don't you think it's good enough to suppose it will go on being like that? You know, when you said you didn't want me to make love to you because you'd rather keep something that was real, you made me think. And what I thought was this—why, we've got the real stuff—it's there—we can't get away from it—it's as solid as wedding cake, but what's the matter with having the almond paste and the sugar icing too?'

This time she didn't speak. The no-coloured eyes were very bright and rather scared. His arm came round her neck, the hand under her chin tipping it up.

'Hate me?'

'Not dreadfully.'

'That's something. Like me?'

'Sometimes.'

'Impassioned creature! Love me a little?'

'No.'

'Sure?'

The scared look went out of her eyes. A sparkle made them brighter than before.

'You haven't said you love me. Do you?'

'Quite a lot, Jan.'

She repeated the words gravely—'Quite a lot.'

It was at this moment that Miss Sophy opened a round blue eye. It rested hazily upon the agreeable spectacle of two young people embracing one another, and closed again. Miss Sophy was no spoil-sport. It was only when the subsequent soft murmurings became so articulate as to make her feel she was eavesdropping that she most regretfully stirred, rustled her cushions, yawned with emphasis, and sat up. The embrace, alas, was over. Dear Janice had a very becoming colour. Dear Garth was also somewhat flushed. She beamed upon them.

'My dears—how nice!'

Garth had the hardihood to enquire,

'What, Aunt Sophy?'

Miss Sophy patted her curls.

'I believe I have had quite a nap,' she said, and beamed again. 'Very pleasant—very pleasant indeed. I had a most agreeable dream—if it was a dream.'

Before she could receive any reply the door was opened. Chief Detective Inspector Lamb appeared—a solid presence, but with an air of haste.

'Beg pardon, Miss Fell.' He came in and shut the door behind him. 'I suppose, between you, there isn't much you don't know about this village. Can you tell me who keeps brandy in the house?'

'*Brandy?* said Miss Sophy in a surprised voice. 'I think we have some.'

Lamb looked past her.

Janice said quickly, 'Mrs. Bush—her aunt has spasms. She lives with them—she's bed-ridden. They always have brandy in case——'

'Is anyone ill?'' said Miss Sophy in a bewildered voice.

Lamb gave a kind of snort. He had an exasperated air. He said testily, 'He isn't ill, he's dead!' and went out of the room and shut the door. You couldn't say that he banged it, but he certainly shut it a little more loudly than he need have done.

Miss Sophy opened her eyes as far as they would go.

'Why did he want the brandy?' she enquired.

CHAPTER THIRTY ONE

Frederick Bush stood looking down from his spare height upon the two London police officers who had summoned him to this interview. Invited to take a seat he did so, retaining an upright carriage and his habitual air of dignified melancholy. He had removed his cap, and held it now in the hand which rested upon his right knee.

Lamb looked shrewdly at him and said,

'Thank you for coming here, Mr. Bush. We are checking up on the events of Tuesday night, and I think perhaps you can help us.' He reached across the table with a paper in his hand. 'This is a transcript of the evidence you gave at the inquest. Will you look it through and tell me if you agree that it is correct.'

Bush took the paper and laid it upon his left knee. He then put down his cap upon the floor, produced a leather spectacle-case from an inside pocket, opened it, and put on the spectacles, all in a very deliberate manner. After which he picked up the paper, read it through without haste, and laid it back upon the table.

Lamb watched him.

'You find that correct?'

Bush was putting away his glasses. When the case was back in his pocket, he said,

'Yes.'

Sergeant Abbott, writing down that single word, made the mental comment that the interview bore a certain resemblance to a slow-motion picture. Shorthand, he considered, was going to be thrown away on Mr. Bush.'

Lamb was speaking.

'Have you anything to add to that statement?'

Bush said, 'No.' He took his time over saying it.

'You're sure about that?'

'Yes.'

'Mr. Bush—it is your habit, is it not, to make the round of the church and churchyard every night?'

With no more hurry and no more hesitation than before, Bush again said,

'Yes.'

'At what hour?'

Frank Abbott thought, 'I'll get something that isn't a yes this time anyhow. I'm about tired of writing it.'

The answer came as the others had come, and without change of voice.

'Ten o'clock.'

'You made this round on Tuesday night?'

'Yes.'

'Then why didn't you say so at the inquest?'

'I wasn't asked.'

'It didn't occur to you to volunteer a statement?'

'No.'

'You answered only what you were asked. If you had been asked, you would have said that you had made this round?'

'Yes.'

Frank thought ruefully, 'We're off again.' His mind played with questions which could not be answered by a mere affirmative.

Lamb said, 'Then we'll get back to this round you made on Tuesday night. When did you start out?'

'A little before my usual time.'

'Why?'

'I'm not bound to a time. I suit myself.'

'And why did it suit you to make an early start on Tuesday night?'

This time there was a definite pause before the answer.

'I don't know that I can say. You don't have to have a reason for everything you do.'

'You say you went out before your usual time. How much before?'

'I couldn't rightly say—a matter of ten minutes perhaps.'

'Did you hear the shot?'

'No.'

'It wasn't because you heard the shot that you started out before your usual time?'

'No.'

Lamb looked at him shrewdly. The melancholy calm of look and manner were unimpaired. He had picked up his cap again and was holding it on his knee as at first, but in a closer grip. A knuckle showed bloodless where pressure tightened the skin.

Lamb said in an easy voice, 'Very well—you went out on your round. Now tell me just where you went and what you did. And don't leave anything out because you haven't been asked—I want the whole bag of tricks.'

Bush put his left hand in his pocket, pulled out a red bandanna handkerchief, and solemnly blew his nose. It was a leisurely affair. So was the return of the handkerchief. So was the measured fall of words which followed.

'I went out of my front door into the street and a bit along till I come to the churchyard gate and in.'

'That would be the gate that opens on the village street?'

'Yes. And along the path on the right, and right round the church, and out by the gate where I come in.'

'Did you see anyone?'

'No.'

'And that was all?'

'I went in, and I did my round, and I come out, and I didn't see no one.'

Lamb said sharply, 'Nothing to add to that?'

'No.'

Lamb made a sudden movement. He leaned forward and thrust out a hand across the table.

'Look here, Bush—you were seen. You didn't see anyone, but two people saw you—a boy and a girl who were under the tree by the Rectory wall. Now what about it? What have you got to say to that?'

All the knuckles of the hand which held the cap showed white as bone. The melancholy face remained calm. Bush said slowly,

'I don't know what they saw. I was doing my round.'

'They saw you come out of the church.'

'They might have seen me come out of the porch.'

'They saw you come out of the door, and they saw you lock it after you.'

There was a long pause. Then Bush said,

'I was doing my round.'

'And your round takes you into the church?'

'It might do.'

'Did it take you into the church on Tuesday night?'

'I won't say it didn't.'

Lamb drew in his hand and sat back. He said,

'Look here, Bush, you'd better make a clean breast of it. If you were in the church you knew Mr. Harsch was dead getting on for about two and a half hours before you went in with Miss Meade and found the body. You can see for yourself that gives you something you've got to explain. If you're an innocent man, you'll be willing to explain it. If you're not you've got a right to hold your tongue, and a right to be told that anything you say may be taken down and used in evidence against you. Now,—are you going to talk?'

There was a prolonged pause. When it had lasted for an indefinite time, Bush said in the same tone that he had used throughout.

'Seems I'd better.'

Lamb nodded.

'That's right! Well, you went into the church——'

'Yes, I went in to do my round. The Rector, he's careless with the windows.'

'Did you see Mr. Harsch's body?'

'Yes, I saw it.'

'Just tell me what you did from the time you went into the church—everything.'

Bush put up his free hand and rubbed his chin.

'I went in, and when I come round the corner where you can see the organ the curtain was pulled back and Mr. Harsch fallen down off the stool.'

'Were the lights on?'

'Only the one he had for playing. And the pistol was fallen down beside him. When I saw he was dead, I didn't know what to do. There wasn't nothing I could do for him, so I thought what I'd better do for myself. Seemed to me it'd be better if it wasn't me that found him when I was by myself at that time of night. Seemed to me he was bound to be missed up at the house and someone 'ud come down to look for him—same like Miss Janice did. So I thought that'd be best, and no getting mixed up with the police.'

'Go on,' said Lamb. 'What did you do?'

Bush appeared to consider.

'I didn't touch him. I knew that wouldn't be right—no more than to put away his key.'

There was a sharp exclamation from Lamb. Bush went on.

'Lying aside of where he'd been sitting on the organ stool.'

'*On the stool?*'

'That's where he'd put it. He'd let himself in and come along with the key in his hand and put it down on the stool. I've seen him do it, and I'd say, "You'll be losing that key one of these days, Mr. Harsch", and he'd shake his head and say "No", and slip it back into his waistcoat pocket. So when I saw it lie there, that's what I done—I picked it up and put it back in his pocket.'

Lamb came in quick and sharp.

'Then why hadn't it got your prints on it?'

Bush looked mildly surprised.

'I took hold of it with my handkerchief.'

Both men stared.

'What made you do that?'

'Seemed as if it was the right thing to do.'

'Why?' The word came back as sharp as a pistol shot.

Bush put up his hand to his chin again.

'I'd no call to leave my prints on it.'

'You thought about that?'

'It come to me.' He dropped his hand.

Lamb said, 'All right, go on. What did you do next?'

'I put out the light, and I come out and locked the door and off round the church like I said.'

'What time was it?'

'Struck ten just as I come to the gate.'

'Was the church door locked or unlocked when you came to it?' The Chief Inspector's eyes were intent and shrewd.

Bush made his undisturbed reply.

'It was open. Mr. Harsch didn't use to lock it, not once in a blue moon.'

Sergeant Abbott thought, 'And there goes our case against Madoc!' He wrote the answer down.

Lamb sat forward in his chair, his jaw hard under heavy muscle and firm flesh.

'You should have said all this before. Holding your tongue like this, you've thrown suspicion on others. When did you see Ezra Pincott last?'

With undiminished calm Bush thought for a moment, and then said,

'Last night—in the Bull.'

'Did you leave together?'

'No.'

'What time did you leave?'

'Seven minutes to ten.'

'What did you do?'

'I went my round.'

'Did you go into the church?'

'Yes.'

'Sure you didn't take Ezra in with you?'

For the first time Bush looked disturbed. He said,

'What would I do that for?'

'You know he had been boasting that he knew something about Mr. Harsch's death, and that it would put money in his pocket?'

'Anyone could know that. He was there in the Bull, saying it for all to hear.'

The next question came very sharply.

'You keep brandy in your house?'

Bush moved in his chair. A slight frown creased his forehead.

'There's nothing wrong about that. Mrs. Bush's aunt, she takes it for her spasms.'

'So I've been told. Did you give Ezra some of it last night?'

The frown straightened out. The grave lips moved into a smile.

'Ezra never needed for no one to offer him drink. What makes you think I'd give him my good brandy?'

Lamb brought down his fist on the table.

'Someone gave him brandy, and someone knocked him out and put him in the water to drown.'

Bush stared.

'You don't say!'

'Yes, I do.'

Bush went on staring.

'Whatever for?'

Lamb gave him back look for look.

'To stop him opening his mouth about who killed Mr. Harsch.'

Bush dropped his cap on the floor. It seemed as if it just slipped from his hand and fell. He stooped to pick it up.

'Whoever 'ud do a thing like that?' he said.

CHAPTER THIRTY TWO

'They would never forgive me if I did not take a visitor to call,' said Miss Sophy. 'I have known them all my life, and Mary Anne is such a sad invalid.'

Miss Silver smiled, and spoke the simple truth.

'I shall be delighted to call on the Miss Doncasters.'

'Then I will just finish the letter I was writing to my cousin Sophy Ferrars. It will not take me long, and it will give them time to finish their tea.'

The afternoon was mild and fair. Miss Silver put on her hat, her gloves, and a light summer coat, and strolled in the garden, where the trees made a shady pattern across Miss Sophy's lawn. It was very agreeable—very agreeable indeed. If her mind had been at rest, she would have been enjoying her visit very much. But her mind was very far from being at rest—oh, very far indeed. She walked up and down upon the grass and considered the unsatisfactory details of the Harsch case.

From somewhere on her left a voice of peculiar shrillness spoke her name. No one who had heard that voice could possibly mistake it. She had made it her business to encounter Cyril Bond that morning. She turned now to see him astride the wall between the Rectory and Meadowcroft, one hand holding an overhanging branch, the other flourishing a stick in a manner which suggested that he regarded it as a spear.

'What is it, Cyril?'

'D'you reckon you know what "Spricken see Dutch?" means?'

Miss Silver smiled benignly.

'You are not pronouncing it correctly. It should be, "Sprechen sie Deutsch?" It means, "Do you speak German?" '

Cyril flourished his spear.

'I arst Mr. Everton, and he said he didn't know any German. There's a boy at our school, his father's a refugee. He's a Jew. He knows a lot of German—he can talk it ever so fast.'

Miss Silver smiled.

'You are a great climber, are you not? I hope you are quite safe upon that wall. Which was the window you climbed out of?'

Cyril drooped.

'I won't 'arf get in a row if Mr. Everton knows.'

Miss Silver continued to smile.

'I shall not tell him. Which window was it?'

143

Cyril reduced his piercing tones to a hissing whisper.

'That one there'—he pointed with the spear—'over the libery. That's how I got down.'

'Were you not afraid that Mr. Everton would hear you?'

Cyril cast her a look of scorn.

'Naow,' he said, making two Cockney syllables of the word and lingering on them. 'I don't do it except when he's out.'

'And he was out on Tuesday night?'

'Acourse he was! Up at Mrs. Mottram's fixing something for her. She can't do nothing by herself.'

'How do you know he was there?'

' 'Cos I heard him say so. Called right out in the hall he did. "I'm just going up to Mrs. Mottram's," he says, "to fix her wireless set." Cook and the other lady didn't 'arf laugh when he'd gone.'

'When did he come back?'

'I dunno—I went to sleep. Oh, boy! When I think I might have heard the shot!'

'How do you know Mr. Everton was not in when you got back?'

Cyril dropped his voice.

'The black-out isn't all that good in the study. I don't say it's bad, but there's always places you can see if there's a light on.'

'Perhaps he'd gone up to his room.'

His tone was scornful again.

'Naow! He sits up ever so late, Mr. Everton does.' He looked sideways out of the corners of his eyes.

'You couldn't be sure,' said Miss Silver mildly but firmly.

'Well then, I could!' He made a sudden cast with his spear into the garden of Meadowcroft and slid down after it.

As she walked with Miss Fell past the intervening two houses to Pennycott Miss Silver had not a great deal to say. Miss Sophy found her a delightful listener. Scarcely drawing breath, she managed to impart a good deal of information about the Miss Doncasters in the short time at her disposal. It went back to their schooldays, and contained some particulars which interested Miss Silver very much.

'But of course it all rather faded during the war—the *last* war—and for some years afterwards. And we all hoped there wouldn't be any more of it.'

'And was there?' said Miss Silver in a most attentive voice.

Miss Sophy stood quite still opposite the Lilacs and said,

'Oh, *yes*.' She leaned towards Miss Silver and fooffled. 'And when it came to such an inordinate enthusiasm for a *house-painter*. . . .'

'It was some minutes before they resumed their interrupted progress towards Pennycott.

They were admitted by an elderly maid and taken upstairs into what had been the best bedroom, now converted into the drawing-room for the convenience of Miss Mary Anne, who slept in the room behind and could be easily wheeled to and fro. She was there when they came in, propped up by cushions in an invalid chair with rubber tyres.

Miss Sophy made the introductions.

'My friend Miss Silver. Miss Doncaster—Miss Mary Anne.'

Miss Silver took a seat beside the wheeled chair and remarked that Bourne was a very picturesque village, and that the weather was delightful. As she did so she was observing the two sisters and their surroundings—the overcrowded room, its walls covered with dark oil paintings in the heavy gilt frames of a bygone day, the floor space contracted by a quantity of ugly, useless furniture which must have cost a great deal some hundred years ago. Curtains of maroon velvet obscured the light. An ancient drab carpet could be seen here and there between the chairs, the cabinets, and the tables which were crowded with gimcracks—a family of wooden bears from Berne; frames carved with edelweiss; a miniature Swiss chalet engrained with dust; other frames of tarnished silver holding faded photographs; little boxes in Tunbridge ware; in filigree, in china; a snowstorm in a glass paper-weight; an Indian dagger in a tarnished sheath. Family history come down to trifles.

A hideous tea-set with a great deal of gilding occupied the mantelpiece, and above it a monstrous overmantel inset with mirror-glass reared itself to the ceiling and reflected a score or so of distorted views of the room.

As a background to the Miss Doncasters nothing could have been more appropriate. She had not been five minutes in their company before she understood why kind Miss Sophy could find no warmer words for either than 'Poor Lucy Ellen', and 'Poor Mary Anne'. There was a strong family resemblance between the sisters, but whereas Lucy Ellen was sharp and ferrety, Mary Anne was heavy and shapeless. Both had sparse grey-white hair and deep lines of discontent.

Without effort on her part Miss Silver found the conversation turning upon Mr. Harsch. It was of course the most dramatic thing which had happened in Bourne since Jedediah Pincott ran away with his cousin Ezekiel's bride twenty-four hours before the wedding and they were both killed in a railway accident, which Bourne considered to be a very proper judgment. It was Miss

Mary Anne who introduced the subject of Mr. Harsch, greatly to Miss Sophy's relief as Lucy Ellen was being what she could only call persistent in cross-examining her about Miss Brown. She hastened to join in.

'I am sure we must all hope that the matter will be cleared up.'

Miss Doncaster gave it as her opinion that it was suicide.

'I said so from the beginning. The jury said so at the inquest. There was never any doubt about the verdict. As I served on the jury I suppose I may be allowed to know.'

Miss Silver gave a slight cough.

'Most distressing for all his friends,' she observed. She inclined an attentive head towards Miss Mary Anne. 'And is it true that he was engaged upon an invention of some value. How doubly distressing if he was not about to finish it.'

'Oh, but he was.'

'Really? How very interesting.'

Miss Mary Anne's voice did not resemble her sister's. It was thick and treacly. She said with unction.

'He finished it that very day—some last experiment, and a complete success. He rang up a Sir George Rendal at the War Office at half past six on Tuesday evening and arranged for him to come down next day. I heard him with my own ears.'

Miss Silver looked mildly surprised.

'You heard him?'

Miss Doncaster said sharply,

'We are on a party line here—you can hear everything. It is most inconvenient.'

Miss Mary Anne went on as if her sister had not spoken.

'You would be surprised at what you hear—people are most incautious. I had lifted my receiver, and I could hear everything he said. I remember I turned to Frederick Bush who was setting up those shelves in the corner—he does all our odd jobs for us—and I said, "*There*—Mr. Harsch has finished his invention —isn't that a good thing? Sir George Rendal will be coming down from the War Office about it to-morrow." And he said, 'Then I expect Mr. Harsch'll be down at the church playing tonight. Last time I saw him he said he'd be down so soon as his work was done." '

'Dear me!' said Miss Silver.

Miss Doncaster cut in with determination.

'Which goes to show that he had planned to take his life. Suicide—that's what I've said all along.'

'Unless there's something in this story about Mr. Madoc,' said

Miss Mary Anne. 'You know, Sophy, they say that he and Mr. Harsch had a quarrel over your Miss Brown.'

Under her best hat Miss Sophy bridled.

'People will say anything. But there is no need to repeat it, Mary Anne.'

It was perhaps as well that at this moment the door should have opened to admit Mrs. Mottram in crimson corduroy slacks and a bright blue jumper, her fair hair encircled by a green and orange bandeau. She looked extremely pretty, and when she saw Miss Silver she uttered a scream of joy and addressed her as 'Angel!'

'Because she was—she really was,' she explained. 'You see, I'd lost—but perhaps I'd better not say what, but it belonged to my mother-in-law, and you *know* what mothers-in-law are—she'd never have believed I hadn't sold it, and then there *would* have been the devil to pay. And this angel got it back for me and practically saved my life.'

She rolled her blue eyes and sat down beside Miss Silver, who patted her hand and said in kind but repressive tones,

'That will do, my dear—we will say no more about it.'

Fortunately all eyes were on the slacks. Miss Doncaster's strongly resembled those of a ferret observing a young and incautious rabbit. She said in acid tones,

'I notice that you have gone out of mourning.'

The blue eyes opened to their fullest extent.

'Well, I only put it on because of my mother-in-law, and it's so long——'

'When I was a girl,' said Miss Doncaster, 'the rule for a widow used to be one year of weeds and crepe, one year of plain black, six months of grey, and black and white, and six months of grey and white, heliotrope, and purple.'

Ida Mottram giggled.

'But then people used to wear crinolines and all sorts of funny things then—didn't they?'

There was a stony silence before Miss Doncaster observed in a pinched voice that it was her grandmother who had worn a crinoline.

Mrs. Mottram gazed affectionately at her ruby slacks.

'Well, when a fashion's dead it's dead,' she said. 'You can't dig it up, or we might all be going round in woad.' She turned to Miss Silver with a marked access of warmth. 'I'm sure I interrupted something frightfully important when I came in—you all had that sort of look. Do go on, or I shall think that you were talking about me.'

'Would that be "frightfully important"?' said Miss Doncaster. The blue eyes rolled.

'It would be to me.'

Miss Silver said gravely, 'We were talking about poor Mr. Harsch, and how sad it was that he should have met his death just when his work had been crowned with success. Miss Mary Anne was being so very interesting. She happened to be on the telephone and she actually heard him telling someone at the War Office that his work was done.'

'Sir George Rendal,' said Miss Mary Anne. ' "Completely successful" was the expression Mr. Harsch used, referring to a final experiment.'

'Oh, yes, you told us.' Ida Mottram was not really interested. 'Do you remember, Mr. Everton had come in to bring you some eggs—isn't he marvellous the way he gets his hens to lay?—and I came with him. You told us all about it then.' Her tone made it quite clear that she didn't want to hear it again. 'And I'm sure none of us thought the poor sweet was going to be snatched away like that. But what's the good of going on talking about it all the time? I asked Mr. Everton this afternoon if he didn't think it was morbid, and he said he did. I mean, it isn't going to bring him back.'

'In fact we are to go through life ignoring what is unpleasant,' said Miss Doncaster. 'I was brought up to face things, and not to put my head in the sand. You seem to see a great deal of Mr. Everton.'

'He's frightfully kind,' said Ida Mottram. 'He made my hen-house out of some frightful old packing-cases and odds and ends. And he's marvellous with the wireless. He knew at once mine needed a new valve, and he got me one when he was in Marbury on Monday, and came over and fixed it up for me and all. He really is the kindest man. But isn't it funny, Bunty doesn't like him at all. It makes it so awkward.'

'Many children object to the idea of a step-father,' said Miss Doncaster in an extremely acid voice.

Ida Mottram broke into girlish laughter.

'Is that what people are saying? What a joke! Of course when there is only one man in the place, I suppose people have to make the most of him. You can't really count the Rector, can you? But I might see if I can get up the faintest breath of scandal about him, just to take their minds off Mr. Everton. Suppose I got something in my eye after church on Sunday and asked him to take it out—it's an old dodge but quite a good one. What do you think?'

he didn't hear the shot. Harsch was shot at a quarter to ten. Bush must have been no great distance from the main entrance to the churchyard—that's the one on the village street—but he persists that he heard nothing. I think he persists too much.'

Miss Silver coughed.

'I have questioned Miss Fell, who really did hear the shot, and she says that the church clock was striking at the time. She says she did not remember this when she gave evidence at the inquest. When she was asked about the time, what came into her mind was that she had looked at the drawing-room clock just before she went out.'

'The church clock was actually striking when the shot was fired?'

'Yes. There is a chime for each quarter. The shot came with the second chime. The sound of the clock striking would, I imagine, tend to obscure the sound of the shot.'

'Yes—that's an idea! But, you see, the first part of Bush's story—all the meat in fact—is absolutely unsupported. He says he came from his own house—he says his wife was upstairs with her aunt—he says he didn't meet anyone on the way to the church. There's no proof that he wasn't there at half past nine or any other time before the shot was fired. Of course there's no proof that he knew Mr. Harsch would be there.'

'The organ stopped just after half past nine,' said Miss Silver. 'And I feel I should tell you what I have learned this evening —Bush was at Miss Doncaster's on Tuesday evening at about half past six fixing some shelves. Miss Mary Anne, who is in the habit of listening in on the party line, overheard Mr. Harsch's telephone call to Sir George Rendal acquainting him with the complete success of his final experiment. She repeated the information to Bush, and also, later on, to Mrs. Mottram and Mr. Everton. She says Bush immediately remarked that in that case Mr. Harsch would be down playing the organ that evening. He said Mr. Harsch told him he would be down as soon as his work was done.'

Frank whistled.

'It doesn't look too good, does it? He knew the experiments had been completed—he knew Rendal was coming down next day—he knew Harsch would be in the church. It's not fair to blame a man for his birth, but he comes of German stock, and there was an attempt to get at him just before the last war, though apparently he turned it down. Suppose there was another attempt this time, with a bigger inducement, and he didn't turn it down— it would explain everything, wouldn't it?'

Miss Silver coughed.

'It would seem to provide an explanation. Pray continue your remarks on Bush's statement.'

Frank swung his leg.

'Well, to my mind the weakest point of the whole thing is his going off and leaving the body in the way he says. I find it uncommon difficult to swallow.'

Miss Silver shook her head.

'Perhaps you have never lived in a village. Village people very much dislike getting mixed up with the police. I find it quite natural that Bush should desire the presence of another witness, and more especially a witness of Mr. Harsch's own social standing.'

'Well—if you say so——' His tone deferred to her.

A smile commended him. She said,

'The point which tells most in Bush's favour is one which you do not seem to have remarked. I refer to the key.'

Frank's eyebrows went up.

'You mean his putting the key back in Harsch's pocket?' I thought that pretty fishy myself.'

'Oh, no.' Miss Silver's tone was firm. 'That is an incident which certainly occurred just as he described it. It is not a thing that anyone would invent, and certainly no guilty man would go out of his way to admit it. It is just one of those meaningless but instinctive things that people do when they are under the influence of shock. He had no reason either for inventing or admitting it. I feel quite sure that it happened just as he said.'

'In other words, you think that he is innocent. I wonder. There's a lot of circumstantial evidence, and it keeps piling up. He left the Bull last night a few minutes before Ezra did—his wife keeps brandy in the house—he has a large and serviceable wheelbarrow in the shed at the bottom of the churchyard—and the dry gravel on Ezra's boots is the same as the gravel on the church paths. He could have had him into the church, given him a tot of brandy, knocked him out, and taken him across the Green in the wheelbarrow to the place where he was found drowned. There was heavy cloud last night, and Bourne goes to bed early. It piles up, doesn't it?'

Miss Silver coughed.

'A man is innocent in law until he has been found guilty by a jury,' she said.

CHAPTER THIRTY FOUR

When Sergeant Abbott had departed Miss Silver glanced at her watch. A quarter to seven! She was afraid Miss Janice Meade—such a charming girl—must have returned to Prior's End. That poor Miss Madoc could not, of course, be left alone for long. A very sad position for her, poor thing—very sad indeed —but perhaps the clouds would lift.

With these thoughts in her mind she opened the glass door into the garden and looked out. A lovely evening, really very mild, but it would not be so warm later on. As she stood there, the door in the wall was opened and Garth and Janice came through.

Agreeably surprised, Miss Silver went to meet them. She addressed herself to Janice.

'I was afraid that I would miss you. If it is not too late, I should be glad of a few words with you.'

Whilst she spoke she was aware that something must have occurred between these two young people. It was plain that they walked on air. Janice came back from a long way off to answer her question. With deepened colour she murmured that she was staying to supper.

'Miss Madoc has an old friend with her. She is staying the night, so I am really not needed. Did you say you wanted to see me?'

'If you can spare the time,' said Miss Silver, and carried her off.

When they were in the study and the door was shut, she said,

'I am afraid this may not be a very good moment, but there is no time to waste. Will you do your best—your very best, my dear—to recall just what Mr. Harsch said to you on that Tuesday evening. There may be something that we have missed. There may be something which seemed unimportant at the time, but which might appear significant in the light of what has happened since. Just throw your mind back and tell me everything you can remember.'

Janice looked at her with startled eyes. It was a long way back from the place where she and Garth had been—all the distance between life and death. She felt a little dazed. Perhaps it was because of this that her answer did not meet the question. She said in a stumbling voice,

'I—don't—know. Miss Madoc said—but that wasn't on Tuesday——'

'What was not on Tuesday?'

'Something he said to Miss Madoc—but it was on Monday, after he was so late getting back from Marbury. I don't think I told you.'

'What was it, Miss Janice?'

'It sounds silly. I don't know why I thought of it just now. Miss Madoc told me, and she spoke of it again today—she was telling her friend about it. She thought it was a warning. Mr. Harsch came back very late because he had missed the train which connects with the bus, and he had had to walk from the Halt. Miss Madoc said he looked dreadful, and he said he had seen a ghost.

'Dear me!' said Miss Silver mildly. 'And what did he mean by that?'

'I don't know. She didn't like to ask him, and he didn't say any more, but she thought he had seen something when he was coming across the fields, and she thought it was a warning.'

'And did he say nothing to you?'

Janice shook her head.

'I was working with Mr. Madoc. I didn't really see him till Tuesday evening—not to talk about anything like that.'

'But on Tuesday evening, when he was talking to you—did he say nothing then?'

Janice sat up straight.

'I don't know—I didn't think about it. . . . Oh——'

'You have remembered something?'

'I don't know. He said—he was talking about coming over here and making a new life when the old one had been destroyed. He said, "You say such things are dead and buried and the door is shut—you think that it will never open again. And then all at once some day you find it is open and someone standing there like a ghost." And then he said, "But we will not talk of things like that—it is not good. You may come to fancy something that is not there, and to see your own thoughts. That is not good." '

'What did you think he meant by that?'

Janice looked at her.

'I thought something had reminded him of the things he didn't want to remember. I said, "Don't think about it any more", and he said, "No—it is not wise—and besides I am not sure." ' She clasped her hands and leaned forward. 'Do you think that something happened when he was in Marbury—something that reminded him?'

Miss Silver said, 'In Marbury—yes——' She paused and repeated, 'In Marbury——' Then, very quickly, 'Did he say any more than that?'

'No, he didn't.'

'Did he say anything about Marbury—anything at all to you?'

'Not after that. But before—oh, when we were having tea, I think it was—I asked how he had got on, and he said, "I missed my train, and so I missed my bus." I said, "How did you do that?" and he said, "I could not make up my mind. That is a very bad fault. I thought I would have some tea because I was tired and thirsty, so I went into a bad hotel which is called the Ram, and I am no sooner in than I come out again, and I have forgotten all about my tea and I miss my train." No, it wasn't when we were having tea—it was later on, after he had put through his telephone call to Sir George. And then he went on to talk about coming away from Germany. He said it was like shutting a door and you thought it would never open again, but you couldn't be sure. He repeated that in rather an odd sort of way—"You can't ever be sure."'

Miss Silver sat in silence for a moment. Then she said,

'Did he mention seeing anyone he knew in Marbury—anyone at all?'

'He saw Bush—I do know that, though it wasn't Mr. Harsch who told me. It was Mrs. Bush. She said Bush had gone over to see his sister who is married to an ironmonger in Ramford Street. She said he saw Mr. Harsch, so I suppose Mr. Harsch saw him.'

'Dear me!' said Miss Silver. 'And is the Ram in Ramford Street?'

'Yes, it is—and very nearly opposite the shop. But quite a lot of Bourne people were in Marbury that afternoon. Miss Doncaster went over because someone told her you could get suet there, but she couldn't find any and she came back frightfully cross. And Mr. Everton was over too. As a matter of fact he goes over quite often. They have all the best films, you know, and he is a tremendous fan. But how I know he was there on Monday is that Ida Mottram told me he got a new valve for her wireless.'

'Yes, she told me that too. And was Mr. Madoc also in Marbury?'

Janice looked startled. She said, 'Oh!' And then, 'I don't know where he was.'

'You mean that he was not at home?'

Janice went on looking startled.

'No, he wasn't. He went out after lunch on his bicycle, and he didn't come home until well after seven.'

'And the distance to Marbury is, I believe, no more than twenty miles by road—he could have been there?'

Janice said, 'I suppose he could.' And then, 'But, Miss Silver, none of these people had anything to do with Mr. Harsch's past. I mean, he wouldn't have called any of them a ghost, would he. He wouldn't have meant any of them when he talked about an opening door.'

Miss Silver said soberly,

'No, he wouldn't have meant any of them. But I think perhaps the door he spoke of opened in the Ram, and it is possible that one of them was there.'

CHAPTER THIRTY FIVE

Sergeant Abbott escorted Miss Silver to Marbury next morning, having slept the night at the Black Bull upon a bed whose mattress, a genuine antique, appeared to be stuffed with period paving stones. To offset this, he had a new-laid egg for breakfast —the Bull keeping its own hens and being very sharply in competition with Mr. Everton in the matter of laying averages. They took the bus to the Halt and caught the 9.40, an exceptionally slow train which not only stopped at everything that could be called a station but occasionally paused by the way and puffed when there was no station at all. They had a carriage to themselves, and beguiled the way with conversation. Miss Silver produced three quotations from Tennyson, two of which were quite unknown to Frank. He was rather pleased with:

'Act first, this Earth, a stage so gloomed with woe
     You all but sicken at the shifting scenes.
 And yet be patient. Our Playwright may show
     In some fifth Act what this wild Drama means.'

and listened respectfully to a eulogy upon the bard. After which Miss Silver opened her shabby handbag and produced an envelope containing half a dozen snapshots which she extracted and handed to him.

'Miss Brown has an excellent camera. I was so pleased to find that Miss Fell had these photographs. They are very good and clear, are they not? The first two were taken at the Mother's Strawberry Tea in the Rectory garden. It has been an annual treat for the last fifty years, but since the war they just have tea and buns, and the fruit is gathered and taken to the Village Institute to be made into jam. Bush has come out very well in the first photograph, but his wife has turned her head away. Miss Doncaster is very good in both of them. Then there are two excellent snapshots of Mr. Madoc. In one of them he is walking with Mr. Harsch. In the other he is conversing with Mr. Everton. It is really very good of them both, I am told. I have not had the pleasure of meeting Mr. Madoc as yet, but Miss Sophy informs me——'

'Yes, it's like him.'

Miss Silver beamed.

'And very like Mr. Everton. Most characteristic.' She displayed the last two photographs. 'The judges in the competition for the best allotment—Miss Fell, Bush, Mr. Everton, and Dr. Edwards. They are all great gardeners. Such a healthy pursuit. Two views, both very good and clear, I think.'

He assembled the photographs fanwise, gazed at her over the top of them, and cocked an eyebrow.

'And what might you be getting at, teacher?' he enquired.

Miss Silver gave her faint dry cough.

'I thought, whilst I was talking to Mr. Madoc, that it might be of interest if you were to show these photographs at the Ram and enquire whether they recognize anyone in them as having visited their establishment on Monday afternoon last week.'

'The Ram?'

'In Ramford Street. Bush's sister is married to a man who has an ironmongery shop across the way. He was visiting her on Monday. The name is Grey. Miss Doncaster and Mr. Everton were also in Marbury that afternoon. Mr. Madoc was absent from Bourne for some hours on his bicycle, but his whereabouts are not known.'

Frank said, 'I know I'm stupid, but do you mind telling me what it's all about? I mean, why Monday, and why the Ram?'

Miss Silver told him.

'Mr. Harsch was also in Marbury that afternoon. He went to the Ram to have tea there, but he came out as soon as he went in. He came home late, and Miss Madoc having apparently been shocked at his appearance, he told her that he had seen a ghost. He did not see Miss Meade at all that night, nor alone until Tuesday evening, when he told her about going into the Ram for tea and coming out again directly. He did not say anything about seeing a ghost, but he made some very interesting remarks which I should like you to read for yourself. I wrote them down, and asked Miss Meade to check them over.' She extracted a doubled-up exercise-book from the handbag and gave it to him, after which she folded her hands in her lap and watched his face whilst he read the pages she had indicated.

'Well?' he said when he had finished. 'What do you make of it?'

Miss Silver was silent. She appeared to be considering her answer. She said at last in a quiet, serious voice,

'He went in to get some tea because he was tired and thirsty, but he came out at once without having any. Afterwards he spoke to one person of a ghost, and to another of an opening door. I have wondered whether he saw that door open before him when he went into the Ram—whether he recognized or half recognized someone connected with his past life in Germany. And I have wondered whether someone else may have been there too—someone connected, not with his past, but with his present life in Bourne. To both these persons recognition would have meant the extreme of danger. They could not afford to remain in uncertainty on so important a point. I think it probable that one of them would have followed him in order to ascertain whether he went to the police. Discovering that he proceeded to the station to wait for the next train, they would conclude that the danger was not immediate—they would separate. But the matter could hardly be left there. Mr. Harsch's death may already have been decided upon. The chance that he might have recognized an enemy agent may, or may not, have precipitated the event. Sir George Rendal believes that a very determined attempt might have been made either to secure the formula of harschite to the enemy, or to deny the use of it to our own war effort.'

Frank whistled.

'If Harsch opened a door in the Ram and recognized an enemy agent, why didn't he go to the police then and there?'

Miss Silver coughed.

'You have not read my notes attentively. Look at them again and you will see that he said, "But we will not talk of things like that—it is not good. You may come to fancy something that is not there, and to see your own thoughts. That is not good." You see, he was not sure. I think he had received a severe shock. When he came to think over what he had seen the shock blurred it—he was not sure. He put his impression into words when he said to Miss Madoc, "I have seen a ghost".'

Abbott surveyed her oddly.

'Look here,' he said, 'the Chief will go batty if you keep on pulling rabbits out of the hat like this. We had a perfectly good case against Madoc until you came along and chucked Bush into the middle of it, and just as we are beginning to pick up the bits and get a good build-up with Bush, you go and drag in our old friend the sinister enemy agent.'

'There are such things as enemy agents,' said Miss Silver soberly. 'I should, of course, be extremely sorry to inconvenience the Chief Inspector in any way, but I would not do him the injustice of supposing that he has any other wish than to arrive at the truth. May I rely on you to see whether those photographs are recognized by anyone at the Ram?'

Frank burst out laughing.

'You may always rely on me, as you very well know. But the Chief will go off the deep end if anything comes of it. Don't say I didn't tell you! And I would like to know whether this is really the fifth Act you were quoting about just now, or whether, to mix the metaphors, you've still got a wilderness of wild monkeys up your sleeve.'

Miss Silver smiled indulgently.

'That remains to be seen,' she said.

CHAPTER THIRTY SIX

Miss Silver sat at one end of a long bare table, and Evan Madoc at the other. They were in a small room with linoleum on the floor. There was no furniture except the table, which was of varnished yellow deal, and a few uncompromising chairs with wooden seats. The air resembled the variety commonly found in post offices and railway waiting-rooms, being cold, damp, and highly charged with disinfectant. The door had an eighteen-inch glass panel at the top, through which the warder standing just outside could watch all that passed. Miss Silver was, however, assured that he was out of earshot.

She had been in the room for some few minutes before Mr. Madoc was brought in. Her first impression was that whether he had or had not shot Mr. Harsch he certainly looked as if he would like to murder her. He had, in fact, begun a somewhat vehement protest, when the warder tapped him on the shoulder. 'Take it easy now—take it easy.' After which he withdrew to his observation post.

Madoc, glaring after him, heard himself addressed by name in a prim, agreeable voice. It was kind, but it held a note of authority.

It reminded him of his Aunt Bronwen Evans whose texts, tips, and toffee had profoundly influenced his early years. He turned abruptly and beheld a little dowdy woman in a black jacket with a bunch of purple pansies in her hat. She said,

'Sit down, Mr. Madoc. I want to talk to you.'

As she spoke, he met her eyes, found in them the one thing he respected, intelligence, and dropped into the chair which had been set for him with no more than a protesting frown. He said,

'I don't know who you are, and I have nothing to say.'

She smiled.

'I have not asked you to say anything yet. My name is Maud Silver—Miss Maud Silver—and I am a private enquiry agent. Your friends, who do not believe that you shot Mr. Harsch, have retained my services, and Chief Detective Inspector Lamb has kindly facilitated this interview.'

Evan Madoc pushed back an untidy black lock which was tickling his nose and said,

'Why?' His voice could not very well have been ruder.

Miss Silver looked at him reprovingly. Her manner indicated that discourtesy relegated one mentally and morally either to the nursery or the slum. A faint flush showed that the intimation had gone home. He said less rudely, but with a show of restrained temper,

'I have nothing to say. And when you speak of my friends, I am at a loss to imagine——'

Miss Silver modified her look. It was still hortatory, but it promised forgiveness—like Aunt Bronwen when she had finished her sermon and the toffee came out of her pocket.

'You have some very good friends, Mr. Madoc—Miss Fell, with whom I am staying—Miss Meade, who was instrumental in calling me in——'

He hit the table with the flat of his hand.

'You are not going to make me believe that Janice Meade is crying her eyes out over me! She told me once to my face that I was the most disagreeable man she had ever met, and that she wouldn't have stayed with me a week if it hadn't been for Michael Harsch!'

Miss Silver coughed.

'Quite so. But she does not believe that you shot him. As a scientist, you should be able to understand that there is such a thing as a passion for abstract justice.'

He gave a bitter laugh.

'And you ask me to believe that she would put her hand in her pocket for that?'

Miss Silver ignored this sordid theme. She gave him a penetrating look and said,

'Miss Janice bases her belief in your innocence upon the fact that you cared a good deal for Mr. Harsch.'

His eyes blazed for a moment. The muscles of his face twitched. He said,

'What has that got to do with her—or with you?'

'Nothing, Mr. Madoc. I mentioned it as the basis of Miss Meade's conviction that you are innocent. But to pursue the question of your friends. Your sister is naturally in great distress, and so of course is your wife.'

His chair was pushed back so sharply as to score the government linoleum. The warder, watching through his glass panel, put a hand to the door knob. But after tensing his muscles as if about to spring up Evan Madoc appeared to change his mind. The impulse failed. He dragged his chair in again and leaned forward with his elbows on the table, propped his chin in his hands, and put up a spread of restless fingers to cover his mouth. He said in a sort of mutter,

'I have no wife.'

Miss Silver coughed.

'Confidence from a client is most desirable. As Lord Tennyson so rightly observes, "Oh, trust me not at all, or all in all." I realize you know so little about me that I cannot expect your confidence, but I do ask you not to complicate the situation by attempting to prevaricate. You were married to Miss Medora Brown on June 15th five years ago at the Marylebone Register Office in London.'

He put his face right down into his hands. The black lock fell forward over twitching fingers. And then quite suddenly, he jerked it back and sat up, a wry grin twisting his mouth.

'Well, it seems a peculiar moment for Medora to claim me as a husband. I suppose you didn't find all this out for yourself?'

'Mrs. Madoc has been in considerable distress. She informed me of your marriage because she was afraid she might be compelled to give evidence against you.'

'And I suppose it's all in the papers!'

'The only persons who know of it are the Chief Inspector, Sergeant Abbott, and myself. Publicity at this juncture would be most undesirable.'

Evan Madoc laughed angrily.

'I quite agree! It would be highly undesirable for her to be known as a murderer's wife! You know she thinks I did it!'

Miss Silver coughed.

'Mr. Madoc, we have no time for these melodramatics. You are in a serious, even a dangerous position. If you can make up your mind to treat me frankly, I believe that I can help you.' She broke into a smile of singular sweetness and charm. 'You see, I am quite sure that you did not shoot Mr. Harsch.'

He flung out his hands as if he were pushing something away and said,

'Why?'

'Because you have such a very bad temper.'

'And what do you mean by that?'

She paused for a moment, looking at him with steady composure.

'Mr. Harsch was shot by someone who had planned to shoot him. The weapon was taken to the spot for that purpose. After the murder it was carefully wiped and Mr. Harsch's fingerprints imposed upon it. I think you might be capable of violence in a moment of passion, but I do not believe you capable of premeditation or of cool after-thought. If you had killed your best friend in the heat of anger you would, I think, stand by your deed and not allow another man to be accused.'

He said in a stupefied voice,

'How do you know?' And then, as if waking up, 'What do you mean—what other man? Is anyone else accused?'

'Frederick Bush is under suspicion. He was seen to come out of the church just before ten o'clock, locking the door behind him. He admits to being there, but says he found the door open and Mr. Harsch fallen down dead by the organ stool. He was afraid of being implicated, so he locked the door and came away. He swears that he did not touch the pistol. By showing that Mr. Harsch had not locked himself inside the church, Bush's statement destroys the most damning part of the evidence against you. As you will see, anyone might have walked in and shot him.'

Madoc hit the table.

'For heaven's sake, stop talking! I tell you Bush didn't do it!'

Miss Silver drew herself up.

'Perhaps you would care to amplify that, Mr. Madoc.'

He pushed long nervous fingers through his hair.

'I tell you he didn't do it—I tell you he couldn't have done it! I've got to make a statement! They mustn't arrest him! Get hold of that Chief Inspector! He was anxious enough for me to talk when I didn't want to! I suppose somebody can produce him now and get me something to write on?'

162

In a calming voice Miss Silver said that she had no doubt it could be managed. She then went over to the door and spoke to the warder. If there was triumph in her heart, no discreetest shade of it was discernible in face or manner. She returned to her place, invited attention by her slight habitual cough, and said,

'Pray, Mr. Madoc, continue. I am deeply interested.'

He stared.

'What do you think I am? I meant to hold my tongue—one isn't bound to hang oneself! There's some work I would have liked to finish. But they mustn't arrest Bush. You see, it's like this. I came back. After I'd got away with the key I walked all out for five or six minutes. I was going home. And then it came over me that I'd better go back. I didn't want that key. If I've got to dot all the i's and cross the t's, I thought I'd made a fool of myself. I was angry. I didn't want to give Medora the satisfaction of thinking I cared whether she went over to the church to talk to Harsch or not. I'd like to say there wasn't any question in my mind about there being anything wrong between them, but she liked talking to him, and when we met we always quarrelled. I thought I'd punish her by putting the key down on the study doorstep for the maids to find in the morning.' His mouth twisted. 'I knew she'd enjoy explaining how it got there.'

Miss Silver sat with folded hands. She made no comment.

Evan Madoc leaned towards her.

'Now listen carefully! I came back across the village street and entered the Cut. When I had come level with the church the clock began to chime for the third quarter.' He hummed the four descending notes. 'It does that three times for the quarter to. It had just got into the second chime when I heard the shot. I didn't know where it came from—there's a good deal of echo there, off the church and off the wall of the Cut. It's difficult to remember exactly how one felt. I think, subconsciously, I was afraid it wasn't Giles shooting at a fox, so I threw up a lot of protective stuff to convince myself that it was. Everything happened very quickly. Immediately after the shot someone in front of me in the Cut began to run. I hadn't noticed him before—the trees keep the moonlight off the path—yews and hollies, very dense—you'll have seen them—but I did see him open the door into the church-yard and run in. It was bright when the door was opened. When I got there it was standing a handsbreadth ajar. I looked in, and this is what I saw. The man who had just gone in was half way over to the door which opens on the Green, running fast, and someone else was just going out of that door. I couldn't see who it was—I couldn't say if it was man or woman—I just saw someone

163

go out and bang the door. And then the second person got there, still running, and went out too.

'Pray continue,' said Miss Silver.

He was frowning gloomily.

'I changed my mind again. I wanted to get home. The police won't understand that, but it's true. I felt sick to death of being angry and wanting to punish Medora. I suppose I really knew that something had happened, but I wouldn't admit it. I just wanted to get home. I went back down the Cut as quick as I could, and just as I came out of it I saw Bush cross over from the left of the main churchyard gate. He didn't see me, because I was in the shadow, but I saw him. So there you are—he couldn't possibly have shot Michael.'

'He couldn't have reached the spot where you saw him in the time?'

He drew with his finger on the table.

'Look—the Cut is the shortest side of a very irregular oblong. I ran down it pretty fast. If Bush was the man I saw leaving the churchyard he couldn't have made it in the time with double the distance to travel. You can measure it up for yourself. It's pretty well twice as far from the gate on the Green to that corner, and then there's all the way along the street to the main entrance, which is much nearer the Cut. Besides, Bush was coming quite slowly and leisurely from the opposite direction. And, to finish up with, if he'd really shot Michael, do you suppose he'd have been such a fool as to go back into the church and stay there till just before ten?'

Miss Silver observed him with attention.

'Your points are very well taken. Now, Mr. Madoc, you say that you did not recognize the first person who left the churchyard. But what about the man who ran—did you recognize him?'

'Yes, I did.'

'Who was it?'

'An old poacher called Ezra Pincott. I saw him quite distinctly. The police had better get hold of him. He probably knows who he was after.'

Miss Silver regarded him steadily.

'I am afraid that is impossible, Mr. Madoc. Ezra Pincott was murdered on Tuesday night.'

164

CHAPTER THIRTY SEVEN

In the Governor's office Evan Madoc wrote a fierce black signature at the foot of his statement.

'There you are!' he said without any respect at all. 'And now, I suppose, you will do your best to hang me!'

Miss Silver gave a faint hortatory cough. She rose to her feet with the air of a teacher dismissing a class. A spark of angry humour came and went in Madoc's eyes. She smiled at him as she came over and gave him her hand.

'I hope I shall see you again very soon,' she said, and felt the long nervous fingers twitch.

She went out, and was presently followed by Sergeant Abbott, who tucked a hand inside her arm and took her out to lunch at the Royal George, which is the gloomiest and most respectable hotel in Marbury. It has a Regency front, a rabbit warren of older rooms with low ceilings and uneven floors all on different levels at the back, whilst its interior decoration perpetuates the taste of the great Victorian age. In the immense dining-room, where before the war Hunt Suppers were wont to be served, only some half dozen tables were occupied. Established by one of the heavily curtained windows, and served with watery soup in tepid plates, they were as free from being overheard or overlooked as if they had been in the middle of the Sahara.

Miss Silver undid her jacket, disclosing the fact that she was wearing a bog-oak brooch in the form of a rose with a pearl in the heart of it. Sergeant Abbott gazed at her with rapture.

'Maudie, you're marvellous!'

The neat, prim features endeavoured to preserve a proper severity. They failed. With the smile which she would have bestowed on a favourite nephew, Miss Silver attempted reproof.

'My dear Frank, when did I give you permission to use my Christian name?'

'Never. But if I don't do it sometimes I shall develop an ingrowing, inverted enthusiasm—an inhibition, or a complex, or one of those things you get when you are thwarted. I've always felt that it was particularly bad for me to be thwarted.'

'You talk a great deal of nonsense,' said Miss Silver indulgently.

Aware that young men do not talk nonsense to their elders unless they are fond of them, her tone did nothing to discourage him. He therefore continued to talk nonsense until the waiter removed their soup plates and furnished them each with a small portion of limp white fish partially concealed by a sprig of parsley and a teaspoonful of unnaturally pink sauace. It all tasted even worse than it looked. Frank apologized.

'They have much better food at the Ram, but we couldn't very well go there in the circumstances. The local Superintendent tells me their Mrs. Simpkins can make you believe that Hitler had never been born, and that you are really eating pre-war food. Simpkins is the proprietor.'

Miss Silver inclined her head.

'Yes. Miss Fell informs me that Mrs. Simpkins used to be old Mr. Doncaster's cook. They were very well off in those days, but when he died they found that his income was largely derived from an annuity.'

Frank looked at her sharply.

'You've been concealing things—you always do.'

Miss Silver coughed.

'I did not wish to prejudice your enquiries at the Ram. Pray tell me if they have had any result.'

He leaned forward.

'Well, I think so. But whether we're any forrader, or what we're heading for, I don't pretend to say. Everybody there could pick out Bush. They know all about him. They know his sister Mrs. Grey, and they say he always comes in for a drink if he's in Marbury. Nobody is prepared to swear that he did come in on the Monday in question, but they all say he'd have been sure to if he was over at the Greys'. Then there's Miss Doncaster. They all recognized her and could name her—said she always came in for tea when she'd been shopping.'

'Yes—Miss Fell told me that. They give very good teas even now. All the food at the Ram is good, though it is such a shabby-looking place.'

Frank shook his head at her.

'Well, well—don't let us dwell upon it—all is over for today. Let us continue—we were doing Miss Doncaster. They are sure she was in on that Monday, because she kept Mrs. Simpkins talking until she missed a bus, and Mrs. Simpkins wasn't at all pleased. She was going out to see a sister at Marfield, and she told me it was just like Miss Doncaster, and that she was a good deal put about. And now we come to Mr. Everton—and that's where we don't get anywhere at all. He might have been in, or he mightn't. They didn't know him. He wasn't a customer, and, as the porter remarked, "One gentleman looks very much like another in our hall''. And that's the truth—it's narrow, it's dingy, and it's dark. He said there was always a coming and going about tea-time. Gentlemen generally had it in the Coffee Room, especially if they wanted something substantial. Mrs. Simpkins would fix them up a sausage and fried vegetables or something like that. But as to who was in on what day at the beginning of last week, he couldn't say. In fact none of them could. When I asked whether Mrs. Simpkins having gone off that afternoon to see her sister was any help, they brightened up a bit and remembered a gentleman who might have been a commercial traveller. And the new kitchen-maid had done him a scrambled egg on toast, and Mrs. Simpkins had put it across her when she came home, because she said those dried eggs wanted handling, and the Ram had got its name to keep up. But though I pressed like mad, no one seemed to be able to reconstruct the gentleman, or to remember who else had been in, and nobody picked Mr. Everton out of any of the photographs. The whole affair is exactly like this revolting sausage—pale, profitless, and imponderable.'

Miss Silver was pleased to be encouraging.

'I think you did very well.'

Frank Abbott shook his head.

'There are just two points—I've saved them up to the end. If nobody remembers Everton at the Ram, nobody remembers Harsch either, yet we know that Harsch went in and came out. Even at midday that hall is like a tomb. But—and this is the second point—as soon as you open the Coffee Room door bright light streams out. There are two good windows there, and they face that door. Suppose Harsch came up to the Coffee Room door and saw it open, he would be facing the light—facing whoever was coming out—facing anyone who was still in the room. But what would he see himself? I tried it out with the porter. The light hits you suddenly. Anyone coming out of the room in the ordinary way appears as a silhouette, but with some light striking the right side of the face and figure. If the opening door of which Harsch spoke to Janice Meade was a real door opening in the Ram, then that's what he would have seen—a silhouette, light striking at an angle on the side of the head, the cheek, the jaw, the shoulder. Not very much to go on, you know—nothing to take to the police—but enough to give you a horrid shock if it was what you had seen before, perhaps many times, when you were in your cell in the dark in a concentration camp and the door opened from the lighted corridor to let one of your tormentors in.' He broke off with a slightly conscious look. 'You know, you'll ruin my career. You're not safe—you're contagious. You start me off enthusing and romancing till I'm not sure whether I'm a policeman or someone in a propaganda film. And what the Chief would say if he heard me just now, I only hope and trust I shall never know. I think we'll switch over to Madoc. What about Harsch's notes and papers—did you get anything out of him?'

Miss Silver inclined her head and said,

'Certainly.'

'You *didn't*! You ought to be a lion-tamer! And not a single scratch? You've no idea how he reared in the air and clawed when the Chief had a go at him. We retired with bowed and bloody heads but no information.'

Miss Silver looked serious.

'Mr. Madoc's temper is regrettable, and he has very bad manners, but fundamentally he is, I believe, an acutely sensitive person who is very much afraid of being hurt. His temper and his rudeness are a kind of protective armour.'

Frank looked astonished. Then he laughed.

'And you dug him out of his armour like a winkle out of its shell! Well, what about those papers? Where are they?'

'I may say that Mr. Madoc displayed a good deal of intelligence. When not clouded by passion his reasoning powers are excellent. Like Janice Meade he was unable to believe that Mr. Harsch had committed suicide. If he had been murdered, the motive which immediately sprang to mind was the possession of the notes and formula of harschite. He collected everything that he could find and went into Marbury by an early train on Wednesday morning. He admits frankly that his motive was partly the desire to get Mr. Harsch's papers out of the way before Sir George Rendal came down. He was not sure what powers the War Office might have. He wanted to see a solicitor, and he wanted time to consider his position—as a pacifist, as a government employee, and as Mr. Harsch's executor.'

Frank Abbott listened with interest.

'What did he do?'

'He visited a local solicitor, Mr. Merevale, after which he proceeded to the Marbury branch of Lloyd's bank where he handed in a large sealed envelope for safe custody.'

'Then the papers are at Lloyd's?'

Miss Silver smiled.

'The envelope contained nothing but blank foolscap, but on his way home he called at the General Post Office and registered a second envelope addressed to the head office of the bank in London—a very intelligent move. The papers are there.'

Frank lifted an eyebrow.

'Has anyone told you that there was an attempt to burgle the Marbury branch on Saturday night?'

Miss Silver said, 'Dear me!' And then, 'I am not surprised. How providential that the papers, thanks to Mr. Madoc's foresight, were in London.'

Frank gazed appreciatively.

'Well, you have him charmed! He'll be eating out of your hand like the rest of us! By the way, I suppose he hasn't had a change of heart about handing harschite over to the government?'

Miss Silver beamed.

'How strange that you should ask me that. We had time for quite a nice long chat whilst we were waiting for you, and he informed me quite of his own accord that, on thinking it over, he had come to the conclusion that as Mr. Harsch's agent he was bound to act as Mr. Harsch himself would have acted, quite irrespective of his own convictions, which he took pains to inform me, remained unchanged.'

'And you had nothing to do with it, I suppose! It's a fascinating subject, but we mustn't dally. I want to talk about Madoc's statement. I don't know what arts you used to get him to make one, but you know the Chief's always expecting to see you fly out of the window on a broomstick. But to come back to the statement—it's a bit of a facer, isn't it? I haven't had time to think it out yet, but if he's right about the distances, then Bush is out of the running as far as Harsch is concerned. And Madoc being out of the running for Ezra Pincott, that leaves us with the person who left the churchyard on the Green side with Ezra hot in pursuit. Madoc says this person may have been male or female, nobody but Ezra being near enough to say which. Difficult to avoid the conclusion that Ezra did not see only that but a damning bit more, that he tried a spot of blackmail on the strength of it, and that he got himself bumped off.'

'That is so.'

'Well then, where do we go from there?'

'With the Chief Inspector's approval, I would suggest a further interrogation of Gladys and Sam. They went for a walk round the Green, probably entering the churchyard at some time after ten minutes to ten. Gladys says she did not take any notice of whether there was a shot or not, which points to their being at some distance from the church at the time. She thinks they had been getting on for ten minutes in the churchyard before Bush came out and the clock struck ten. They must have got there after Bush, as they did not see him enter the church. Now I would like very much to know whether they started out for their walk by the road which passes the houses, or whether they took the round in reverse and came back that way. If this was the case, I think it possible that they may have met the person Mr. Madoc did not recognize—the person who left the churchyard almost immediately after the shot was fired.'

'Wouldn't they have said?'

Miss Silver coughed.

'Anything very familiar may easily be disregarded. For instance, the church clock at Bourne chimes the quarters. How many of the people in those houses round the Green really hear it? I have asked a number of them, and they say they hardly ever notice the chimes. In the same way, I think it is possible that Gladys and Samuel might have encountered someone whom it would be quite natural to see at that time and in that place without really noticing them at all. There is a pillar-box just opposite the Rectory gate. If, let us say, Mrs. Mottram, or Dr. Edwards, or Miss Doncaster, or Mr. Everton, or the Rector, were observed either coming or going between his or her own house and this pillar-box, what would be the natural conclusion? You see, it is as easy as that—those young people would not have attached the slightest importance to such an encounter.'

Frank looked dubious.

'I should have thought they would have mentioned it.'

Miss Silver smiled.

'Have you found that village people are at all apt to volunteer information? That is not my experience. They may, or may not, answer a direct question, but they rarely volunteer anything. There is an instinct of secrecy which is bred into their very bones. There are well known cases where what was common knowledge on the subject of a crime has never reached the authorities even after a couple of generations. In the present case, however, we have to deal with goodnatured, artless young people, and I think a direct question or two might elicit the facts.'

Frank nodded.

'It shall be done. Now what about these times? They run pretty fine. I'd like to go over them with you.' He paused as the waiter took away their plates, and got out his notebook. When the stooping elderly figure had gone away down the long room, he bent the book back to make the pages stay open and leaned across the corner to Miss Silver. 'I've roughed it out here from the statements. Some of the less important times are guesswork.

8.50—Cyril gets out of the window.

9.20—Cyril to Cut (approximate).
9.30—Medora Brown to Cut.
9.31—Madoc to Cut. Row between them. Organ still playing. No evidence that it was heard after this.
9.34—Exit Medora to house, and Madoc with key.
9.35—Cyril to bed.

Now this is where Madoc's statement comes in.'

He wrote upon the opposite page, and then read out what he had written:

'9.43—approx.—Madoc re-enters Cut. Ezra already there.
9.45—Harsch is shot, on the second chime of the quarter.'

He looked up.

'Madoc says he stood where he was until the third chime had gone. Says he didn't see Ezra till after that. He thinks they both of them waited as long again before they moved. Then he saw Ezra run, and come to the door and open it. Now how long would that take? Madoc was level with the main block of the church—that would give him about a hundred yards to go, and Ezra perhaps eighty. The chimes take five seconds each—say twenty seconds before either of them moves, and twenty seconds for Ezra to reach the door and get it open. Well, there he is, looking in—and it's forty seconds since the shot was fired. What has the murderer to do in that forty seconds? He has fired the shot, and Harsch is dead. He's got to wipe the pistol, get Harsch's fingerprints on it, let it drop, and scoot back the way he came. None of that would take more than forty seconds, would it? Ezra might have seen him coming out of the church. I think he must have, but we'll have to pace it and time it on the spot. Well, Ezra sees him, but he doesn't see Ezra—he wouldn't have come out of the church if he had. He runs for the gate on to the Green. That's the really dangerous part of the whole show, but he's got to risk it. There's a diagonal path from the church door to the gate, and it's not very far. Ezra would have to go across country or a long way round. He hears Ezra running, but he gets to the gate and slams it. But Ezra has recognized him, and presently he tries a spot of blackmail and gets bumped off. So now we don't know who the murderer was. I don't think it was Madoc, because, *a,* it would be absolutely pointless for him to incriminate himself by saying he came back if all the rest of it was a string of lies; and, *b,* he certainly didn't kill Ezra, because he was under lock and key in Marbury jail.' He

171

looked up and grinned. 'Nice to have something you can feel sure about, isn't it?'

Miss Silver was giving him a very flattering attention.

'Pray continue.'

'Well, I don't think it was Bush either. It can't be if Madoc's statement is true. And why should Madoc go out of his way to incriminate himself by admitting that he came back, unless he really couldn't hold his tongue and let an innocent man be arrested? Which brings us back to the timetable again.

9.46—approx.—Madoc looking into churchyard.

That gives him three minutes to walk back along the Cut and see Bush enter the churchyard by the main gate, and Bush one minute to come round the church and in at the side door.

9.50—Bush finds the body.

9.52 approx.—Gladys and Sam to the churchyard.

9.58—Bush comes out of the church and locks the door. How's that?'

'Excellent,' said Miss Silver.

CHAPTER THIRTY EIGHT

Frank Abbott burst out laughing.

'And it doesn't get us anywhere at all! Exit Madoc. Exit Bush. Enter invisible murderer, sex unknown. Nobody saw him except Ezra, and Ezra is no more. Please teacher, who did it?'

Miss Silver remained silent.

He quirked an eyebrow at her and said,

'Strictly off the record and between ourselves?'

Miss Silver coughed.

'There is so little to go on—just a few straws in the wind—nothing that could be called evidence.'

He gazed imploringly.

'*Strictly* off the record, teacher?'

She said gravely, 'I think it was one of the people who went to the Ram on Monday afternoon.'

His eye brightened.

'Do you include Bush?'

'I do not think that it was Bush.'

Frank whistled.

'Who's left? Miss Doncaster, and possibly Everton, but there's no evidence to show that he was ever near the Ram. Oh, by the way, the Chief has checked up on him, and it all sounds according to Cocker. Stockbroker. Gregarious friendly soul. Often said he would like to settle in the country. Shell-shocked in the blitz—bad nervous breakdown—ordered a country life. Dropped out—you know how people do in London when they retire. Sounds all right, doesn't it?'

'He has never had anyone down to stay,' said Miss Silver. 'He is said to have gone over to meet a cousin in Marbury a little while ago, but that is the only evidence of contact with friends or relatives. For a friendly, gregarious person that seems a little strange.'

'Nervous break-downs do leave people strange, don't they? And, you know, it's quite easy to drop out.'

'That is very true.'

'Then, for what it's worth, Mrs. Mottram gives him an alibi. She says he was with her until a quarter to ten on Tuesday night, and that the shot was fired just as he said good-bye.'

Miss Silver coughed.

'A very good example of the unreliability of evidence. She told me the same story, but with a difference. She said Mr. Everton heard the shot and thought that it was Giles shooting at a fox. He had just looked at his watch and said he must go, as it was a quarter to ten and he was expecting a trunk call.'

Frank Abbott's eyes narrowed.

'Not quite the same thing, as you say.'

Miss Silver coughed again.

'Not quite. Mrs. Mottram was one of the people I was thinking of just now when I said that those who live round the Green are so accustomed to hearing the chimes they no longer notice them. Just before I left her I asked whether she could remember hearing them when Mr. Everton was saying good-bye, and she said she thought she could, but she wasn't sure, because she hardly ever did notice them unless she was listening. She thought she heard something just as he went out.'

Frank Abbott frowned.

'Something odd there, isn't there? Everton looks at his watch and says it's a quarter to ten and he must be going because he's expecting a trunk call. Then he remarks on the shot—''Hullo, there's Giles shooting at a fox!'' or words to that effect. And then he says good-bye, and Mrs. Mottram hears something which she thinks may have been a chime. Well, there simply wasn't time for it to happen like that.' He turned his wrist so that they could both see the second hand of his watch. 'Look here—ding, ding, ding, ding—five seconds dead. The shot came just into the second chime—another two seconds. Everton has only got three seconds to hear the shot, say his piece about Giles shooting at a fox, say good-bye, and get going. Well, it simply can't be done in time for Mrs. Mottram to hear the remaining chime. The only drawback is she doesn't seem sure enough about anything to make it worth while trying to build up a theory on what she may or may not have heard. I suppose she's telling the truth?'

'Certainly—as far as she knows it herself. She would make a very bad witness. Her mind is extremely inconsequent, and she would be very easily confused. We had better check the whole thing over with her again and see whether there is any variation from what she said to me.'

Frank nodded.

'All right—so much for Everton. Now, what about Miss Doncaster? You say you think it was one of those people who went to the Ram on Monday afternoon who shot Harsch. As far as I can make out, you get there by what I can only described as one of your broomstick methods, and it's going to make the Chief feel very uncomfortable. You know, I'm beginning to suspect that he's got a medieval streak under all that beef and brawn, and that there are times when he gets a shiver down his spine about you. I must watch and see if I can catch him crossing his fingers, or secreting a sprig of rowan in his pocket.'

Miss Silver reproved this levity, and received an apology.

'All right, I'm back on the trail. Well, we do know for certain that Miss Doncaster was at the Ram. We haven't any evidence at all that Everton was, and for the moment we're not considering Bush. Well, that leaves you Miss Doncaster as first murderer, and I quite agree that she would do very well in the part—she's cram full of envy, malice, and all uncharitableness. But we're going to want something a little more specific than that. What can you do about it?'

'Not very much,' said Miss Silver. 'She and her sister were at a finishing school in Germany for two years. They came back with a great enthusiasm for everything German. During their father's lifetime they used to go every other year to one of the German spas. This was discontinued on his death in 1912. About 1930 the sisters began their trips abroad again—Switzerland, the Tyrol, Germany. Miss Doncaster developed a violent admiration for Hitler—Miss Sophy says she was really very trying about him. But in 1938 Miss Mary Anne became paralysed and the trips had to be abandoned. Since the war broke out Miss Doncaster appears to have had a complete change of heart. She is by way of being very patriotic, and Hitler is never mentioned. Miss Sophy said it was really the greatest possible relief.'

Frank Abbott whistled.

'Does she know how to use a revolver?'

'I believe so. Mr. Doncaster was fond of shooting at a mark. Miss Sophy says he made his daughters' lives a burden to them about it, and it was very noisy and uncomfortable for the neighbours.'

'None of which is evidence,' said Frank Abbott gloomily. 'Let's see—we checked up on everybody in those houses. What was she doing on Tuesday night?' He flicked over the leaves of his notebook. 'Here we are! Pennycott—Doncasters. Maid in kitchen—heard nothing, didn't go out. Invalid sister upstairs, back room—wireless on—heard nothing. Miss Doncaster—with sister except for five minutes somewhere between half past nine and ten, when she went to the pillar-box opposite the Rectory and posted a letter—cannot fix time exactly—thinks it was nearly ten o'clock—met nobody, heard nothing. Well, there you are. As far as opportunity goes she had it. What about motive? I suppose she might have had that too. A violent enthusiasm for Hitler might have made her willing to work for the Nazis. It doesn't seem credible, but she wouldn't be the only one. I don't know how it gets them, but it seems to. I suppose there wasn't anything else—any private feud with Harsch? He hadn't been treading on her toes?'

'I have not heard anything. It would not, of course, be at all difficult to offend her.'

Frank burst out laughing.

'I should call that a masterpiece of understatement!'

CHAPTER THIRTY NINE

Mrs. Mottram rang the bell of Pennycott. At the Rectory she would have opened the door and yodelled, but the Miss Doncasters were sticklers for what they called the forms of civilized

175

society, and what was the good of putting their backs up? It was so easy, and you did it so often without meaning to, that you couldn't even get a kick out of it. Besides, poor old things, what a life! Year after year, with nothing happening to you—just withering up and going sour. Her heart, which was as soft as butter, really pitied them, and however rude and disapproving they were, she always turned up again, with an egg, or a cabbage-leaf full of raspberries, or one of the bright unsuitable magazines showered upon her by her friends in the Air Force. She had one tucked under her arm now with a colour-print on the cover depicting a damsel in a wisp of scarlet bathing-dress about to take a header into a bright blue sea.

Admitted by the elderly maid, she pranced gaily upstairs, pleasantly conscious of being young and very much alive. She found Miss Mary Anne alone in the drab room with its litter of rubbish and its dead, stale air. It was rather a relief only to have one of them to deal with. She shook hands, felt the slack, cold fingers slip away, and saw the pale glance slide disapprovingly over her yellow jumper and her rather bright blue slacks to the scarlet bathing-girl.

'Lucy Ellen is out,' said Miss Mary Anne in a grumbling voice. 'I'm sure I don't know what she goes out *for*—morning, noon and night, until you'd think she'd be worn out. And at the end of it I don't know what she's done. Shopping is what she says, but what is there to shop in Bourne? Picture postcards at Mrs. Bush's, I suppose. And off to Marbury every week. And what does she do *there*—that's what I'd like to know. It's my belief that she just walks about looking in at the shop windows, and then she has tea at the Ram and comes home again.' The thick complaining voice was like treacle gone sour.

Ida Mottram thought it all sounded too grim for words. She sat down on the hearth in front of the languishing fire and began to poke at it with a bit of stick.

'No wonder you're cold,' she said. 'I'll have this up in no time. I may be a fool about some things, but I'm the world's smash hit with fires. You just wait and see!'

'Lucy Ellen doesn't like anyone to touch the fire but herself.'

'Well, she can't do it when she's out, can she? Look, it's coming along like anything!' She pulled one log forward, tilted another, blew upon a brightening ember, and with a rush the flame came up.

Sitting there with the firelight on her face, she began to tell Miss Mary Anne all about Bunty's encounter with a bumble bee.

'And she brought it in sitting on her hand and wanted me to stroke it.'

'How very foolish! I suppose she got stung?'

Ida giggled.

'Oh, no, she didn't—it loved her! But I made her put it back on one of the roses. She was so disappointed. She wanted to take it to bed with her. Don't you think it was rather sweet?'

Miss Mary Anne sniffed. She was not in the least interested in bumble bees or in Bunty Mottram. She wanted passionately to find out whether Garth Albany and Janice Meade were engaged, and to find it out before Lucy Ellen did. Silently and resentfully, this was the game she was always playing against her sister. Tied to her sofa she might be, and Lucy Ellen free to go about and gather up the news—free to go into Marbury and have tea at the Ram—but all the same, once in a way it was she who scored. If she could get in first about Garth and Janice, Lucy Ellen would be properly taken down. Ida Mottram might know something——

She began to ask questions which circled the subject, drawing in gradually, getting nearer and nearer. It was an art in which she excelled, and Ida was no match for her. Having, in fact, nothing to conceal, she was as open as the day. Oh, yes, she thought they liked each other—why shouldn't they? It would be very nice. Didn't Miss Mary Anne think it would be very nice? And Miss Sophy would be so pleased—didn't she think so?'

'If his intentions are serious,' said Miss Mary Anne in her gloomiest tone.

Ida giggled.

'People don't have intentions now—it's not done. They just go off and get married.'

She began to look round for something to screen her face from the fire. It was fairly blazing now, and her skin scorched so easily. She could feel her left cheek burning. She reached out to the small table by Miss Mary Anne's couch and took a paper at random from a pile which cluttered the lower tier. Turning it over, she saw that it was a garden catalogue with a cover displaying apples, pears, plums, gooseberries, raspberries, and blackcurrants, all at least twice as large as life and much more brightly coloured. She was about to say, 'Oh, are you getting any fruit trees?' when Miss Mary Anne remarked that young men in the Army were notorious for the way in which they flirted, and that she believed Garth Albany's mother had been very *rapid* when she was a girl.

The moment passed. Ida with the catalogue spread out to shield her face, listened to the scandalous account of how the late

Mrs. Albany had actually kissed Garth's father under the mistletoe at a Christmas party at the Rectory—'And they were not even engaged then, so it shows you what she was like.'

Sitting back on her heels, Ida turned the pages of the catalogue. She was listening as you listen to something which you have heard before, and which doesn't matter at all. She flicked the pages over—red currants as big as sixpences—beans a foot long—a page with a nick in the edge and a list of apple trees—apple trees. . . .

She stopped hearing Miss Mary Anne's voice. There was something very odd about the page with the nick in it. Faint brown writing coming up where the paper was hot—getting more distinct as she looked at it. At the top and at the bottom of the list of apple trees—words very odd words. Now she could read them. At the top of the list two words, *'Am Widder'*. And at the bottom of the list three more words, *'Montag halb fünf.'*

She stared at the writing, and quite unaccountably her heart began to thump. She didn't know why. She hadn't really begun to think what the words might mean, but they frightened her, coming up like that out of the blank spaces on the page of Miss Doncaster's catalogue.

They frightened her because they came up so suddenly out of nothing, and because they were German words. A secret message written in German—that was enough to frighten anyone. All at once the crowded room with its dead air was like something you dreamed about and waked up shaking. Almost without thinking what she did she doubled the catalogue over and pushed it up under her jumper. She had her back to the couch. The littered table screened her. Her hands were quick and deft—much quicker than her thoughts, which were confused and lagging.

Miss Mary Anne said in her treacly voice,

'So it all goes to show you can't trust anyone.'

Ida Mottram got up. Her legs had a funny disjointed feeling. She kissed her hand to Miss Mary Anne and said she must really go.

'Because Bunty is having tea with Mary Giles and Mrs. Giles will be bringing her back. She sees her through the hedge on their side of the Cut and in at our garden door. There's a gap in the hedge that Bunty can get through. So convenient.'

Miss Mary Anne looked very huffy indeed. She expected you to stay for hours and hours and hours, poor old thing. Ida shut the door on her with relief and fairly ran down the stairs and out of the house.

Outside in the road she stood still and wondered what she ought to do. It was all very frightening and very horrid, and she didn't

178

know what to do. She must tell someone who would know. Miss Silver would know. She must tell Miss Silver.

She ran all the way to the Rectory, to be told by Mabel that Miss Silver had gone to Marbury and she didn't know when she would be back, and Miss Sophy and Mr. Garth were gone up to Prior's End to have tea with Miss Madoc, but they would be coming back soon, and Miss Janice would be coming back with them.

When Mabel was telling Janice and Garth about it she said Mrs. Mottram seemed as if she was upset about something—'Not at all in her usual, Mr. Garth—looked for all the world as if she was going to cry. I hope she hasn't had bad news or anything like that, poor thing.'

'It was then that Janice said, 'Oh, I'd better go round and see.'

Ida Mottram went away very much discouraged. She went back to her own house, which was next door to Pennycott, and rang up Mr. Everton. She didn't feel like standing on anyone else's doorstep and being told they were out. So she rang up, and there, almost at once, was Mr. Everton's kind, cheerful voice saying, 'Dear lady, what can I do for you?'

'You're sure I'm not interrupting?'

She was feeling better already. Men were such a comfort—they always knew what to do. Mr. Everton would know. He was being most polite in his kind, old-fashioned way. 'If all interruptions were as pleasant as this one——' He would be coming round at once. This was in answer to her 'I'm so terribly worried about something.'

She hung up the receiver. Then she pulled the catalogue out from under her jumper and unfolded it. The faint brown lettering was just legible and no more. She began to think about what it might mean. Two years in a Swiss finishing school had left her with a fair knowledge of French and German. She slanted the shiny page and stared at the words on it, '*Am Widder*'. *Widder*—the word puzzled her for a moment. And then, like a picture on the screen, there popped into her mind Polly Pain wriggling, and twisting from one foot to another as she recited a list of animals under Fraülein Lessner's sardonic eye:—'*Der Schaf*, the sheep. *Die Kuh*, the cow. *Der Widder*, the ram.'

Yes, that was it. *Widder* was a ram. '*Am Widder*—at the Ram'. '*Montag halb fünf*—Monday at half past four.' Why did Miss Doncaster have a catalogue with a secret message in it which said, 'At the Ram, at half past four'?

Mr. Everton came into the room just as she remembered that

Miss Doncaster's old cook and her husband kept the Ram at Marbury, and that Miss Doncaster always had tea there when she went in to shop.

CHAPTER FORTY

He noticed at once how pale and disturbed she looked. The blue eyes which he admired had an expression of distress. She was certainly a very pretty woman. And then his eye fell on the catalogue. She was holding it out to him with both hands.

'Oh, Mr. Everton, I'm so glad to see you! I was getting so frightened. It's so dreadful, and it seems to be getting worse every minute—but you will know what to do.'

'Dear lady, what is it? I can't bear to see you like this.'

'Oh, you are so kind! And it's such a relief to tell someone, because I don't know what to do.' She pushed the catalogue at him and said, 'Look!'

He took a moment to adjust his glasses.

'Well, well—now let me see—a list of apple trees. Are you thinking of putting any in?'

'No—no. Look! Oh—oh, don't you see, there's some writing—here—and there!' She pointed with a scarlet fingernail. 'It's fading out, but it was quite clear. It came up when I held it to the fire at Miss Doncaster's. I wanted something to screen my face, and the writing came up. It's German. It says, "*Am Widder—Montag halb fünf*".'

'I don't know any German,' said Mr. Everton. 'I don't suppose you do either. Do you?'

'Oh, *yes*! We all learnt it at Miss Braun's. I was quite good. It means "At the Ram—Monday, at half past four". And Miss Doncaster always has tea at the Ram when she goes into Marbury to shop. Isn't it *dreadful*!'

Mr. Everton gazed at her, kind but bewildered.

'I'm afraid I really don't quite take it in. Are you sure there isn't some mistake? There doesn't seem to be anything on this page except a very ordinary list of apple trees.'

Ida felt a sudden obstinacy.

'It was there all right, but it's faded. If we hold it to the fire, perhaps it will come up again.'

He said in a soothing voice, 'Well, well, we can always try,' and she went over and switched on a small electric fire which stood in front of the empty grate.

No one would have guessed what desperate thoughts whispered and clamoured behind that kindly, puzzled air. The millionth chance, and it was going to trip him up—that damned old magpie the Doncaster woman picking up the catalogue and going off with it! He knew when it must have happened—the day she had come into the garden and he had left her to find her own way out through the house. Just for such a small, small slip, to lose everything. She must have gone peering and prying into the study and taken it then. He ought to have destroyed it as soon as he had read the message. Yes, and have the servants wonder why he was burning paper, when everyone had it drummed into them morning noon and night that every scrap must be saved. He could have put it out for salvage. And have someone take it to light the fire with! No—all that he had done had been right and prudent. He had left it lying on his table amongst other catalogues as if it were no matter at all. And it had been the right thing to do—he would always maintain that it was right. Because all the way through, his position, the whole scheme, had depended on everything being just what everyone would expect. The moment there was the least variation from the normal, the least little thing of which anyone could say 'That's odd,' the plan was in danger. No—what he had done was right. It was only the millonth chance that had tripped him up.

These things were in his mind all together, speaking loud, speaking low. And amongst them, wary and poised, his inner self, the will to survive, to pluck safety out of defeat.

He watched the bar of the electric fire grow red. The inner self saw a small bright picture rise—the page held to the fire, curling in the heat, breaking into flame, falling back into harmless ash. He could do that, but it would not save him. Ida Mottram would swear to what she had seen, and the very destruction of the page would damn him.

No deeper than he was damned already. He was in two minds whether to destroy the page or not. It wasn't the page that had to be destroyed—it was Ida Mottram. If he were to shoot her now, he could put her body in the cupboard under the stairs. That would give him an hour or two to get away. The car laid up in his garage could be on the road in a quarter of an hour. If he could reach Marbury he would have a chance. But he must make Marbury before they found her.

His hand went into his pocket and felt the little pistol wadded in a handkerchief. A tiny, deadly thing, not at all like the cumbersome old weapon he had been clever enough to use for Harsch. It would make very little noise. Nobody in the country turned their heads when they heard a shot. He had gambled on that with Harsch, and it had come off.

There was hardly any interval between the click of the electric switch, the reddening of the bar, and Ida Mottram turning round to say,

'I think it's hot enough now.'

Until she came to die she would never again be so near to death as she was just then. He had the pistol free of the handkerchief. The hand in the pocket moved, withdrawing itself. Janice Meade came into the room.

Neither of them heard anything until she was there, just across the threshold. Ida Mottram said, 'Hullo!' Mr. Everton's hand came out of his pocket empty.

And now what? He must wait and see. If Mrs. Mottram held her tongue—but she wouldn't—she never did. As long as she believed that the message in the catalogue was for Miss Doncaster he had a chance, but the moment Miss Doncaster knew she would speak. He could imagine the furious zest with which she would denounce him.

He turned with his pleasant smile.

'How do you do, Miss Janice? Shall I put out the fire, Mrs. Mottram? Our little experiment can wait till afterwards. Yes, really—I think it would be better, dear lady.'

But Ida Mottram was opening the catalogue.

'Oh, I haven't any secrets from Janice,' she said. 'Jan, the most extraordinary thing!' And there she was, pouring it all out—her visit to Miss Mary Anne—the catalogue used to screen her face—the message which had come up on the blank white spaces and faded again. 'And Mr. Everton won't believe it was ever there at all. And it said in German, "At the Ram—Monday, at half past four." Isn't it dreadful—*Miss Doncaster*!'

Janice had got as far as the middle of the room. She stopped there by the folding table which Ida used for Bridge. It was folded now, and a bowl of old moulded glass full of September roses standing on it. The scent of the roses came up. She knew they were there, but she wasn't looking at them. She was looking at Ida on the hearth-rug with the catalogue in her hand, and she couldn't take her eyes away, because she had seen it before, not in Ida's hand but in Miss Doncaster's. And Miss Doncaster had said, 'I never bother to write for these things myself—I borrow my neighbours'. This is Mr. Everton's. I daresay he'll never miss it—you never saw such a mush as he's got on his table. So I just picked it up and brought it along.'

Mr. Everton went softly across to the door and shut it. Then he went back almost as far as the glass door into the garden and stood there looking at the two girls. It was a good position. He could see them both from there, and the light was right.

Ida Mottram looked round over her shoulder.

'Oh, it's coming up beautifully!' she said.

Mr. Everton said, 'Miss Meade——' and Janice turned. He saw something in her face. He said softly,

'What is it, Miss Meade? Won't you tell me?'

She put up her hand to her head and said in a faint, steady voice,

'It's so hot in here. Please turn the fire out. I think it would be nice in the garden.'

Ida dropped the catalogue.

'Jan—aren't you feeling well?'

'Not very. I'd like—some air.' She couldn't think of anything else, but it wasn't going to be any good.

Mr. Everton did not move.

And then, whilst Ida Mottram's eyes went round and surprised, something else moved beyond him in the garden. The head of Cyril Bond emerged from a lilac bush. He held a small bow and arrow, and his eyes were fixed upon imaginary Indians.

Janice felt a warmth rise up in her. It wasn't true that she was hot—she was deadly cold. She hadn't known how cold she was until that warmth touched her, and she knew that it was hope. She began to pray with all her might. The cold was the cold of thinking that she would never see Garth again. It began to go away.

Cyril Bond, glaring at the enemy he meant to scalp, was suddenly aware that he was closer than he had meant to be to Mrs. Mottram's drawing-room windows. He wasn't really supposed to be there at all, but when you are tracking an enemy you have to follow him. All the same he was too near the window, and—jeepers!—there was Mr. Everton no more than a yard inside it. Lucky he wasn't looking this way, but he might turn round. Cyril prepared for flight.

And then something stopped him. He could see Mr. Everton's back, and Miss Meade standing up in the middle of the room, and Mrs. Mottram down by the fire. Miss Meade looked funny somehow. Mr. Everton had his hand in his pocket, and then it came out with a pistol in it. Oh, boy! Just for a moment Cyril felt excited, and then something began to heave inside him and he wondered if he was going to be sick, because Mr. Everton was pointing the gun at Miss Meade, and Cyril heard him say, not loud but very distinctly,

'Don't move, either of you!'

He must have crawled clear of the lilacs, but he didn't remember doing it. He was running, sobbing whilst he ran. He thought he was going to be sick, but he kept on running. He barged into Major Albany and gasped through chattering teeth,

'He's shooting them! Mr. Everton's shooting them—in Mrs. Mottram's drawing-room! Ow, Major!'

Garth Albany dropped him and ran.

Mr. Everton stood with his pistol levelled and considered his plan. If he shot one of them, the other girl would scream. You couldn't stop a woman screaming unless you gagged her. He couldn't risk a scream. He said quite pleasantly,

'My dear lady, nobody is going to hurt you, but I want a little time to get away.' Then, as Ida blinked bewildered blue eyes at him, 'Miss Meade, you've got a head on your shouldlers. I don't want to hurt either of you, but you must see that I can't risk your giving the alarm. If you will do what you are told you will be quite safe. I don't think Mrs. Mottram has as much self-control as you have, and I want you to gag her. There is some nice pink silk in her work-basket there which will do very well. Hurry, please!'

Hurry—— She had seen Cyril's horrified face. She had seen him crawl away. Hurry—— He wouldn't go on crawling—he would run. Hurry—— How long to reach Garth? How long for Garth to come? She had got to make time. And Mr. Everton had the pistol. He mustn't have a chance to shoot at Garth.

The scent of the roses came up from the heavy glass bowl.

'Hurry!' There was a dangerous urgency in Mr. Everton's voice.

Her head felt stiff. She turned it a little, and saw Ida Mottram kneeling up on the hearth-rug and staring blankly at the pistol. She said in a surprised voice,

'I don't understand——' and Mr. Everton said, 'I'm afraid you will have to be gagged, but nobody is going to hurt you.'

That wasn't true. Janice looked back at him. For a moment that had nothing to do with time it was just as if she was looking through a window into his mind. He would make her gag Ida, and then he would kill them both—her first, before she could scream, and then Ida, who couldn't scream because she would be gagged.

Something in her said 'No!' and her mind went cold and clear. She said in a slow, considering voice,

'I'm sorry—would you mind saying it again? What do you want me to do?'

He began to tell her all over again, but before he had said more than half a dozen words she saw Garth come round the corner of the house. He was running. She picked up the heavy glass bowl with the roses and pitched it at Mr. Everton as hard as she could. It wasn't for nothing that Garth had taught her to throw. It took him full in the face with a scatter of roses and water, and the bowl smashing home. His glasses broke, and he cried out with a horrible animal sound of pain. Ida Mottram screamed at the top of her voice, and for half a split second Janice wondered whether the glass door to the garden was locked, because if it was, Mr. Everton was going to kill them all. And then, before she had time to remember that Ida never locked it in the daytime, Garth turned the handle without any sound at all and stepped into the room.

He made a long reach over Mr. Everton's drenched shoulder, took him by the wrist, and jerked his right hand up. The pistol went off, and a little plaster came pattering down on to the table where the bowl had stood.

The next thing she knew, she was at the telephone calling up the police. Mr. Everton was on the ground with Garth sitting on him, and Ida was saying between her sobs, 'Oh, you've broken my bowl! And it's cut his face—it's bleeding! Oh, poor Mr. Everton!'

CHAPTER FORTY ONE

A day or two later there was a gathering at the Rectory to bid Miss Silver good-bye—Miss Sophy, Garth and Janice, Sergeant Abbott, Ida Mottram, and Miss Medora Brown who was really Mrs. Madoc.

This disclosure had so gone to the Miss Doncasters' heads that, forgetting their ancient grudge, they were as one woman in saying that they had always felt that there was something strange about her, and as for Mr. Everton, if any one had cared to ask their opinion, they would have said at once that the shape of his head was German.

Frank Abbott, who appeared to be off duty, and was sitting

reverentially on a fat Victorian stool at Miss Silver's feet, said in a coaxing voice,

'Come along—tell us all. You suspected Everton from the first—didn't you? Why?'

Miss Silver coughed.

'My dear Frank, you are so impulsive. I did not begin to suspect Mr. Everton until Wednesday—the day before we made our expedition to Marbury.'

Frank pricked up his ears.

'What happened on Wednesday?'

Miss Silver regarded him with complacence.

'Very little—very little indeed. If I had mentioned it, you would have thought that I was exaggerating the importance of a trifle. When I was waiting in the garden for Miss Fell, who was very kindly taking me to call on the Miss Doncasters, the evacuee child, Cyril Bond, was up on the wall. As you may have observed, he has a considerable thirst for knowledge. He leaned suddenly out between the overhanging branches and enquired, "What does *Sprechen sie Deutsch* mean?"—mispronouncing the words in a most afflicting manner. However, the sense was clear, and I told him it meant "Do you speak German?" He had apparently picked up the phrase from another evacuee, of Austrian-Jewish extraction.'

Ida Mottram said in a puzzled voice,

'But why?'

Miss Silver smiled, patted her hand, and continued.

'Cyril informed me that he had approached Mr. Everton before asking me, and that Mr. Everton had said he did not know any German. It seemed incredible to me that an educated man who was aware that the language in question was German should have been unacquainted with the meaning of so common a phrase. And I wondered why he should have been at so much pains. After that the circle kept narrowing. I had never been able to believe in Mr. Madoc's guilt, and his testimony cleared Bush. Everything else apart, Mr. Madoc could not have killed Ezra Pincott, since he was then in Marbury jail. And Bush could not have killed Mr. Harsch if Mr. Madoc's statement was correct.'

Frank Abbott nodded.

'No—we checked it all up—he couldn't have got to the place where Madoc saw him in the time.'

'It was abundantly clear,' said Miss Silver, 'that Ezra met his death in an attempt to blackmail the murderer. The type of gravel found on his boots showed that it had been picked up on a path in the churchyard or on the drive of one of the houses along the

Green. The fact that this gravel was dry and clean was a proof that Ezra did not walk to the miry place where he was found drowned. From the moment Miss Janice informed me of the conversation in which Mr. Harsch used some such phrase as "A door opening upon the past" I had a strong conviction that this door had opened in the Ram. Mr. Harsch went in there to have tea, and he came out without having it. Why? He missed his train, and when he got home he told Miss Madoc that he had seen a ghost. Where? It was clear to me that he had had an encounter which gave him a severe shock, that this encounter was connected with his past life, and that he was not entirely sure that his mind had not been playing him tricks. It was not, of course, someone from Bourne who startled him, but it occurred to me that two persons may have been present, and that one of them may have come from Bourne. If this was the case, both these persons had reason to be very uneasy, and fear lest they should have been recognized may have precipitated the murder.'

Garth Albany said, 'I don't think it did. Sir George was coming down next day—they were bound to bump Harsch off before he delivered the goods. Look here, Ida—Miss Mary Anne told you that she had overheard Harsch's call to Sir George. Did you repeat that to Everton?'

Ida Mottram opened her eyes as wide as they would go.

'Oh, no, but he was there—we were there together. He was always so very interested about Mr. Harsch.'

'You bet he was!' said Garth. 'And you bet he'd have collected the papers if Madoc hadn't got them off to his bank. He didn't have to risk getting them on the night of the murder, because he could count on Madoc being pretty sticky about handing them over to Sir George. Sorry, Mrs. Madoc, but anyone who knew him could have counted on that.'

On being addressed by what was, after all, her legal name, Medora Madoc blushed painfully. She looked suddenly a good deal younger and, to Garth's amazement, shy.

Miss Silver inclined her head.

'I think that is quite true, Major Albany. I believe the plan was to allow Mr. Harsch to complete his experiments, and then murder him before he could hand the results over to the government. They knew that the time was running short and they must be ready to act at any moment. The meeting at the Ram may have been for the purpose of handing over a weapon very carefully chosen with a view to suggesting suicide. It is, I think, instructive to look back and see how very near the plan came to succeeding. If it had not been for the fact that Mr. Madoc's conduct exposed him to suspicion, the verdict of suicide would almost certainly have stood, since but for Mr. Madoc's arrest I doubt very much whether Ezra Pincott's death would have received the attention it deserved. It is reassuring to reflect that criminals so often come to grief over some small happening which they could not have foreseen. All through, Mr. Everton's success and safety depended on his never being suspected. Actually, the very pains he took to avoid suspicion convinced me that there was something to suspect. When Mrs. Mottram told him that I was to be called in, there is, I think, no doubt that he took steps to discredit Miss Janice. I have never been able to regard the conversation I heard behind me in the Tube station as fortuitous, I am quite sure that it was carefully planned. He is known to have gone over to Marbury on the Saturday evening, and I have no doubt that he telephoned from there to a confederate in London. It has not, unfortunately, been possible to trace the call. As we now know, Mr. Everton's name is not Everton at all, but Smith. His parents were Germans of the name of Schmidt. He was born and brought up in this country, but paid frequent visits to Germany and became a fanatical Nazi. But——' she turned graciously to Frank— 'Sergeant Abbott is better qualified than I am to deal with this.'

'Well, it's no secret now. He was up before the magistrates yesterday. The real Everton is still having a nervous breakdown somewhere in Devon. They picked him carefully. He doesn't seem to have any relations, and his friends were the sort you pick up doing business over a drink or a lunch—easy come, easy go. It was "poor old Everton" for a bit, and then nobody bothered. He's too bad to write letters. He just dropped clean out. I gather there's no real likeness between him and Schmidt, but a superficial description of one would fit the other—height, figure, colouring. He seems to have played the part of the cheerful little man with country tastes and a liking for having a finger in everybody's pie, and to have played it very well indeed.'

Miss Sophy sat up and said,

'I don't believe it was a part. I believe it was what he might have been if that wretched Hitler had left him alone. When you think how many, many people were killed in the last war, it does seem a pity Hitler shouldn't have been one of them.'

Frank Abbott turned an appreciative eye upon her.

'Thanks for those kind words, Miss Fell.'

With a faint cough Miss Silver resumed.

'From the moment I had talked with Mrs. Mottram it was, of course, clear to me that Mr. Everton's alibi for Tuesday night was no alibi at all. He called Mrs. Mottram's attention to a shot which she did not hear and, looking at his watch, remarked that it was a quarter to ten. Actually, I believe that it was then half past nine. He ran very little risk, as Mrs. Mottram does not wear a watch and has no clock in her drawing-room.'

'Watches won't go on me,' said Ida, looking round for sympathy. 'They say it's electricity or something. And I can't sit in the room with a clock—it worries me. But I'm practically sure I did hear something chime—and of course I thought it was a quarter to ten like he said.'

Miss Silver smiled at her.

'Yes, my dear—I think he counted on that. He left you at half past nine, and four or five minutes later he entered the church. I felt sure all along that the murderer was on friendly terms with Mr. Harsch, and that some conversation preceded the shot. You see, the curtain which screens the organist was pulled back, and no one seems to have heard the organ later than a very few minutes after half past nine. Unless the murderer makes a statement, we shall never know quite what happened. But since the appearance of suicide was aimed at, it would be necessary to put Mr. Harsch off his guard, and to hold him in conversation until the next set of chimes fell due at a quarter to ten. Schmidt would be watching the time, standing close up to the organ stool. To pass as suicide, the shot must be fired at point-blank range. The three chimes for the quarter begin. At the second he fires. Mr. Harsch falls down. Schmidt has only to wipe the weapon, clasp his victim's hand upon it, and let it drop again, releasing the pistol. If Ezra Pincott had not been in the Church Cut upon his own affairs that night, there is no doubt that a very wicked plan would have succeeded.'

Garth laughed.

'Ezra was after Giles's rabbits!' he said. 'He could get rabbits anywhere, but it tickled him to get Giles's—he'd been doing it for years. And a clever old poacher like him wouldn't be foxed over which side of the road that shot came from. There wasn't anything about sounds that Ezra wasn't up to—I've been out with him and I know. He told me once he could hear an earwig walking on a leaf, and I believe him.'

'That is very interesting, Major Albany. To continue. Hearing the shot, Ezra ran to the door in the churchyard wall and opened it. He saw Schmidt leave the church, and ran after him. We know that he caught him up, since Sam and Gladys now say, what would have been more useful if said at once, that, returning from their walk by way of the road which passes the houses, they observed Mr. Everton and Ezra in conversation at Mr. Everton's gate. They heard Ezra say, "Drunk or sober, it'll be something to talk about in the morning", and he then went off laughing.'

'Fit to bust himself,' said Frank Abbott. 'They also say that a little later on they saw Miss Doncaster come out and post a letter. As soon as she'd gone in they went into the churchyard. When I asked them why they hadn't said all this when it was some use, they said it was only old Ezra and Mr. Everton, and that old Miss Doncaster that's always posting letters, and Gladys giggled and said, "You wouldn't think she'd have a boy friend, would you?" He turned to Miss Silver, sitting on the footstool with his arms locked about his knees. 'Reverend preceptress, why don't you say, "I told you so"?'

He got an indulgent smile, but before Miss Silver could speak footsteps were heard in the hall and the door was flung open. Striding past the indignant Mabel, Mr. Madoc bounced the door shut and comprehended the assembled party in a scowl of greeting. There was some kind of an inclination of the head in the direction of Miss Sophy and Miss Silver, after which his frowning regard came to rest upon his wife, who sat there as if she had been turned to stone. He addressed her in a series of angry jerks.

'If you're coming home you had better pack your box! Pincott's van will call for it in half an hour!'

Without waiting for an answer he turned and went out. The door banged after him. The front door banged.

Medora Brown got up. Her marmorial pallor seemed to have gone for good. She was very much flushed, and she looked as if she might be going to cry. She came over to the sofa and said, 'Dear Miss Sophy—may I?' and then fairly ran out of the room.

Garth said, 'Gosh!' And then, 'How long will it last?'

Miss Silver gave him a glance of mild reproof.

'They have both been so very unhappy,' she said. 'I do not really think she will find him difficult to manage. Tact and affection should cure him of expecting to be hurt. I saw at once that that was the trouble, and I believe she will be able to deal with it.'

Garth just gazed, until Miss Silver turned back to her audience. Then he leaned over Janice, on the arm of whose chair he was sitting, and murmured, she hoped inaudibly,

'Darling—*swear* to be tactful and affectionate.'

Miss Silver coughed.

'There is very little more to say. I think that Ezra received some money on account. He seems to have stood drinks all round at the

Bull, which was not his habit. But he showed the usual mounting appetite of the blackmailer, and—he began to talk. He became too dangerous to be tolerated. I think he was asked to call at a fairly late hour, met by Schmidt himself, and invited—probably —into the garage. Yes, I feel sure that it would have been the garage. Being a converted coachhouse, it is very roomy, and it houses a most convenient wheelbarrow. Ezra was offered brandy, which he accepted with avidity. He was then knocked out, placed in the wheelbarrow, and conveyed—probably across the Green, the shortest and safest way—to the place where he was found. There was some risk about this, but not very much—Bourne goes early to bed, and I recall that the night was cloudy. Returning home and unobserved, Schmidt must have considered himself safe. The case against Mr. Madoc must have seemed very strong to him, and he would confidently expect a verdict of accidental death in Ezra's case. I cannot praise too highly the acumen of Sergeant Abbott in detecting the dry specks of gravel which had adhered to the mud on Ezra's boots, and his brilliant deduction that Ezra had not walked but been carried to the miry place where he was found.'

For the first and only time in his history Frank Abbott was seen to blush. The colour, though faint, was quite discernible, and it may be said that it filled Garth Albany with joy.

Miss Sophy heaved herself up from the sofa and announced that she must go to her poor Medora. Ida Mottram embraced Miss Silver, rolled her eyes at Frank, and announced with a faint scream that she must fly to Bunty.

But at the door she turned.

'Oh, Mr. Abbott, I suppose you can't tell me, but it does seem such a pity—those lovely hens of Mr. Everton's—I suppose he wouldn't divide them among us?'

'I'm afraid I couldn't suggest it, Mrs. Mottram.'

'Oh, well——' She kissed her hand to the room and departed.

Miss Silver looked after her with affection. Then she turned to Garth and Janice.

'I have a few things to put together in my room. My taxi should be here in about ten minutes time. Sergeant Abbott will be travelling with me as far as Marbury. It is always a little sad to say good-bye at the end of a case, but if the guilty have been discovered and the innocent cleared, I am cheered and encouraged. There is no greater cause than justice, and in my humble way I try to serve that cause. May I offer you my very best wishes, and my earnest hopes for your happiness?'

She went out—a little dowdy person in garments of outmoded

style, the bog-oak rose at her throat, her hair, neatly controlled by a net, piled high in a tight curled fringe after the fashion set by Queen Alexandra in the nineties and now just coming in again, her feet in woollen stockings and bead-embroidered shoes, a brightly flowered knitting-bag depending from her arm.

She went out, and Frank Abbott shut the door after her. As he turned back he was again seen to be slightly flushed. In a tone so far from official that it actually sounded boyish he exclaimed,

'Marvellous—isn't she!'